THE DOPPELGANGER'S DANCE

A Jewish Regency Mystery

LIBI ASTAIRE

ASTER PRESS

First published 2013

Copyright 2013 by Libi Astaire
Cover photo: Copyright Maria Dryfhout/
Shutterstock.com

ISBN: 978-0-9885809-6-1

This book is a work of fiction. Names, characters, places, and incidents are either the product of the author's imagination or are used fictitiously.

Published by:
Aster Press
Kansas-Jerusalem
asterpressbooks@gmail.com

PROLOGUE

HOW VERY MUCH can happen in a year! Not long after the unpleasantness at the Jewish orphanage was resolved to the satisfaction of all, Miss Taylor and Mr. Oppenheim were married, to the great joy of their friends and well-wishers.

If there was one blot on the otherwise delightful day, it was the absence of a young lady who had played such an important part in smoothing the way for the marriage to take place. I refer, of course, to the Narrator of these chronicles and, dear Reader, if you recall the events of *Tempest in the Tea Room* you will understand why I would not have willingly missed this wedding for the world.

But as my father, Mr. Samuel Lyon, clockmaker to the fashionable world, has informed me on occasions too numerable for me to count, it is the Almighty who rules the world—and decides, at least in this instance, which young ladies shall travel to Manchester for a wedding and which shall remain in London to help their mother nurse back to health their younger siblings, who had most inconsiderately gone for a walk in the rain, which led to their coming down with a sore throat only a few days before we were scheduled to depart.

Despite my protests that I will most likely be twenty-five and an old woman before I shall have another chance to see something of the world, Mr. Lyon assured me that we mortals cannot foresee the future. And the truth of his wise words was soon revealed! Within the year I was seated in a carriage bouncing down a country road, on my way to Leeds.

Although I must admit, now that I am an experienced traveler, that the *thought* of bouncing down a country road is much more pleasant than the actual experiencing of it, I trust there will be no such disappointment with the tale I am about to narrate; it should be of interest to any person of sensibility — including admirers of Mrs. Ann Radcliffe and her *horrid* fiction— since it recounts the strangest series of events to occur in the history of London's Jewish community, at least that I can recall.

Therefore, without further introduction, I bid my pen to play chorus and verse to the discomposing mystery of *The Doppelganger's Dance*.

Devonshire Square, London, England
Chanukah 5574/December 18, 1813

CHAPTER I

"I SUPPOSE YOU are right, Mr. Melamed. The thing must be done, though it is inconvenient. Not to mention the expense, the cost of traveling such a great distance being what it is."

Mr. Samuel Lyon returned the letter he had been given to peruse to his fellow member of London's Great Synagogue, Mr. Ezra Melamed. Mr. Melamed was not just a member of that illustrious institution but a *parnass*, or benefactor, of London's Jewish community, due to his great wealth and numerous connections, which extended as far as the upper reaches of English society. Yet even though all agreed that Mr. Melamed could expect others to defer to his leadership (and, to be truthful, there were those who wished that he *would* perform his duties single-handedly and not bother them with tiresome communal affairs), Mr. Melamed insisted upon soliciting the advice of other well-regarded members of the community, such as Mr. Samuel Lyon, clockmaker to the fashionable world, whenever an important decision had to be made.

"I would go to Leeds myself, but I must travel to Brighton for business," said Mr. Melamed. When Mr. Lyon did not reply, Mr. Melamed added, "Of course, you have your business concerns as well. But I thought that your assistant might be able to take care of your shop while you are away."

"Mr. Warburg is a most capable man," Mr. Lyon reluctantly agreed. "I have no uneasiness about Mr. Warburg. But why is the woman in Leeds?"

"I suppose you will hear the full story before the rest of us."

Mr. Melamed took a final look at the piece of paper, upon which a few brief lines had been written with a hand that displayed education, elegance and economy—three virtues that could not but make an impression upon a person who valued excellence in both taste and character. He then returned the letter to his coat pocket and his attention to Mr. Lyon, who was still looking unhappy about the prospect of traveling to Leeds to escort a Jewish woman back to London.

"I will do all in my power to make your journey a comfortable one," said Mr. Melamed. "You and Mrs. Lyon may make use of my carriage. You may take one of my servants, as well, if you prefer not to take your own. The other expenses of the journey will be paid for out of the communal fund."

Mr. Lyon could not quarrel with such generous terms. Yet still he hesitated. "I first must speak to Mrs. Lyon and obtain her consent. A journey from London to Leeds—and back again—is no small undertaking."

"That is precisely why I am sure Mrs. Lyon will agree to your going. Mrs. Salomon cannot possibly make such a journey alone."

The two friends parted, one certain that a communal duty had been disposed of, the other just as certain that a conjugal disagreement was about to ensue.

When Mr. Lyon returned to his family abode in Devonshire Square, he was met with a scene of family tranquility that was all the more arresting for being so rare. Mrs. Rose Lyon, the matriarch of the family, was seated on the settee by the fire, reading to Esther and Sarah, the family's two youngest daughters.

Joshua Lyon was, as usual, busy with his toy soldiers, planning the next battle. General Wellington's forces had achieved a tremendous success that summer in Spain, at the Battle of Vitoria, and in the autumn Wellington had crossed the Pyrenees and brought his army to France. That mountainous performance had been reenacted many times in the Lyon family's drawing room, to the consternation of Mrs. Lyon, who, at the sight of the furniture rearranged to form a suitable mountain range, would declare with an aggrieved tone of voice that, in her opinion, war ought to be abolished by all civilized nations. But her opinion had gone unheeded, and after England's Austrian, Prussian, and Russian allies suffered a crushing defeat at Dresden, it was clear that the war with "Boney," as we Englishmen call Mr. Napoleon, was far from over. Mrs. Lyon therefore had to be contented with the soothing words of her husband that at least Wellington had not crossed any large bodies of water, and so for the moment the furniture and carpets were safe from a watery recital of the British army's latest adventures.

As for Miss Rebecca Lyon, the chronicler of this narrative and the eldest daughter at home, now that her sister Hannah was happily married to Mr. David Goldsmith, she was seated by the window overlooking Devonshire Square, thinking how nice it would be if a mysterious carriage painted all in black, except for the gold trim, and pulled by a team of sleek black horses would clamber into the square at that moment. The owner of the carriage, a man whose black looks signaled that he was from foreign parts — Italy or Sicily, she had not yet decided which — and up to no good, would jump down from the carriage, followed by a beautiful but pale-looking young woman (his daughter? his wife?), who was clearly in distress. The two would disappear into one of the square's apartments (the recently vacated rooms above the residence of Miss Harriet Franks, Rebecca's best friend, would suit nicely), and thus would begin a lovely mystery story for Rebecca to solve, in the style of Mrs. Ann Radcliffe, the well-known authoress of Gothic novels.

When she was thus employed in such pleasant daydreams, Rebecca had no desire to scatter Joshua's regiment with a well-aimed swirl of the hem of her muslin dress, or complain that Sarah and Esther had cut up one of her old straw bonnets without permission, to make new bonnets for their dolls, even though they had done so that morning. Besides, she was already much too old to stoop to such childish displays of perverseness and temper, at least when she was feeling grown up of her own accord. It was another thing entirely when adults reminded a young person that they were no longer a child, a reprimand that somehow always seemed to have the opposite of its intended effect.

Mr. Lyon stayed in the doorway for a few moments, to savor the homey scene. Then his presence was discovered and the tranquility was exchanged for the bustle of the family's removal to the dining room, where the table was already laid for their supper. It was only after the soup course had been eaten and cleared that Mr. Lyon broached the subject of the journey to Leeds to his helpmeet, Mrs. Lyon.

"Why you, Mr. Lyon? What have you to do in Leeds?" asked that good woman, who disliked traveling even as far as Mayfair, since she preferred the comfort of her own home to all other places in the world.

"I have nothing to do in Leeds. But someone from the community must escort Mrs. Salomon to London."

"I do not see why. Why cannot her husband arrange for her return to London, without bothering the community? And what about our children? We cannot possibly leave them here in London on their own."

"I am sure that Mr. and Mrs. Franks would take them in. It is just for a few days."

"I think it would be much better if the Franks went to Leeds and we took in Harriet," said Mrs. Lyon, glancing over at the far end of the table, where Esther was busy braiding a string bean into Sarah's hair. "Harriet is no trouble at all."

"Yes, but Mr. Melamed asked me to make the journey. He must have had his reasons for making the request."

"And I have my reasons for declining that request. No, I cannot give my consent to such a venture, Mr. Lyon. The roads at this time of year, the lack of proper kosher accommodations along the way—Mr. Salomon should have considered that before he allowed Mrs. Salomon to embark upon such a hazardous journey alone."

Mr. Lyon was silent, but not defeated. Mrs. Salomon might have been in America for almost twenty years, but he had not forgotten that in the waning years of the previous century there had been a great rivalry between Mrs. Salomon and Mrs. Lyon, who were then young ladies of marriageable age. The fact that they had both married well had done nothing to dispel their antipathy to one another; and so, when the Salomons were ready to embark upon that long-ago journey to New York, the two ladies had said their good-byes with frigid politeness, quite content to have an ocean between them.

Knowing all this, Mr. Lyon, who had by now accepted the necessity of the journey to Leeds, had kept undisclosed one important detail, which he intended to reveal only after his wife had had time to express her initial displeasure. This having been done, he said, "Mr. Salomon has met with a tragic end. Mrs. Salomon is a widow."

Mrs. Lyon opened her mouth to speak, but once the full meaning of her husband's words sank in, she quickly closed it. A few moments later, though, she said, "What about her son? I am positive that when

Mrs. Salomon left London, there was a little boy. By now he must be a grown man."

"I cannot say. Mrs. Salomon did not mention him in her letter."

"Do you think he has met with a tragic end as well, Papa?" asked Rebecca, who had been following the conversation with great interest.

"I hope not."

"If he did, Mrs. Salomon will be like Naomi, returning to Bethlehem without husband or sons," said Rebecca, vividly visualizing the Biblical scene described in the *Megillah of Ruth.*

"She did not mention a daughter-in-law, Rebecca," said Mr. Lyon, "and we should not anticipate misfortune. For all we know, Mrs. Salomon's son is quite healthy and still in America."

For a brief moment, it did occur to Mrs. Lyon to say that if that were the case, the son should have accompanied the mother to England. But she held her tongue. A widow must be treated with charity, both in thought and deed, no matter what had happened in the past.

"I suppose, then, that Mr. Melamed is right. Someone must accompany Mrs. Salomon," she therefore conceded. "But I cannot possibly accompany you, Mr. Lyon. You know the state of my health, how delicate my digestion has become during this last year. Yet you must not travel alone. Surely Mr. Melamed would agree that you and Mrs. Salomon cannot travel such a distance alone."

"I agree with you entirely," he replied. "That is why I thought that Rebecca could come with me. And Perl could help us prepare our food, and serve as

Rebecca's maid—if, of course, you can spare Perl, my dear."

Mrs. Lyon did not know what to protest first—the absence of her daughter, or her housemaid. Rebecca had no such hesitations. She leaped from her chair and flung her arms about her father's neck. "Oh, Papa! May I really come with you? Shall we travel by the Royal Mail, and stay at a coaching inn, and be accosted by bandits, and ..."

"We shall not travel in a Royal Mail coach, and with God's help we will not meet with any bandits," said Mr. Lyon, extricating his neck from his daughter's arms. He then said to his wife, "Mr. Melamed has offered us the use of his carriage. He also offered us one of his servants. But I thought Rebecca might be more comfortable if Perl accompanied us."

"I would," said Rebecca. "Perl is so very capable, I am sure we will not go hungry. If we pack a few of our cooking pots, she will think of a dozen ways to cook an egg."

This interesting discussion continued all the way through the meat course. When it had been decided which kosher provisions and cooking utensils would be brought along, and that they would bring their own bed linens, since one could not possibly rely upon those provided by a strange inn, Mrs. Lyon gave her reluctant consent to the plan.

"I must tell Harriet at once," said Rebecca, as the family returned to the drawing room for tea, since she could not conceive of keeping such exciting news from her best friend overnight.

"At this hour?" Mrs. Lyon protested, glancing out the window.

"It is still light out," said Mr. Lyon. "And the Franks home is just a few steps away. And we shall then be able to drink our tea in quiet. But do not stay long, Rebecca," he added, giving a nod in Mrs. Lyon's direction. "Your mother is correct to insist that you be home before it is dark."

When Rebecca returned, it was earlier than either Mr. or Mrs. Lyon expected — and she did not return alone.

"I hope you do not mind our barging in like this," said Mr. Franks, whose entrance was followed by his wife and daughter. "When I heard you were planning a trip to Leeds, it occurred to me that we might make a party of it."

"Have you business there?" asked Mr. Lyon.

"Not yet. But you must have heard about the experiments being made there with steam locomotives. Blenkinsop and Murray seem to be making great progress with their two-cylinder machine. I should like to see it for myself."

Mrs. Lyon smiled indulgently at Mrs. Franks. It was commonly known that Mr. Franks had a great interest in all things scientific. Mrs. Lyon thought it must be very tiresome to have a husband who was forever talking about gas lighting and water pumps and, now, locomotives, and so she handed Mrs. Franks a larger than usual slice of cake.

"How fast can they go?" Mr. Lyon asked.

"According to the newspaper accounts, ten miles an hour."

Mrs. Lyon nearly dropped the tea pot. "So fast? Why so fast, Mr. Franks? I am not against progress, but surely that must be very dangerous!"

Mr. Franks smiled. "A fast horse can travel that distance in an hour, Mrs. Lyon. Even the Royal Mail can do it, on certain roads."

"Then what is the advantage?"

"A horse cannot keep up the pace for very long. But a locomotive will not tire. As long as it has fuel, it can travel day and night at ten miles an hour. One could travel from London to Leeds in a day, instead of in four or five."

"I cannot imagine it either," said Mrs. Franks, giving an astonished Mrs. Lyon a reassuring smile.

Mr. Franks stood up and began to pace up and down the room, something he often did when he was excited about a new scientific venture. "I predict," he said, pointing a prophetic-looking finger in the air, "I predict that the day is not far off when we will not have to imagine traveling by locomotive; we shall do it. It's the coal mine owners who are behind the race to build a better machine, and they shall not rest until they have found a way to transport their coal quickly and inexpensively." Having reached the settee where Rebecca and his daughter Harriet were sitting, he said to them, "You may not think it possible now, but I predict that when you are my age you will travel by locomotive, and you will look back with fond amusement at our cumbersome and drafty coaches and wonder how you ever tolerated traveling at such a slow pace."

Rebecca and Harriet exchanged glances. It was impossible, of course, to laugh at Mr. Franks. He was an adult, and one did not laugh at one's elders. But it was also impossible to think of themselves as ever being as old as their fathers and mothers, and so they hid their smiles behind their teacups.

Meanwhile, Mr. Lyon was looking worried. "I do not know what to say. Mr. Melamed has offered me the use of his carriage, but it can seat only three comfortably and I have already promised Rebecca. And we must have a servant to see about the meals."

Rebecca's heart skipped a beat as she saw, for the first time, the danger. Mr. Franks intended to go with her father to Leeds!

"Yes, so Miss Lyon informed us," said Mr. Franks. "But if I hired a carriage, and brought Harriet and one of our servants along …"

Before he could finish his sentence, the two young ladies sprang up from their seats as one, and began to thank Mr. Franks for thinking of this most excellent plan.

Mr. Lyon glanced over at Mrs. Lyon. He knew that, despite her protestations to the contrary, she did disapprove of Mr. Franks's enthusiasm for progress and mechanical advancements. After several moments of tense consideration, she said, "I give my consent, Mr. Lyon, only if you promise me that the carriages will not travel faster than five miles an hour. Otherwise, I cannot possibly agree."

"I shouldn't worry," said Mrs. Franks. "After the girls have loaded their trunks with their clothes and their sketching supplies and whatever else they intend to bring, I doubt there is a team of horses in the world that could travel any faster."

CHAPTER II

NORMALLY, REBECCA WOULD have been very interested in hearing more about Mrs. Salomon, since a newcomer to the community was always a topic worthy of notice. But her thoughts were too full of the upcoming journey for her to think of anything else. Therefore, Rebecca daydreamed about melancholy ruins, and grand stately homes, and picturesque wooden bridges suspended over dappled streams, all of which would be perfect for sketching, while her mother conversed with Mrs. Miriam Baer—a woman who was as renowned for her matchmaking skills as the good food she served in the coffee house she owned with her husband, Mr. Asher Baer.

"A tragic end is so very vague," Mrs. Baer was saying. "You are certain the letter did not say more?"

"I did not see the letter. I can only report what Mr. Lyon told me," replied Mrs. Lyon, uncharacteristically unforthcoming. Although she usually enjoyed a good chat as much as the next person, she could not yet bring herself to be happily interested in the affairs of Mrs. Salomon. And the fact that there had been an endless stream of visitors to Devonshire Square ever since the news of that lady's imminent arrival in London became commonly known, only made her less eager to discuss the subject.

"America is so very big," Mrs. Baer continued, "so very, very big. A person could quite disappear in it, or so I am told."

At last, Mrs. Lyon comprehended where Mrs. Baer's thoughts were leading, and her interest was sparked. "You do not think?"

"I would like to think otherwise. If someone had actually seen Mr. Salomon die, if Mrs. Salomon knew for a fact the cause of her husband's demise, would she not have written, 'Mr. Moses Salomon was struck down by a fever,' or 'Mr. Moses Salomon was drowned at sea'? Why would she choose to be so mysterious, if there were no mystery concerning her husband's death? Why write that he has met with a *tragic end*?"

Mrs. Lyon thought back to earlier days. "She did have a tendency for drama, a need to be the center of attention. Of course, we were young girls," she added, recalling her resolve to be charitable, "and girls do so wish to be noticed, once they reach a certain age."

Mrs. Lyon shot an accusing glance in her daughter's direction. For once she had no cause for complaint. Rebecca was sitting demurely in her chair, with her cap neatly arranged over her brown curls and the ends of her sleeves free from blotches of ink. However, although Mrs. Lyon did note that Rebecca was not yet at the age to start thinking about finding a husband, she knew that the years were passing and that that interesting time in a young lady's life was not far off.

"There could be a practical reason," said Rebecca, who was of course unaware of her mother's thoughts, but whose own interest in the conversation had been sparked by the words "drowned at sea." Those few words had made her imagination fly at once to the

Atlantic Ocean, where a frail vessel was being tossed and turned upon the deep and darkly turbulent waters. Just as quickly, though, her thoughts returned to England and more prosaic matters. "A letter is so expensive to receive. Perhaps she thought it best to be brief."

Mrs. Baer gave Rebecca a grateful smile, since her nature was to be cheerful, rather than morose, and the desire to economize would happily resolve all doubts. Then her pensive mood returned. "If only one knew for sure. It would be a terrible thing if Mr. Salomon met his end in the wilderness, without a reliable witness to see it. Without proof that her husband is, indeed, dead, poor Mrs. Salomon will not be able to remarry."

"I should not be overly worried. I am sure we shall hear the full story when Mrs. Salomon is in London," Mrs. Lyon said curtly. She did not at all savor the vision of Mrs. Salomon surrounded by an attentive circle of female admirers, all eager to hear each word of the thrilling tale.

"You are right," said Mrs. Baer, hearing the reassuring words more than the tone. "Worry accomplishes nothing, and I cannot think why I feel so uneasy. It is much more likely that Mrs. Salomon will be able to remarry. And Mr. Melamed has been a widower for far too long."

"Mr. Melamed?" gasped Mrs. Lyon, nearly choking on her tea.

"Of course, until we meet the woman it is impossible to know if they will suit one another. We must hope that her years in America have not had an adverse effect on her manners and speech. But their ages are similar, and a man does need a woman to look after him. It makes all the difference when there is a woman in the home." Mrs. Baer began to smile, apparently seeing these happy changes already in place in Mr. Melamed's home on Bury Street.

Mrs. Lyon tried to return her friend's smile. But the thought of her former rival making a triumphant match with one of the most important men in the Jewish community was too bitter a medicine for her to swallow.

When the exciting day of departure arrived, it seemed that half the congregation of the Great Synagogue had come to Devonshire Square to say good-bye. The post chaise hired by Mr. Franks arrived first, and everyone commented on the bright yellow color of the carriage and the liveliness of the horses, as though they had never before seen a hired coach in their life. Mr. Melamed's carriage was an even more familiar sight, yet its elegance, as well as the magnificence of his team of horses, shone all the more brightly when seen in comparison to its humbler, hired cousin.

The many trunks were handed up, the two young ladies and Perl were handed in to their carriage, while Mr. Lyon and Mr. Franks took their seats in the carriage of Mr. Melamed. And then, amidst a multitude of good wishes for a safe trip—as well as many tears from Mrs. Lyon and a few last words of calm advice from Mrs. Franks—they were off.

The first day was glorious. Once they had left the crowded, noisy streets of London behind them, Rebecca and Harriet flung open the carriage window and eagerly breathed in the fresh country air. They laughed at the jolts that nearly sent them crashing into the carriage's roof, an often enough occurrence, since the road seemed to have been fitted with an endless supply of ruts for their amusement. There were serious moments as well, as they studied the passing scenery and discussed the merits of the various views. They both agreed that it was a pity that they could do no sketching while they were in the bouncing carriage. At Harriet's suggestion, they tried their hand at composing an 'Ode to Nature' instead. But the exercise was soon abandoned as it was much more pleasant to talk about everything they were seeing than try to confine a small part of it into a few lines of verse.

Then came the final exciting moment of the day, their arrival at the coaching inn where they were to stay for the night. The inn was everything that Rebecca had hoped it would be, and she was determined to impress all that she saw upon her memory, so that she could recall every detail on later days, when her life had returned to its dull routine. She was particularly enthralled by the way the inn hummed with activity when another carriage rumbled into the courtyard and the stable boys accomplished the change of horses with lightning speed. Then the unknown carriage went on its way and the stable boys disappeared into the gathering darkness, by which time her own luggage needed for the night had been unloaded and she and Harriet followed Mr. Lyon and Mr. Franks into the inn.

The inn's proprietor was a broad-shouldered, hearty, welcoming man — and happy to let Perl have a place in the kitchen to warm their meal, once Mr. Lyon had pressed a few extra coins in his hand.

On their way to the private sitting room that they had engaged, Rebecca took note of the travelers who were sitting in the public space. Although it was never polite to gape, and certainly not acceptable for a respectable young lady to gaze too long at a man, there was a young man sitting in the back of the room who did make Rebecca stop and stare. There was nothing exceptionable about the way that the young man looked, except for the fact that he looked familiar. But before she could comment to her father that another member of their synagogue was at the inn, the young man got up and disappeared through a door into another room — and Rebecca forgot about the incident in her own excitement of eating a meal in a coaching inn for the very first time. That meal was a simple one, but since it was spiced with the charm of new and unusual surroundings — including ancient oak beams overhead and a wood floor that creaked and sagged in the most delightfully atmospheric way — Rebecca thought it one of the most delicious meals she had ever eaten.

Later, when she and Harriet were in their bed chamber, her thoughts returned to all the heretofore unknown people she had seen and she commented, "Is it not odd, Harriet, how we are in this inn this evening together with all these people and tomorrow we shall all go our separate ways, perhaps never to meet again?"

Harriet yawned. "Why is it odd? That is what an inn is for."

"Yes, but just think, we do not know them, they do not know us, yet for these few brief hours our lives have become joined. We all have the same concerns ..."

"Fleas in the mattress!" said Harriet, laughing as she scratched her arm.

"I am serious. Do you not wonder at all about those other people and their histories? Who they are? From where have they come? Where they are going? What will happen to them and their hopes and their plans?"

But Harriet had drifted off to sleep.

CHAPTER III

THE CHARM OF travel had lost much of its luster by the last day of their journey. Rebecca was therefore lost in a drowsy half-sleep—and dreaming of traveling through a dangerous mountain pass in the wilds of northern Italy, where she was being chased by agents of the Roman Inquisition—when the carriages lumbered into Leeds, a town that was becoming renowned as a center of English commerce and manufacturing. Jolted back to the present by the sudden halt of the horses, she opened her eyes to the prospect of an ordinary red brick house that had an ordinary English-looking husband and wife standing on the doorstep, all of which made her correctly surmise that she had arrived at her destination and so, regrettably, the opportunity for a real adventure had passed.

Mr. and Mrs. Deare, their hosts while they stayed in Leeds, welcomed the travelers with broad smiles and cheery entreaties to come sit by the fire, change their traveling clothes, have some tea, peruse the books in the library, and try out the spinet in the drawing room, each outdoing the other in their attempt to make their visitors feel at home.

"Please forgive us," said Mr. Deare, laughing after he realized that despite their good intentions, their effusiveness had left the newcomers still standing on the doorstep. "We have so few visitors from London. But do come in. I expect you will want to wash away the dust of your journey before anything else."

When the little party had reassembled in the drawing room, they were greeted by the sight of a side table laden with cold meats and savory pies and bowls filled with fresh fruit. "You will want some refreshments before supper," said Mrs. Deare, beckoning to the two girls to come fill their plates.

"We don't often have mutton or beef," Mr. Deare added. "There are only a few Jews living in Leeds, as you probably know, and a butcher familiar with the laws of kosher slaughtering comes only a few times a year. We were fortunate to have such a visitor just last week, in time for your visit and that of Mrs. Salomon and her son."

Mr. Lyon looked up from the meat platter with its tempting delights; after nearly a week on the road and eating a kosher traveler's fare of mainly vegetables and eggs and grains he was grateful to see food more to his liking. But the mention of a son almost made him lose his appetite. Had the uncomfortable journey been unnecessary, after all?

"I did not realize that Mrs. Salomon's son is in Leeds," said Mr. Lyon, doing his best to mask his irritation. "Did he accompany her on the ocean journey, or does he now live in your town?"

"They traveled together. I cannot imagine that Leeds would hold much attraction for a young man like Mr. David Salomon. He is musically inclined."

Mr. Deare made no attempt to mask *his* apparent irritation with Mr. Salomon, although he did not elaborate upon how, exactly, the young man had managed to offend him in such a short amount of time. However, it seemed that Mrs. Deare had not taken a similar offense, since she turned to the two young ladies and said, "Mr. Salomon is a composer, as well as an accomplished musician. I believe he was quite sought after in New York. He has graciously agreed to perform at a musical evening arranged by the Leeds Musical Society. I have arranged for all of us to attend, if, of course, you wish to go."

The last comment was directed to Mr. Lyon and Mr. Franks, who both immediately asserted that they were delighted with the idea. Although neither man was particularly musical, a refusal on the part of the London visitors might be interpreted as looking down upon provincial entertainments and they had no wish to possibly offend their hosts.

Neither Mrs. Salomon nor her son made an appearance at the nuncheon that had been prepared for the newcomers, and so the pleasure of making their acquaintance had to be delayed. The visitors from London decided that a rest after their long journey would be the wisest course of action and retired to their rooms. But sleep eluded two of them. Rebecca therefore took up her sketchbook, while Harriet went to explore the Deares' library. When she returned a short while later she brought with her two volumes, with the intention of reading aloud from one of them.

"I have found a book written in America," said Harriet, showing the first volume to her friend.

"*Kelroy*, a Novel by a Lady of Pennsylvania," Rebecca read out loud, studying the book's title page. "Do you suppose Mrs. Salomon brought it with her?"

"I cannot see how it could otherwise have appeared in this house. The only other book of interest is this one — *Pride and Prejudice*. It is a new novel by the author of *Sense and Sensibility*."

"I suppose, then, there will be no castles or bandits," said Rebecca. "Kelroy sounds like the name of a castle, does it not?" she added hopefully.

"Yes, though I do not know how many castles there are in America."

"Well, perhaps Mr. Kelroy's fortune has been stolen by a wicked uncle and so he has gone to America to make a new fortune, so that one day he can return to England and reclaim his ancestral home."

"Really, Rebecca, you should write a book yourself one day."

"Perhaps I shall. I often think it must be much easier to paint a story with words than tell one with paint."

Rebecca returned to her drawing, and Harriet began to read. Although there were no castles or bandits in the novel *Kelroy*, the story about doomed love was of sufficient interest to make the time pass quickly and they were amazed when Perl appeared in the room and began to scold them for not having changed their frocks for dinner.

"I cannot be in two places at once," Perl good-naturedly grumbled as she went to the wardrobe where she earlier had hung up the girls' dresses, to select what they would wear that night. "I am sure that Mrs. Lyon would have wanted me to help with the preparation of this evening's meal, rather than leave everything to a strange cook, so I cannot be blamed for your tardiness."

Fortunately, Perl's nimble fingers were expert at doing up buttons and tying bows. And since neither young lady was of an age to request an elaborate dressing of her hair, Rebecca and Harriet appeared in the drawing room in time to note that they were not the last of the guests to arrive.

Mrs. Deare, who knew that her husband disliked being kept waiting for his meal, gave the girls a grateful glance. But her eyes kept flitting from the door to where Mr. Deare was conversing with Mr. Lyon and Mr. Franks. When she saw her husband glance surreptitiously at the mantelpiece, where a clock was chiming the hour, she said, "I'll go see if Mrs. Salomon needs help."

"That will not be necessary, Mrs. Deare," said a pleasant voice, and all eyes turned to the doorway, where a handsome woman dressed in an elegant lavender silk gown—lavender being the color worn when a woman was in half-mourning, according to the non-Jewish world's traditions—was standing. Beside her was a young man, also striking in appearance, who lent the woman his arm as the pair floated into the room.

"I trust I have not kept you and your guests waiting too long," the woman continued. "But I was so engrossed in the pamphlet you lent me, Mr. Deare, the one about mechanical science on the factory floor, that I quite lost track of the time. Of course, I did not understand much of what I read, so please do not quiz me. But I do believe a person should try to improve their mind, even when they have reached my age and sad station in life."

She paused in her recital. Illuminated as she was by the soft candlelight that showed off to perfection the still rosy bloom of her cheeks and the sparkle of her deep blue eyes, the woman was, Rebecca thought, anything but the picture of a middle-aged widow mourning the death of the husband of her youth.

"This is Mrs. Salomon," Mrs. Deare said to the newcomers, apparently too in awe of her guest to formulate a proper introduction. "And Mr. David Salomon, her son."

The mother nodded to the group, while the son gave a short bow. Then, accompanied by Mrs. Deare, they glided into the dining room, while the others followed. Rebecca found herself both attracted and repelled by the older woman, who, upon further inspection, reminded her of a deposed queen holding court in some provincial hamlet where a few loyal subjects danced attendance upon her royal person.

"It was so good of all of you to come," Mrs. Salomon beamed at the party from London, when they were all seated around the table. "I feel quite overwhelmed by this attention, especially since it has turned out to be so unnecessary. My dear David was able to make the trip after all."

"I wonder that you did not think it necessary to apprise Mr. Melamed of that fact," said Mr. Lyon, with uncustomary bluntness.

Mrs. Salomon leaned back in her chair and smiled. "Ah, but then you would not have seen Leeds, Mr. Lyon. As a person of science and culture, I am sure you would not have wished to miss seeing Leeds. Why, I am quite convinced, after reading that pamphlet, that Leeds, with its steam engines and moveable bobbins, is quite the eighth wonder of the world."

Rebecca noticed that Mr. David Salomon was attempting to hide a smile by taking a sip from his wine goblet. However, she was not sure if he was silently laughing at the provincial pride of people like Mr. Deare or the overdone worldliness of his mother who had, after all, been living in New York for many years — and New York was most certainly not London!

"Yet we citizens of Leeds are not so wondrous that we are insensible of the honor of having Mr. Salomon perform for us," said Mrs. Deare, whose simple, open nature made her immune to ironic barbs, whether intended or not. "Have you decided upon the program yet, Mr. Salomon?"

Before the young man could reply, Mr. Lyon voiced a disturbing thought that had just occurred to him. "Are you not in mourning for your father, Mr. Salomon? Is a musical concert appropriate at such a time?"

"It would not be appropriate for me to attend a concert until the year of mourning has come to an end," David Salomon replied. "But since music is my profession, I am allowed to teach and perform. Otherwise, I would be left without a way to earn my livelihood, and I have no wish to become a burden on the communal coffers."

"Of course, there is no real danger of that! David does not have to sing for his supper," Mrs. Salomon quickly interjected. "Fortunately, Mr. Salomon left us very comfortably off. But it is the American way for even a gentleman to work at some profession, and so David insists on teaching and performing, even though he really should be at work composing. That is his real genius! They called him another Beethoven in New York. Have you the notice with you, David? I am sure Mrs. Deare would like to see it."

"No, Mother," Mr. Salomon said, smiling. "I am not in the habit of carrying my reviews upon my person."

"It is his one fault," Mrs. Salomon whispered loudly to Mrs. Deare. "He is much too modest."

"You will perform one of your own compositions at the concert, won't you, Mr. Salomon?" Mrs. Deare gushed. "It would be such an honor — a premiere in Leeds!"

Mr. Salomon bowed in her direction. "I hope to be able to gratify your request."

"He is so patient," said Mrs. Salomon. "He has been working with your Leeds musicians for three days now and still ..." She raised her napkin to her lips, as though to stop any uncharitable words from slipping into the conversation. "But miracles do still occur, do they not? And David is such an expert teacher that I am sure that the fellow who calls himself a pianoforte player will finally get the notes right."

"What instrument do you play?" asked Mr. Franks.

"In concert, the violin," replied the young man. "I am qualified to teach most stringed instruments, including the harp and the pianoforte."

"It is a pity we cannot convince you to remain in Leeds, Mrs. Salomon," said Mrs. Deare. "You and your son would be such ornaments for our little town."

"That is so very kind of you to say so. But surely even you would agree that it would be a crime to bury a person with such talent in a place like Leeds.

Even New York was not worthy of his accomplishments. That is why we have returned to England. London is the place for a composer like David. And after we have conquered London ... Vienna, Bonn, Paris ..."

"There is a war going on," Mr. Lyon interrupted, rather ungraciously. "But if you do conquer Paris, I am sure General Wellington and all England will be much obliged."

Mrs. Salomon was superbly unruffled by the comment. Indeed, she beamed benevolently at Mr. Lyon, as though he were a child too small to properly understand the great matters of the world. "The sonata is more powerful than the sword, Mr. Lyon. Paris will welcome us, just as London will. You'll see."

"Well, she certainly does not lack confidence," Mr. Franks commented, after the party had returned to their respective rooms for the night.

"Too much, for my taste," replied Mr. Lyon. "I wonder if her son is as good as she claims."

"We shall soon find out. He seems to be a nice enough fellow. A bit quiet, but that's not a fault."

"Why could they not have sent word that he was able to escort his mother to London? It would have saved us so much inconvenience and expense."

"Really, Lyon, can you imagine a woman like Mrs. Salomon slinking into London unnoticed? A woman like that requires a grand entrance, a stage full of people to attend her."

"I only hope she does not intend to rent rooms in Devonshire Square. Mrs. Lyon and she will not get along."

"Bury Street will be her objective, if I am not mistaken."

"Bury Street?"

"Come now, did you not notice that moment of disappointment when she saw that only you and I — two happily married men — were there to greet her?"

"Who was she expecting to see, the Prince Regent?"

"She was expecting to see Ezra Melamed."

Mr. Lyon looked at his friend with amazement, and then he began to grin. "So that was her plan! To ensnare poor Melamed before they even got to London! You astound me, Franks. How did you pounce upon the plot so quickly?"

"I cannot take the credit," said Mr. Franks, laughing. "Mrs. Franks mentioned something, before we left. Women understand these things better than we men do."

CHAPTER IV

THE NEXT DAY Mr. Franks proposed an outing to see the new locomotive, and Mr. Deare heartily agreed to the idea.

"You don't have that in London, I dare say," he said, unabashedly proclaiming his pride in his city. "There are also some factories on the outskirts of town that visitors find interesting. Some are four and even five stories high and the windows are lit up half the night. It's quite a sight to see."

"It's a new world," said Mr. Franks with enthusiasm, happy to find a congenial companion in Mr. Deare, who by profession was a cabinet maker who specialized in the production of metamorphic furniture. Mr. Deare's chosen work was not something new—for years clever craftsman had been transforming chairs into day beds or library steps with a few well-placed hinges and screws, as well as hiding secret compartments within tables and cupboards—but the interest in new inventions that the two men possessed formed an instant bridge of friendship between them and soon they were engaged in lively conversation. That left Mr. Lyon to perform the role of convivial chaperon to the two young ladies, which he accomplished by promising some time for shopping after they had seen the locomotive machine.

Martin Roth was thinking a thought similar to that of Mr. Franks as he stood on a hill overlooking the long strip of rail that joined the Middleton collieries and Leeds. At the moment, the landscape that stretched before him was empty of mechanical interest. But the increasing number of people clambering up to the hilly vantage point—some by carriage and some on foot, and all of them eager to see "the new world" that was embodied in the new machine—told him that soon the show would begin.

"Martin," a familiar voice whispered in his ear.

"What are you doing here?" the young man replied, without bothering to look at the speaker.

"Is that any way to greet an elder brother?"

"It's my way. From now on I do things my way."

Nathan Roth, a young man of twenty-six or twenty-seven, gave a low laugh. "You will find such an approach to life quite useful, now that Father has decided to disinherit the two of us."

Martin turned to face his brother. Nathan was the taller of the two and, crowned as he was by auburn-colored locks, the more striking in appearance. To look into Nathan's steely blue eyes, Martin had to look up at his elder brother, which was a thing that he no longer cared to do. But his brother's news was too distressing to pretend that he was unconcerned. "I thought you were going to fix things, obtain his forgiveness."

Nathan shrugged. "You know how Father is. One cannot reason with him when it comes to certain topics." He paused for a moment, to survey the crowd. "I thought you should know, before it becomes public knowledge."

"Much obliged, but you could have sent a letter. It would have been cheaper."

"Yes, but you might have sent a reply to London, which would have been a waste of good lucre since it wouldn't have found me."

"Why not? Have you given up your rooms?"

"Don't fence with me, Martin. You know why I am here. I haven't more in the world than what I am presently carrying on my person, so if you will not let me lodge with you, I shall have to make my bed on this hill. It is a charming enough spot, as hillsides go, but ..."

Nathan's voice trailed off, and Martin looked to see what had attracted the attention of his older brother. Standing to one side of the crowd was a party from London that he recognized, since he had been a member of the Great Synagogue before his removal to Leeds. Martin raised his hat to Mr. Lyon and Mr. Franks, in acknowledgement of their similar gesture. He then bowed slightly in the direction of Mr. Deare, his employer, and hoped that Mr. Deare would not be too angry at his disappearing from the workshop for a few hours.

Nathan also acknowledged the other party from London, but under his breath he uttered a short, blunt expression of exasperation. In reply to his brother's questioning glance, he said, "I hoped that I had seen the last of them when I successfully eluded them at an inn along the way."

"What does it matter if they see you?"

"I would have preferred that none of Father's acquaintances knew I was here. We must do something, Martin. We must put our heads together and come up with a plan."

Martin groaned. "I want no more part in your plans."

"I can understand how you feel, dear brother, after what happened last year. But we are in a serious predicament. We simply cannot let Father make a new will."

Nathan would have said more if he had not noticed that his younger brother's attention had drifted down toward the line of rail. Indeed, almost everyone was looking in the direction of Middleton, where a cloud of dark smoke could be seen in the distance. The locomotive designed by Mr. Blenkinsop and Mr. Murray was approaching.

The excitement of the crowd mounted as the engine, pulling behind it some thirty wagons of coal, neared the lookout point, announcing its presence with more smoke and a fearsome racket. Some of the smaller children, terrified by the din, clung to their mother's pelisse and began to wail, their shrill voices adding to the electrifying sense of amazement and confusion. Older boys began to whoop and wave their hats in enthusiastic greeting of the ungainly mechanical monster, while some of the more somber gentlemen took out their pocket watches to time the engine's speed. Mr. Franks was one of these people, and he remarked to Mr. Deare, shouting over the noise, "It is not as fast as I thought it would go."

"It depends on the load the engine must haul, and there are four tons of coal in each of those wagons," replied Mr. Deare. "Even at three or four miles an hour, think of how much coal it can transport in a day."

Rebecca was also looking intently at the approaching machine. She had made a promise to her brother Joshua that she would draw him a sketch of the locomotive, and so she tried to fix the odd-looking contraption in her mind: *A large black cylinder resting on its side, held up by six large wheels (three on each side). Attached to the front of the cylinder is a long black chimney-like pipe reaching upward, like an arm raised in greeting.*

Yet even as she carefully observed what was going on around her, she also observed what was going on within her — the fact that she could not understand why sensible people were so excited about such a dirty and noisy thing. True, the locomotive might be practical and improving for people engaged in commerce and manufacturing. But it was not beautiful. Indeed, its scrawling black line of smoke and metal was in total opposition to the serene valley view daubed in soul-pleasing greens and browns. And although she was still young, she felt a pang of nostalgic regret for a fast-fading world that had never known such things as locomotives and factories lit up halfway through the night.

When the locomotive and its wagons had passed by, the crowd began to disperse. Mr. Deare escorted his visitors back to his coach, which was old-fashioned and therefore quite roomy and able to accommodate them all. In his desire to play the role of gracious host, he quite forgot about his errant assistant. But his departure was watched by the two Roth brothers, whose financial circumstances made walking back to town a necessity.

"I suppose you understand how that machine works," said Nathan, after a few minutes of silent walking had placed them in a part of the road where he could speak without fear of being overheard.

"I have my ideas," Martin replied. "They are keeping the details a secret. They do not want Boney to learn how it is done, I suppose."

"Would you say that the man that can invent a machine that can travel twice as fast would be able to sell his invention for a good-sized fortune?"

"Very likely. It would take a tidy sum to do the work, though. One fails many times before he succeeds when it comes to these inventions."

"It is a pity, then, that you have no desire to be reconciled with our father," said Nathan. "I myself have no ambitions, other than to live comfortably with as little effort as possible. But for someone like you, a lack of funds is a crime."

Nathan cheerfully swung his walking stick before him, as though tramping back to Leeds was the most delightful way to spend an afternoon. From the corner of his eye he could see that Martin was lost in bitter thought, a sight that made him smile.

The seed had been planted. Now all that was needed was to watch it grow.

David Salomon removed the gloves from his hands with regret. The room was too chilly for his taste — he still had not become accustomed to the dampness of the English weather — but if it was difficult to play the violin with stiff fingers it was impossible to play with gloves on.

Yet it was not just the weather that cast a gloomy chill on the room. He had offended Mr. Karl Grimm—the German-born player of the pianoforte who never hesitated to inform people that in his youth he had performed before almost all the crowned heads of Europe—by refusing to perform one of Mr. Grimm's compositions at the upcoming musical evening. A cold war had therefore arisen between the two men. Since the other players were afraid of Mr. Grimm, who had a quick temper that was often made even more caustic by too much drink, they were inclined to follow his lead in all things. And since David Salomon would soon be departing for London, there was even less incentive to bow to his requests.

But Mr. Salomon could be obstinate when it came to musical matters. And even though this was only Leeds, a provincial town hardly worthy of his notice, he was not about to give in to a drunken player long past his prime. He therefore took a place before the other musicians and said, "We will begin with Clementi, the Sonatina in G major."

Mr. Grimm shot the younger man a nasty look; it was his job to announce the order of the rehearsal and not some violin player, even if the violin player in question was providing the financial backing for the concert. But since his mouth was already feeling dry and his thoughts were on the refreshments waiting for him at the gin house, he decided that it was best to get the rehearsal over with as quickly as possible, rather than argue the point of honor. He did not wait, though, for a signal from Mr. Salomon to begin. *He* was ready and with a flourish he began to attack the keys.

Mr. Salomon did not try to stop the assault on the helpless instrument. He had to concede that the older man had agility and speed, but there was very little true musicality to be heard underneath the barrage of sound. He might have tried to instruct a younger person, someone who would listen and profit from his advice. With Mr. Grimm there could be no such interchange, and so he let Mr. Grimm have the first movement, and the second as well. It was the Rondo where he intended to make his stand — and astonish.

"Mr. Grimm, if you please," he said in the slight pause between the second and final movement. "I will play the lead here."

"You intend to take my place at the pianoforte, sir?"

"No, you will remain where you are — and accompany me."

"*I* will accompany *you*?"

"Yes."

Mr. Grimm rose from his seat and glared at the young man. "Where I come from, the violin player knows his place. And so do the Jews."

"Then go back there, sir, if you are nostalgic for the scenes of your youth. This is Leeds and I have assumed the financial responsibility for this concert. You will do as I say, or you will not play."

The other musicians held their breath, waiting for the outburst they were sure was about to ensue. What they could not know was the state of Mr. Grimm's pockets, which happened to be in a sadly diminished state. Since he had been counting on this performance to replenish the stock of coins, Mr. Grimm bowed sullenly to his opponent and said, "And you will discover that Leeds is not New York."

Again not waiting for the signal to begin, Mr. Grimm attacked the Rondo with his usual speed. This time, Mr. Salomon stopped him.

"I would like a slower tempo, sir."

"This is a Rondo, sir."

"I know."

"A Rondo is always played quickly."

"Tomorrow night the audience will hear something new."

Mr. Grimm slowed down his speed. It was evident from the sour expression on his face that he was not pleased.

"Even slower, Mr. Grimm."

"What?"

"Let me show you."

Mr. Salomon began to tap out a stately tempo with the back of his violin bow, oblivious to the surprised looks of the other musicians.

CHAPTER V

MR. DEARE FOUND that he so much enjoyed his London guests that he did not want to deprive himself of even an hour of their company. He therefore left his furniture workshop in the hands of his assistant, after warning Martin not to go off to see the locomotive again—at least not until the visitors had returned to London. Martin accepted the admonishment without complaint, and he was hard at work when his brother strolled into the workroom.

Nathan Roth had the true connoisseur's eye, even though he lacked the pocketbook that made the collecting of fine things a possibility. As he made a tour of the place he nodded his approval at the graceful pieces of furniture in various stages of manufacture. "Show me one of your designs, Martin. I am certain it will be the best."

Although Martin's instincts told him to maintain a frosty distance, the proud artisan in him gained the upper hand. He therefore led the way to a narrow table leaning against a wall, the sort that might be used as a stand for an elaborate flower arrangement or a small collection of curios.

"It turns into a tea table?" said Nathan.

"Of course, there's that," Martin replied, moving the table to a more central location so that he could take out the third, supporting leg from behind the table. He lifted up the top surface of the table and when it rested upon the supporting leg the rectangle was turned into a square, suitable for the placement of a full tea service and places for four guests. "Now, watch this."

Martin restored the table's top to its original position. Then he lifted a double layer of wood, which he again rested upon the back leg. A surface suitable for writing, including a leather blotting pad that had been attached to the walnut tabletop, was revealed.

"I suppose that somewhere you have hidden drawers for pen, ink, and paper," said Nathan, running his fingers over the surface. "Yes, I think that here ..." Placing both hands on either side of the table's back edge, he pressed down and released a hidden spring mechanism. A length of drawers of various sizes popped up from their hiding place. Nathan opened a few of the drawers, which were of course presently empty but would one day be filled with the writing implements and correspondence of the table's future owner. Then Nathan said, "This has been done before, if I am not mistaken. I am almost certain that I saw one of these at the home of Sir George Hampton."

"Perhaps you did. I did not say that a table with three uses was new."

"Have I missed something?"

"Yes," replied Martin, smiling.

For the next quarter of an hour Nathan examined every inch of the table. He could discover no more secrets hidden within the wood. "I give up," he said, genuinely pleased to be outsmarted by his younger brother. "What is the real secret of this piece?"

Martin removed one of the small drawers, placed his finger upon the bottom edge of the drawer's back and exerted a slight pressure. A thin interior compartment, which had been flawlessly concealed within the piece of wood, fell into his hand.

"One could hide a letter — a will, perhaps — or some jewels or coins inside this compartment, and no one would ever find it," said Martin, handing the thin box to his brother. "Unless," he added, "they were very, very lucky."

"This is clever," Nathan replied, admiring the trick. "Your talents are wasted in this honest enterprise."

Martin felt the heat rising to his cheeks. He took back the compartment and returned it to its place. "I learned my lesson, if you did not. I have no desire to end up on the gallows."

"We failed, because we were inexperienced. Now that you know how to construct this confounded furniture, we would know all the hiding places."

"I won't help you steal back more of your promissory notes, Nathan. Your gambling debts are your concern, not mine."

Martin lifted the table and put it back against the wall. By then his cheeks were burning red, but not from exertion. Whenever he thought back to the incident, he became overcome by shame and embarrassment. In those days, which really weren't so long ago, he had been in awe of his elder brother, who was so clever and so well-acquainted with the fashionable world. Martin was then too young to frequent the gambling dens that were like a second home to Nathan, but he eagerly drank in the stories that his brother told him — the thrill of fortunes won and lost and won again, all at the toss of the dice. Then there were the card tricks that Nathan had mastered, as well as the latest slang that made them both laugh. Martin could not imagine his brother ever doing anything that was seriously wrong, which is why when Nathan presented the idea of stealing back a promissory note he had been forced to give to a moneylender as a "lark," an adventure, Martin had believed him.

"It's really the moneylender who is the criminal," Nathan had assured his younger brother. "His rates of interest are exorbitant, much higher than what ought to be allowed. If we can get back the note and destroy it, we will be heroes."

Things turned out otherwise. The promissory note was not in the cupboard drawer where it was supposed to have been. While they were absorbed in rifling through the other drawers the moneylender appeared, armed with a pistol, and loudly raised the hue and cry.

There was only one way the moneylender could be persuaded to not press charges: Mr. Samson Roth, the widowed father of the two boys, had to pay back all the money Nathan owed, plus a hefty sum to soothe the distressed feelings of the aggrieved moneylender. Mr. Roth did it, to avoid the scandal, but he made his disgust known to his two sons. "And next time, I will let the two of you hang," he had told them.

Martin had believed him. His parents' marriage had not been a happy one and there had never been much affection between the father and his sons. After this incident there was even less. When Martin expressed an interest in leaving London and learning a profession, other than the one that his father was engaged in — buying and selling silk cloth for ladies' dresses — Mr. Samson Roth turned to Mr. Melamed. Mr. Melamed sent letters to his acquaintances. Mr. Deare replied that he needed an assistant who was clever with his hands — a quality that Martin possessed — and for the past year the young man had been happily employed in learning his new trade.

Nathan, however, had continued to place his faith in cards and dice. For a while, he won enough to live upon. Then the wheel turned, as it always must, and he tried to become reconciled with his father's affections and pocketbook. The meeting was poorly timed. The wheel of fortune had turned for the elder Mr. Roth as well, in the form of an unfortunate investment in some wormy timberland in Sweden and other misadventures. During the intended scene of reconciliation the incident with the moneylender was recalled, stormy words were exchanged, and the meeting ended with the promise that Mr. Roth was determined to make a new will, one which would disinherit both of his sons.

Surprisingly, this news had not unduly distressed the elder son, who now explained to Martin, "Brother, I wouldn't think of involving you in my gambling affairs, and I am surprised you think me such a dunderhead to even try. When I said earlier that I have come to Leeds with the intention of benefiting both of us, I meant it. And thanks to your ingenuity with this furniture, I think now I know how to do it. But if you truly have no wish to hear me out, I will be silent. Although it would be so easy to slip a will of our own — which would naturally be in our favor — into one of your clever hiding places, and then deliver the table to Father as a gift. No one would know about our will until after Father's death, when we would conveniently discover it and present it to the lawyers."

"We're not prophets, Nathan. A will has a date. How can we know how long Father will live? A will needs a signature, too."

"I'll take care of the signature. And we can add the date afterward. We just need the table. How much does this masterpiece of yours cost?"

Martin was silent, while a struggle raged inside him. Never before had his future looked so utterly inescapably grim. He knew that he would never find a place in his father's affections, but he had clung to the hope that if he one day proved his mettle his father would invest in his career as a solid business venture. He had so many ideas for new inventions coursing through his brain, ideas that he had hoped to one day be able to put to the test in the world of action and accomplishment. But all that took money. Without money there was no time to dream and sketch and tinker, no place to work, no means to purchase materials to experiment with, to throw away when the experiment failed, and purchase again for the next try.

Mr. Deare's workshop, which had felt so homey and satisfying an hour ago, seemed now to be a prison, looking at it as he now did through the despairing eyes of a disinherited son. He could see himself growing old and withered there, wasting his life thinking up ever more ingenious ways to hide a secret compartment for the amusement of idle noblemen. Instead of producing new things that would better the world, his life would be wasted in the production of clever, puerile tricks. The thought made him sick.

"Well, Martin? Are you with me?"

Martin turned and gazed at his brother's face — the charming smile, the sparkling eyes, a face that was a perfect lie — and the sight of that visage, and the sort of life it promised, made him feel even sicker.

"No, Nathan, I am not," he said rising from his chair and going to the door, which he opened for his brother. "I am staying in Leeds, and so is the table."

"Very well, I wish you luck."

Nathan walked out of the workroom, swinging his cane with a jaunty air as he disappeared down the street.

CHAPTER VI

REBECCA STARED UNHAPPILY at her reflection in the mirror. "I do wish we had known beforehand that there was going to be a concert. I would have brought my nicer hair ribbons with me."

Harriet, who was already dressed, pinned down another curl on the side of her friend's head. "I am surprised there was not more selection at the shop we visited this afternoon," she said, by way of consolation.

"It was not the fault of the selection, Harriet. I do not wish to speak disrespectfully about my father, but I do not think a man, even the most generous of men, can ever properly understand that a young lady can never have too many hair ribbons."

Rebecca sighed. Her father usually did not quibble over the price of a ribbon. But this afternoon, after he had learned that the ribbon was being bought specifically for the concert, he became unaccountably irritable and refused the purchase. She would therefore have to compensate for the loss with extra curls and she only hoped that she, who was from London, would not disgrace her city in front of the ladies of Leeds.

Fortunately, by the time they reached the concert hall Rebecca, who had never been to a public concert, was much too excited about the event to think about how she looked. Their party was seated with Mrs. Salomon, and so they had an excellent view of the stage, where the musical instruments had already been arranged. The evening promised to be a great financial success, since the hall was completely filled with ladies dressed in their finest gowns and jewels, accompanied by their husbands and sons, who were also smartly attired.

Rebecca thought to count the number of candles that illuminated the room—she had never seen so many before—but gave up when the musicians took their places. To her surprise, Mr. Salomon was not there. Since Mrs. Salomon did not appear to be perturbed by the absence of her son, Rebecca—who was a novice in the mysteries of the grand entrance—assumed that there was nothing seriously amiss.

The program began with the Clementi Sonatina, a piece that Rebecca was familiar with. Like most young ladies, she had been instructed in the art of the pianoforte; like many, if the real truth were to be told, she had given her instructors more grief than pleasure. It was not the fault of the young lady, of course, at least not in her opinion. In far too many compositions there were so many musical notes on a page that it was nearly impossible to keep track of them all; and during an especially difficult passage, composers did have a distressing tendency to change their minds about whether or not to flat the B or sharp the C.

Tonight, though, it was not she who must do battle with Mr. Clementi and his Sonatina. She was free to watch the pianoforte player, which she did with pleasure since she had never before seen ten human fingers fly about the keyboard at such an amazing speed.

During the brief interval between the second and final movement, she and Harriet whispered their thoughts about the playing so far, both agreeing that it was wonderfully quick and lively. Then the first notes of the Rondo were sounded. Rebecca turned with wonder at the slow rhythm of the opening notes. For a moment, she worried that the musician seated at the pianoforte had taken ill.

She was not alone. From the sound of the murmurings, it seemed that everyone in the audience feared that something had gone wrong. Mr. Grimm gave a quick glance in the direction of the ladies and gentlemen. Rebecca noticed that his lips began to curl into a sort of sardonic smile.

And then she heard it. A sweetly plaintive note, rising from somewhere in the darkness at the back of the stage—a sound that seemed to come from a place that was not in this world. One heavenly note followed after another, and then the player began to slowly emerge from the shadows.

It was Mr. Salomon—for who else could it be playing the violin?—and yet it was not he. Rebecca could not find words to adequately explain the phenomenon. She thought she knew the Mr. Salomon that she had observed seated at the Deares' supper table: a young man with proper, albeit somewhat reserved manners, who might be considered handsome if a person's taste ran to chestnut-colored hair that was a little too long and a complexion that was a little too pale. This person standing on the stage seemed not to be a man, but music itself. His entire body bended and swayed in graceful movement, as each wistful note of the Rondo's melody was magnificently revealed by the unexpected slower tempo.

Gentlemen raised their quizzing glasses to their eyes and ladies fluttered their fans as the initial murmurings of disapproval gave way to excited whispers of pleasure. The whispering soon faded into silence as all were transported willingly by the elegant player to the Kingdom of Song. The sweet longing of the opening refrain was repeated, and then it dissolved into something more passionate—a dazzling crescendo, an outpouring of musical fire. One woman fainted, overcome by emotion. Another followed. They were left to revive on their own, without their vials of hartshorn, which remained in their reticules, for no one could tear away their eyes from the mesmerizing musician and his enchanted violin.

Then the final note sounded, poignant and plaintive.

Slowly, Mr. Salomon lowered his violin. Slowly, the ladies and gentlemen returned to life. Then there was music of a different kind, the thunderous applause and cheers of the crowd. Mr. Salomon acknowledged the adulation with a graceful bow and turned to salute the other players. Only one did not return the gesture, Mr. Grimm, whose face was a perfect reflection of his name.

"He must take care of the receipts and pay the players," said Mrs. Salomon, explaining her son's absence after the performance, as the group waited for their carriages. "A concert is much more than what you see on the stage."

"And that was exceptional," said Mr. Lyon, who wished to make up for his past abruptness now that he had seen with his own eyes that David Salomon was a true artist.

"I think I liked Mr. Salomon's own composition the best," said Rebecca.

"Yes, it is wonderful," replied Mrs. Salomon. "Of course, that piano player made a muddle of the Adagio, but what can one do? I don't think too many people noticed."

"Is the score available for purchase?" asked Harriet.

"That is one of the business matters we must apply ourselves to when we reach London, finding a publisher."

"I assume Mr. Melamed will be able to help you with that," said Mr. Franks.

Mrs. Salomon smiled. "Do you think so? It would be wonderful if David could receive help with establishing himself. He is quite clever at business, not at all like his mother in that area, but I begrudge every mundane act that takes him away from his art."

Their carriages arrived and soon they were on their way to the Deares' home, for the final night before the entire party's return to London.

A man dressed in shabby clothes watched them go, and then he turned into the dark alleyway. He already knew that there was a back entrance to the building—he had scouted out the area before the concert—and he correctly surmised that at the present hour the entrance would be unattended. He entered the building and noiselessly slipped down a corridor which led to a still brightly-lit room. Inside the room, the treasurer of the Leeds Musical Society, Mr. Miller, was counting out the proceeds of the concert's ticket sales. The shabbily dressed man did not enter the room. Instead, he found a spot where he could see and hear without being seen or heard himself.

"A very successful evening, Mr. Salomon," remarked Mr. Miller, as he straightened the columns of shiny coins. "Should your path ever bring you back to Leeds, you will be very welcome, I am sure."

David Salomon glanced at the other musicians. Despite the concert's success, it seemed that the treasurer's sentiment was a minority opinion. Yet he knew that, as the organizer of the evening, he should end the venture with a few words of praise for each of the musicians. Therefore, as each man stepped forward to receive his pay he forced himself to recall some musical phrase that the player had executed well.

When it was the turn of Mr. Grimm to receive his money, Mr. Salomon hesitated. The animosity between them had been too bitter to be sweetened by a few meaningless words. He therefore said, "If we should meet again, sir, I hope it will be a more agreeable experience for both of us."

Mr. Grimm pocketed his money and placed his hat on his greying head. "I very much hope there will not be a second meeting, Mr. Salomon. I was brought up to always remember that the player is the faithful servant of the composer. He must never trample upon a composition's intended tempo just to make a shameless exhibition of himself—and make a few foolish women faint. Good night, sir."

Mr. Salomon watched the pianoforte player leave the room, and he too hoped it would be the last time he would set eyes on the man. Then it was his turn to take possession of his money.

"Can we lock up the building, Mr. Salomon?" Mr. Miller inquired. "Have you got everything?"

The young man realized that he had left his music in his dressing room and he went to retrieve the manuscript. It was then that the man keeping a silent watch saw his chance, and he followed Mr. Salomon down the dimly lit passageway.

The pages of music were still sitting where they had been left. Mr. Salomon was in the act of picking them up when he happened to glance in the mirror and saw, to his surprise, that there was another man in the room.

"Don't pretend you don't know me," said the man, quietly closing the door.

At first, David Salomon was about to protest that he did not know the wreck of a man that was confronting him. But the voice, with its American accent, was strangely familiar, as was the scar on the man's upper lip.

"Jonas?" he said, finally. "Jonas Street?"

"So you do remember me."

"What are you doing in Leeds?"

"What do you think, Davey?"

"My father is dead, Jonas."

"And ain't that just too bad. I was right sorry to miss the funeral. I've never seen a man go to his grave all dressed up in furs."

"I don't know what you're talking about."

"I think you do, Davey. Where are they, boy? Did you sell them? Is that how you and that mother of yours managed to slip out of New York without paying me for my work trapping them? Those furs were top quality. You must have gotten a pretty penny for them."

Before Mr. Salomon could reply, Mr. Miller opened the door and entered the room. "It is getting late, Mr. Salomon," said the treasurer. "Have you found what you were looking for?"

Mr. Miller then noticed the other man, regarding the stranger with a mixture of surprise and distaste.

"I believe he has mistaken his way," said Mr. Salomon. "If you would be so good as to show him to the door, I will follow in a few minutes."

Mr. Miller nodded and said, "This way, if you please."

"I'll see you in London, Davey," Jonas said, before being shoved through the door. "And remember me to your mother. Tell her I'll see her, too."

CHAPTER VII

THE NEXT MORNING brought with it a sky that was grey and dreary.

"I do hope it will not rain," said Mrs. Deare, glancing anxiously up at the dark clouds, while the coachmen loaded the trunks on top of the two carriages. With her own hands she placed in the hired carriage a picnic hamper filled with good food, so they would have nourishing, kosher meals while on the road.

Then it was time to say goodbye. While the guests were thanking their hosts for their hospitality and their hosts were thanking their guests for such an enjoyable time there was a sudden moment of confusion. In London, Mr. Lyon and Mr. Franks had reckoned on there being only six passengers traveling during the trip home. This time the two gentlemen would travel in the hired coach, since it was the less comfortable of the two, and Harriet and Rebecca would switch places as the third passenger. Mrs. Salomon was to have Mr. Melamed's coach, with Perl in attendance, and one of the young ladies as the third passenger in that vehicle. But despite the excellence of this arrangement, an unforeseen difficulty had arisen: There was no room for Mr. Salomon in either carriage.

As the gentlemen were discussing the problem, Mrs. Salomon solved it in her own way. "Come, David, help me into the carriage," she said, standing before the one belonging to Mr. Melamed. Once inside, she grasped her son's hand and pulled him inside, too. "Perl, you will come with us, and be quick about it. Coachman, close the door and you be quick, too."

The carriage set off before the rest of the group fully realized what had happened.

Mr. Lyon could think of several things he might have wanted to say, as Mr. Melamed's carriage disappeared around the corner, but since he was a gentleman he restrained his tongue and said nothing. Instead, he nodded toward the hired carriage and said to his daughter, "You and Harriet must share the third seat. There is no other way."

Thankfully, both of the young ladies were slim. Yet they were not made of air and so it was impossible for the two of them to sit comfortably on a seat that had been designed for just one. Somehow, though, they all managed to squeeze into the carriage. After a cheerful word from Mr. Franks, which lightened the gloom, they became determined to make the best of an uncomfortable situation.

Now that their guests were gone, Mr. and Mrs. Deare returned to their normal routine. For Mrs. Deare that meant giving her housemaid and cook their instructions; afterward, she sat down at her desk to write a long letter to her sister, for it is always a pleasurable experience to share pleasant news with people we love—and the week spent in the company of Mrs. Salomon and her son had been pleasant, indeed. For Mr. Deare, it meant exchanging his good coat for his everyday one and going to his place of business.

He arrived at the workshop early and began his morning by taking a look at the orders book. Having satisfied himself that all was as it should be there, he next took out his money box. To his surprise, it felt strangely light. The reason for this state of affairs was soon discovered. The lock had been forced and the box was empty.

At that moment, Martin entered the room.

Mr. Deare showed him the empty box. "Can you explain this, sir?"

Martin, who had turned pale at the sight of the empty box, thought he could. He was almost certain that Nathan had repaid his hospitality by breaking into the workroom and stealing the money. But he could not be the one to accuse his brother.

"I cannot, Mr. Deare. If you are willing to forgo an explanation, I will repay you the amount that has been taken."

"If you cannot provide me with an explanation, sir, you must consider yourself no longer in my employment."

"I understand, Mr. Deare. If you please, write up the promissory note and I will sign it."

Mr. Deare wrote up the note and pushed it and a pen in the young man's direction. Martin glanced down at the sum—fifty pounds—and tried to fight back the tears that were starting to form in his eyes. Fifty pounds was a full year's salary for him, provided that he could find skilled work. It would take him many years to pay back such a sum.

He signed his name to the note and walked out of the workroom.

The minute after the door closed, Mr. Deare regretted the hastiness of the transaction. He had liked Martin. Perhaps if he had not been so abrupt, the young man would have been more willing to confide in him. Yet it was certain that Martin had known something about the theft, otherwise he would not have responded as he did.

Mr. Deare sadly shook his head. Then he took out another sheet of paper. He would write to Mr. Melamed, who had recommended the young man, and enclose the promissory note, with his compliments. Mr. Melamed could afford to hold such a note until the young man found the means to repay his debt. Mr. Deare could not.

While Mr. Deare was composing his letter to Mr. Melamed, the rain began to fall. By the afternoon the road had turned into a mess of mud. The horses pulling the hired carriage of the travelers returning to London did their best to struggle onward, but their valiant attempt was not helped by the extra weight within the carriage and the extra baggage loaded on top. It seemed to the now dispirited party that their pace had slowed to a crawl, and that things could not get worse. They did. The horses unknowingly drew the carriage into a hole that was so deep that they could not pull it out.

The coachman, who had jumped down from his perch to try to encourage the horses, gave up and came to the carriage window.

"The weight is too much for the horses, sir," he said, looking from one gentleman to the other.

"What shall we do?" asked Mr. Lyon.

"We must unload either some of the passengers or some of the trunks."

"And leave them behind?"

"It's either that or we stay here until the weather clears and this hole dries out. That could take days."

The two gentlemen climbed out of the coach and gazed up at the roof, where the trunks were stored.

"Lyon, are any of those trunks yours?" asked Mr. Franks.

"No."

"They must all belong to Mrs. Salomon and her son, for I don't see any of mine either. The coachmen must have loaded our trunks onto the other carriage."

"This poses a serious problem," said Mr. Lyon, pulling the capes of his overcoat closer about his neck, in a vain attempt to shield his person from the pouring rain. "If the trunks were ours, we could say what to unload. We cannot give away what does not belong to us."

"What can we do?"

"Shouldn't there be a Royal Mail Coach?" Mr. Lyon asked the coachman.

"There might be."

"We must wait, then."

Rebecca was not sure how long they waited on that forlorn and rain-drenched road, but she was certain that it must have been a very long time. If the day had been fine, she and Harriet could have climbed down from their carriage and gone for a stroll outside. Then again, if the day had been fine, they would not have found themselves in this predicament.

Finally, they heard the blast of a coachman's horn in the distance, and never did a horn sound sweeter. A few minutes later the horses of the Royal Mail Coach came lumbering down the road. Fortunately, the coachman was a jolly fellow who thought that stranded carriages were a fine adventure. But since he, himself, had to travel according to a strict timetable, his friendly offer of assistance was tempered by a true need to be on his way.

"There is one unoccupied seat, an outside seat on the top," he called out to the stranded travelers, after he had been apprised of the situation. "Two of your trunks can go above and one can go below."

"That should be enough," said their coachman, who hurried off to start removing the luggage.

Both Mr. Lyon and Mr. Franks looked up at the travelers seated on the outside seats. Their mournful faces and shivering, rain-drenched bodies told them all they needed to know about the comforts of that mode of travel.

There was an uneasy moment of silence. When it looked like it would remain unbroken, Mr. Lyon said, "I'll take the mail coach."

If Mr. Lyon hoped that Mr. Franks would insist on *his* traveling on the outside seat, exposed to the stormy weather, those hopes were not fulfilled. After he gave Rebecca a quick kiss on her cheek, Mr. Lyon was hoisted up to the roof of the carriage by the coachmen, and the Royal Mail's coachman climbed back onto his perch.

"Wait!" Rebecca shouted. She ran to her father and handed him the picnic basket so that at least he would have kosher food for the journey, for in their hurry they had forgotten to ask if the Royal Mail Coach would be traveling along the same route.

"Thank you, Rebecca. I'll ..."

She could not hear her father's last words, since his coach had set off. She could only wave goodbye to his forlorn figure, which was clutching with one hand the basket and with the other hand hanging on for dear life to the coach's roof. And all the while the rain continued to pour down.

"I shall never forgive her. Never!" Mrs. Lyon placed a hot brick under the covers, at the foot of the bed where Mr. Lyon was lying in a feverish state. "To leave you stranded on the road like that, while she and her son traveled comfortably and snugly in Mr. Melamed's coach—I don't care if she is a widow, that was no way to behave."

Mr. Lyon was in too weakened a state to reply, and so Mrs. Lyon was free to continue to express her anger as she fussed about the sick room.

The travelers had eventually all arrived home safely, thanks to the great kindness of the One Above, but it was doubtful that any of them would look back upon the experience with fondness. Mr. Lyon, as mentioned, had developed an ague as a result of that ride in the rain. Neither the Franks nor Rebecca had been able to enjoy their ride, since all of them were thinking of Mr. Lyon. As for their meals, Rebecca was sure she would never be able to look at another egg again, no matter how it was cooked. Even Perl, who should have enjoyed her journey since her coach was the most comfortable, had fumed all the way to London, speaking to Mrs. Salomon only when she absolutely must make a reply.

"And to think that she has not even bothered to inquire after your health," Mrs. Lyon continued, fluffing up the pillows on the sickbed for the dozenth time. "She could have at least left her card. And I know what you are thinking, Mr. Lyon. It is true that her son did call upon us and he did convey his mother's regards. I have no quarrel with Mr. Salomon, at least not about that. But I shall not invite them to dinner, so do not try to convince me."

Actually, Mr. Lyon was in no state to convince anyone of anything, since in addition to gaining a fever he had lost his voice. And if Mrs. Lyon thought that Mrs. Salomon was distressed by the lack of an invitation to dine at Devonshire Square, she was mistaken. The silver platter that sat in the entry hall of the rooms that Mrs. Salomon had rented was overflowing with visiting cards and invitations. Everyone, it seemed, wished to make the acquaintance of the newcomers to London's Jewish community.

However, there was one card that Mrs. Salomon would rather have not received, which arrived a few weeks after their arrival in London.

"David, did you meet a man named Jonas Street in Leeds?" she asked, carrying the scribbled, nearly illegible note into the library.

"I did. He came round after the concert."

"You should have told me."

"I did not want to distress you. I know how painful any remembrance of Father and New York must still be."

"Nonsense. It is you, David, who must not be distressed. But I am surprised you remember him. You were still a boy when he went out to Michigan."

"He was always a colorful figure."

"I suppose that is one way to describe him." Mrs. Salomon took another look at the note. "Did he say why he has come to England?"

"If I understood him correctly, he claims that Father owed him payment for some furs, and so he has followed us across the ocean to get his money. I assume he is mistaken. The lawyer did settle all of Father's accounts before we left New York, didn't he?"

"Of course he did."

"Then if Jonas comes here and tries to make trouble, I will show him the receipt for the money we gave him and send him on his way. By the way, where did you put the receipt book? I don't think I have seen it since we left New York."

"It must be in one of the trunks that haven't yet been unpacked," said Mrs. Salomon.

"Tell the servants to take care of it today. We do not want Jonas popping up like a jack-in-the-box at an inconvenient moment and finding us unprepared, at least not if we wish to establish ourselves in London society."

If Mr. Salomon had hoped to assuage his mother's anxiety with his words, the attempt did not succeed. Mrs. Salomon nervously fingered the fur trim of the morning jacket she wore over her muslin dress while she pondered the problem of Jonas Street. When she did come to a decision, her usual confidence returned.

"David, let me speak to Jonas when he calls. I know you were friendly with him when you were a child, but that was a long time ago and the American frontier changes a man."

"You forget, Mother, that I saw him in Leeds. I saw what he has become."

"You saw only the outer shell, what a harsh climate and rough living can do to a person's face and skin. I am speaking of the inner changes that occur when a man lives in the forest amongst the animals and the Indians for too many years."

"That is all the more reason why I should be the one to speak with Jonas and not you."

Mrs. Salomon shook her head. "I fought to protect you from that world, so that you could cultivate your talent unsullied by the brutality of your father's business and the sordidness of his employees and acquaintances. I will continue to protect you, David. As long as there is breath in my body, you shall know nothing of the Jonas Streets of the world."

CHAPTER VIII

MRS. MIRIAM BAER had not yet made the acquaintance of Mrs. Salomon, since that lady was out whenever she called. Yet that unfortunate state of affairs had in no way diminished her hopes of making a match between Mrs. Salomon and Mr. Melamed. Indeed, she had been working behind the scenes to accomplish a meeting between the two people, which was supposed to have occurred the previous night. Therefore, when she saw that Mr. Melamed had entered the coffee house she was consumed by curiosity.

Since he had become a widower, Mr. Melamed had often taken solace in the comfortable surroundings of Baer's Coffee House, a kosher establishment located in the City on Sweeting's Alley that offered strong coffee and tasty food prepared by Asher and Miriam Baer, as well as interesting conversation provided by the merchants and financiers who treated the coffee house as a second home.

When Mrs. Baer saw that Mr. Melamed had taken his accustomed seat at the back of the room, she hurried over with a plate of freshly-made potato kugel, arriving at the table just ahead of her husband, who brought over a pot of coffee and a cup and saucer.

"Well, Mr. Melamed, you have outdone yourself this time," she said. "All of London can speak of nothing but your act of gallantry."

"Then it is strange that I am not aware of what you are referring to, Mrs. Baer."

"Why, I am referring to your lending your carriage to Mrs. Salomon and her son. It was so generous of you and done for such a good cause. I hear they are such fascinating people."

Mrs. Baer waited expectantly for Mr. Melamed's reaction. She did not expect him to gush—a man of his age and position would never fully reveal the secrets of his heart in public. Yet she had been arranging marriages for so many years that she was an expert at interpreting those tell-tale signs that signaled whether or not one party was interested in the other. She therefore felt confident that within the next minute or two she would know where things stood with Mr. Melamed.

That gentleman, for his part, was wishing, for the first time in his life, that he had walked past the coffee house without stopping. "I am glad to hear that you approve of them," he said, finally and without conviction.

This was not the response that Mrs. Baer had hoped for, but she did not lose heart. "I have not yet had the privilege of meeting Mrs. Salomon," she admitted, "so I cannot give *my* opinion."

"Since I am in the same position as you, Mrs. Baer, neither can I," replied Mr. Melamed, smiling for the first time.

"But ... last night ... Mrs. Sofer's dinner party ..."

"A pressing business matter at the last minute prevented me from attending."

"Oh," said Mrs. Baer, her crestfallen face speaking the volumes that her shocked-into-silence tongue could not. She and Mrs. Sofer had spent hours planning that dinner party, going over the guest list dozens of times. As people guided by the sound moral principles of the holy Torah, they could not just throw Mr. Melamed and Mrs. Salomon together at the dining table, even though their objective was matrimony. Instead, they had labored to bring together an interesting array of Jewish London's finest citizens, people who would provide the elegant setting where the widow and the widower could shine and admire each other's sterling qualities. Afterward, Mrs. Baer would take care of the rest.

"Mrs. Baer, shouldn't you be seeing to the roast beef?" said Mr. Baer, hoping to bring an end to the awkward moment of silence.

She took the hint, but did not leave without first giving her husband a look that said, "You must get to the bottom of this, Mr. Baer."

Mr. Melamed motioned for Mr. Baer to take a seat, which that worthy man did, being an expert in interpreting his wife's looks and smiles.

"I do not object to Mrs. Baer's wanting to marry me off," said Mr. Melamed. "But the situation is becoming intolerable. Granted, the vast majority of London's citizens have never heard of either me or Mrs. Salomon, and so when I am in Mayfair or Piccadilly I am safe. But I cannot walk about our small corner of the city without being the recipient of a multitude of unwanted winks and stares."

"Well, if everyone thinks it could be a match, perhaps there is something to it," said Mr. Baer, trying to be loyal to both his wife and his good friend.

"You heard what happened in Leeds?"

Mr. Baer shifted uneasily in his seat. "I may have heard something."

"Mr. Lyon has not yet fully recovered."

"I know. But you could hardly expect Mrs. Salomon to leave her son behind."

"Why not?"

"Well, they are strangers to England."

"And Miss Lyon and Miss Franks are accustomed to traveling the length of England alone?"

"Of course, the young ladies couldn't have been left behind."

"You see that, so why did neither Mrs. Salomon nor her son?"

"Really, Mr. Melamed, I think you are being unfair. There may be a reason for the lady's behavior. You should give her a chance to explain."

"I left my card this morning."

"At an hour when you knew that she would not be receiving visitors?"

Mr. Melamed laughed. "Your wife will never forgive me, I know."

"You will have to make the lady's acquaintance someday."

"In the meantime I have made the acquaintance of the son. He is a more sensible young man than I expected. Do any music publishers ever come into your coffee house?"

Mr. Baer glanced about the room, filling it with the memory of customers past. His regular clientele ran to more prosaic professions—cabinet makers, milliners, and the like. Yet there were also the infrequent customers, who came from all walks of life, including the arts. The shadowy image of a face began to dance tantalizingly before his eyes. "There is someone," he said slowly, "if I could only think of his name. Shall I call for Mrs. Baer? She'll know."

"No," said Mr. Melamed. "Please, let Mrs. Baer remain where she is. If the two of you do think of someone later, send me the name. If I can, I will help Mr. Salomon — for his sake."

Mrs. Baer did recall the name of the music publisher, but she did not send a messenger to Mr. Melamed's house on Bury Street. Instead, she ordered the driver of her hired carriage to take her to the residence of Mrs. Salomon.

"Tell Mrs. Salomon that I have a message from Mr. Melamed, if you please," she said to the housemaid.

When the housemaid returned, Mrs. Baer was admitted to the drawing room — at last! Mrs. Salomon warily greeted her. She did not recognize Mrs. Baer from her youth, since Mrs. Baer had grown up in Manchester and arrived in London after Mrs. Salomon had set sail for American shores. In addition, the lady of the house at first did not know how to correctly place this unknown woman socially. The visitor did not have the appearance of a servant, yet if she was not employed by Mr. Melamed why was she running errands for that gentleman?

The object of these wary musings relieved Mrs. Salomon of any further anxiety. "I am Mrs. Miriam

Baer," she announced, "matchmaker of London's Jewish community."

Mrs. Salomon relaxed and beamed back. Gesturing to her new friend to please take a seat beside her, she said, "Thank you for seeking me out. The kindness of you and your community quite overwhelms me. However, although someday I would like to remarry, I do not know if ... so soon ..."

Mrs. Salomon removed a handkerchief from her sleeve and dabbed her eyes.

"I understand," replied Mrs. Baer, not at all dismayed since she maintained her own private definitions of words such as "soon" and "later" and "perhaps." "I would not think of rushing you. That is why the message I bring is on another matter entirely."

Mrs. Salomon lowered her handkerchief. "Another matter?"

"I believe your son asked Mr. Melamed for advice about music publishers."

"David!" Mrs. Salomon exclaimed, the sunshine returning to her world. "Did he do that? I would not trouble Mr. Melamed for the world about our little domestic matters. But I am sure you know how impetuous young men can be, Mrs. Baer. My David is so anxious to make his way in the world. I hope Mr. Melamed did not take offense?"

"To the contrary, he is most eager to assist your son," said Mrs. Baer, exaggerating the true state of affairs, but doing so for what was in her eyes a worthy cause. "That is why he begged me to bring you this message, without delay. Mr. Herman Kimml is a very well-respected publisher of musical scores.

He has an establishment on Cornhill Street. It is not far from the clock-making shop of Mr. Lyon."

Mrs. Baer paused, realizing too late that she had unwittingly touched upon an awkward topic.

"Do not be distressed, Mrs. Baer," said the lady of the house, giving her guest's arm a gentle squeeze. "The people of your community have been so kind, yet I know there has been some talk about that unfortunate incident in Leeds. Could you, if you can spare the time, stay for a little while longer and hear my side of the story?"

Mrs. Baer assured the lady that she could.

"Of course, I do not expect that you will understand. Someone who has never experienced what I have ..." Mrs. Salomon raised the handkerchief to her eyes a second time.

"If the topic distresses *you*, perhaps another time would ..."

"No, please, I do so need to speak with someone. Will you have the patience to hear the sad tale of a heartbroken woman?"

Mrs. Baer assured the lady that she would.

"Have you ever, Mrs. Baer, seen an Indian — an American Indian?"

Mrs. Baer, who was about to settle comfortably into her chair, sprung back to attention at this unexpected development and said, "No, Mrs. Salomon, I have not."

"Have you ever heard ... I hesitate to even mention it ... have you ever heard what an American Indian does to a person who is unfortunate enough to fall into his bloodthirsty hands?"

"No," whispered an enthralled Mrs. Baer.

"He has a knife, Mrs. Baer, and with that knife he removes the scalp of his victim — all of it, the hair, the skin, everything. That is how he kills his quarry. That is how my late husband — my dear, dear husband — that is how he died, at the hands of an Indian who was supposed to be his honest guide and trusted companion. That is how my husband was repaid for his kindness and generosity!"

Mrs. Baer was too shocked to speak. When she recovered the use of her tongue, she asked, "Are there many Indians in New York, Mrs. Salomon? I never realized."

Mrs. Salomon gave the other woman a sharp look. Then she softened and said, "It did not happen in New York, Mrs. Baer. My husband's business was trapping and selling furs. Although we lived in New York, there were times when it was necessary for him to personally oversee the men who caught the animals out in the wilds of the American continent. He was murdered in the Territory of Michigan, far, far away from any semblance of civilization."

Enthralled as she was, a warning bell still went off in Mrs. Baer's head. "Did anyone see the ... the ..."

Mrs. Salomon understood her intention. "One of the trappers saw. He managed to save his own life, but not the life of my husband." The handkerchief returned to Mrs. Salomon's eyes a third time. "I try not to be bitter. I do try not to blame that man for not saving my husband from such a horrible death. And I try not to be afraid, Mrs. Baer. But when I close my eyes at night, I see that scene ... my poor husband, on his knees, at the mercy of that heartless savage. I see the knife, the ..."

"Oh, do stop, Mrs. Salomon! Please, do not distress yourself!"

"I am sorry. Do not pay attention to my anguish. More important to me is that you understand—that I regain your good opinion of me. Not that I deserve it, I know. I am ashamed of myself for what I did in Leeds. But sometimes I am so overcome by fear. I know, of course, there are no Indians in England. Yet when the fear comes over me, I quite lose my ability to reason. That is why I ordered the carriage away so quickly. I was suddenly so afraid, I could no longer think, except to think that I must get away, at once ... before ... before ... Oh, can you forgive me?"

"Of course, I can," replied Mrs. Baer. "And I will explain everything to Mr. and Mrs. Lyon. I am sure they will forgive you, too, once they understand."

"Yes, do explain to Mrs. Lyon," said Mrs. Salomon, without enthusiasm. Her warm smile returned, though, when she said, "And please do thank Mr. Melamed for his kindness to my son. I shall give David the message when I see him next."

Mrs. Salomon escorted her visitor to the front door. She was pleased to see that Mrs. Baer was hurrying in the direction of Bury Street and Mr. Melamed's rooms, and not toward Devonshire Square!

"Well done, Mother. It is you who should be on the stage and not me."

Mrs. Salomon turned to face her son, who had joined her in the front hall. "Listening in on private conversations does not become a person with your gifts and education, David."

"I had no intention of listening when I came to the drawing room door. But once there, I was as enthralled as your visitor. Who was she, by the way?"

"A foolish woman, but she could be useful. She is a matchmaker. You would not mind, would you, if I remarried? Not at once, of course, but in the future?"

"Of course not, Mother. It would relieve my mind immensely to know that you have someone to protect you from those Indians."

He laughed, and she laughed as well.

"I had to say something," she said, drying her eyes with her handkerchief. "I suppose it was rude of me to run off like that in Mr. Melamed's carriage, but the thought of having to travel all that distance and listen to the chattering nonsense of those two girls quite overpowered my sense of propriety."

"Still, it's not quite the thing for a person with your gifts and education to tell a lie, Mother."

"Touché. I promise to tell no more lies if you promise to not listen behind any more doors."

"Seriously, someone from New York might come here, someone who knows how Father really died."

"We'll worry about that then. Meanwhile, at least Jonas Street and the sob story he told the lawyer have been of some use."

The smile disappeared from Mr. Salomon's face. "We shouldn't laugh at Jonas. It must have been horrible for him to see that other trapper get scalped. I suppose it's no wonder that Jonas seems to be half out of his mind, after seeing a thing like that."

"Thankfully, we have nothing more to do with the Territory of Michigan," said Mrs. Salomon. "What did you come to the drawing room for, David? Did you wish to speak with me?"

"I asked the servants about the receipt book. They say that all of the trunks have been unpacked, and they haven't seen it."

"How very strange, I am almost certain I remember seeing it in one of the trunks before we left New York. But let us not worry about that now. Mr. Melamed has found a music publisher for you — a Mr. Kimml of Cornhill Street. If you hurry, there may still be time to call upon him today."

On Bury Street, Mrs. Baer concluded her tale and waited to see the reaction.

"That does put a different complexion on the incident," said Mr. Arthur Powell, a friend and business associate of Mr. Melamed. Mr. Powell had been seated in Mr. Melamed's library when Mrs. Baer called. Although Mr. Powell was not himself Jewish — he was the youngest son of Lord James Powell — he had come to the aid of London's Jewish community so many times that Mrs. Baer felt free to speak before him, with Mr. Melamed's permission, of course.

Unbeknownst to Mrs. Baer, Mr. Melamed had confided his misgivings about Mrs. Salomon to his friend, after he first heard about the incident in Leeds.

Mr. Powell, a widower himself and therefore the target of numerous matrimonial plots within his own social circle, had been the one to advise Mr. Melamed to absent himself from the Sofer dinner party, going so far as to provide a pressing business matter to discuss for the occasion. Never mind that the two men had spent an agreeable evening in Mr. Melamed's library playing chess, instead. It had prevented Mr. Melamed's name from being linked too closely to that of Mrs. Salomon too soon.

"Indians, well," Mr. Powell continued. "A woman would be easily frightened after something like that. I am not saying that I approve of her behavior in Leeds, but it does make it more understandable — and forgivable."

"Yes, I suppose it does," said Mr. Melamed, with reluctance. "Thank you, Mrs. Baer, for relaying the information."

Mrs. Baer had to content herself with that, for the moment. It was a small opening, to be sure, but she had worked wonders with little more than this before. Mr. Melamed must now think more kindly about Mrs. Salomon. Mrs. Salomon must be pleased by Mr. Melamed's having gone to the trouble of finding a music publisher for the lady's son. It never hurt for each party to think that the other one was more interested than they were — which was precisely why an experienced matchmaker was needed when it came to such delicate negotiations.

With that happy thought, she returned to Sweeting's Alley and the coffee shop to tell her husband the thrilling tale she had heard. By the end of the day the story of Mrs. Salomon and the Indians had traveled from Sweeting's Alley to the Great

Synagogue—and from there to the supper tables of almost every Jewish home. Along the way, at least in some versions of the story, Mrs. Salomon had been transported to Michigan and witnessed the terrifying incident with her own eyes. In others, it was she who had almost been scalped, and it was her son her rescued her in the nick of time. In all the variations Mrs. Salomon was declared a heroine of almost Biblical proportions, and the next day her calling card tray was once again filled to overflowing.

CHAPTER IX

"HOW DOES IT work?"

The Earl of Gravel Lane was out on one of his rare visits to a client — rare because he conducted most of his unfortunately illegal business from his establishment located near Petticoat Lane. He was accompanied by his second-in-command, General Well'ngone. It was this second person who had voiced the question that intrigued them both.

They were standing in the curio shop of Mr. Herbert Kimml, examining a lady's sewing box shaped in the form of a piano. The Earl of Gravel Lane had turned a small key and a musical tune had begun to play. Picking up the box to examine it from all sides, and still not finding an answer to General Well'ngone's question, the Earl graciously admitted that he had no idea how the thing worked.

"We can either leave it and accept it as one of life's more beautiful mysteries," said the Earl, "or we can smash it to pieces and try to discover the truth in that way."

The Earl smiled sweetly at the proprietor of the shop. This Mr. Kimml was the brother of the previously mentioned Mr. Herman Kimml, the publisher of musical scores. There was yet a third brother with a business establishment on Cornhill Street, Mr. Harold Kimml, who manufactured pianos.

Mr. Herbert Kimml looked with alarm at the sewing box, which was worth a great deal of money not only because of its graceful design and musical virtues, but because inside it was a complete set of sewing implements embellished with mother of pearl decoration.

Meanwhile, the Earl waited, the very picture of patience — albeit a picture from an earlier century. By virtue of necessity, his taste in clothing was dictated by what could be found in the more miserable second-hand establishments found on Petticoat Lane. Determined to turn that necessity into a virtue, he ignored the bland castoffs from his own era and selected the more extravagant fashions from the 1700s: satin coats trimmed with lace and richly embroidered waistcoats, which he topped off with a powdered wig. Of course, by the time these articles of clothing graced his still young person the satin was torn and stained, the lace was shredded to pieces, and the embroidered threads had lost their sheen. Yet he wore his rags proudly, and no one who knew him dared laugh.

In his own way, the Earl was an important man, since he headed one of the more successful rings of youthful thieves. It was also his way to avoid violence whenever he could. He therefore returned the exquisite sewing box to the counter, saying, as he did so, "My business is not a charity, Mr. Kimml. I performed a service for you. I expect to be paid for that service. Have you the money, sir?"

Mr. Kimml nervously fingered the folds of his cravat. "No, Earl, not at the moment. You know how young gentlemen are. They're fine ones when it comes to buying little presents for their young ladies, but when it comes time to pay they demand to receive the goods on credit."

"No, I do not know. Fortunately, in my line of business I do not deal with gentlemen," replied the Earl, removing his snuff box from his coat pocket and taking a pinch of the powdery stuff. After giving a sneeze, he said, "I will repeat my question. Do you have the money?"

"No."

The Earl turned to his companion. "General Well'ngone, what do you suggest we do?"

The General was a less imposing figure than the Earl, since he was a few years younger and therefore not much older than a child. Yet, he too was a picturesque denizen of London's streets, dressed as he was in an oversized military greatcoat, his costume crowned by a battered bicorne hat.

"Earl, won't you be having a birthday soon?"

"Possibly," replied the Earl. Since the young man had been orphaned at birth and grown up on the streets, where birthday celebrations were a rare event, he could not say for sure on what day he had been born. Yet, all men must be born on some day and so he said, this time with more conviction, "Yes, it is very possible. What of it?"

"Have you taken a fancy to this sewing box, sir?"

"It is a pretty trifle."

General Well'ngone picked up the sewing box and presented it to the Earl. "Please accept this little token of esteem with my compliments, Earl. May you live to be 120." Having bestowed upon his commander the traditional Jewish birthday greeting, for the two thieves were members of London's Jewish community, he turned to Mr. Kimml. "And you, sir, may have my credit."

The Earl of Gravel Lane and General Well'ngone strolled toward the door, with the sewing box. They knew they had no cause to worry that Mr. Kimml would stop them. If that gentleman had tried to do such a foolish thing, his triumph would have been transitory. The Earl would only have hired a gang of thieves who were expert at break-ins, and who would remove much more than one sewing box from the premises.

As they were leaving a gentleman entered the shop, Mr. Salomon. Not being familiar with the Earl and General Well'ngone, he openly showed his surprise at their appearance. The General considered repaying the stranger's rudeness by removing the gold watch from Mr. Salomon's pocket. But since the Earl was already out the door he let the opportunity—and the gold watch chain glinting in the light—slip by.

Mr. Salomon's puzzlement did not cease even after he was inside Mr. Kimml's shop. Glancing around at the assortment of work boxes, albums and other curios, he strongly suspected that he was in the wrong place.

Mr. Kimml, spying the violin case that the gentleman was holding in his hand, understood the mistake and quickly set about to correct it. "If I am not mistaken, sir, you are either looking for my older brother, Mr. Herman Kimml, publisher of fine music, or my younger brother, Mr. Harold Kimml, who manufactures fine pianos."

"Yes, I am looking for Mr. Herman Kimml. I understood his business was located on Cornhill Street."

"You understood correctly, sir. Allow me to introduce myself. I am Herbert Kimml and my shop of musical curios is here. If you cross the street and continue a few doors to your left, you will find the pianos manufactured by my brother; and I assure you, if you happen to be in the market for a new piano, that you will not find an instrument with a sweeter sound anywhere in England. As for my brother who publishes music, his shop is next door, but it is on the second floor, which is perhaps why you missed it. Let me show you the way."

Mr. Salomon protested that he did not wish to take the shop proprietor away from his business. Mr. Kimml protested just as energetically that it was no inconvenience at all, since his assistant could watch the shop for the few minutes he was gone. The assistant was duly called for and the two gentlemen left the shop.

"You are new to London, sir?"

"Yes," replied Mr. Salomon.

"You are a composer, as well as a musician?"

"Yes, I am."

"Could I be so bold as to ask you for your name? It is an impertinence to ask such a question, I know. But there is something in your face that tells me you will one day be famous. I should like to be able to tell my grandchildren that I, Herbert Kimml, was one of the first men in London to welcome you to our city."

Mr. Salomon bowed in acknowledgement of the compliment. True, his first impression of Mr. Kimml had been less than enthusiastic — Mr. Kimml's round face, mass of unruly curly brown hair that was now streaked with grey, and wide-eyed expression that suggested he was in a permanent state of childish, astonished delight rarely inspired admiration upon first acquaintance. But Mr. Salomon was now ready to view the shop owner in a more favorable light. "My name is David Salomon. And I am very pleased to make your acquaintance, Mr. Kimml."

"The pleasure is all mine, I assure you. And here we are."

Having already arrived on the upper floor, Mr. Herbert Kimml opened a door and motioned for Mr. Salomon to enter before him. Mr. Salomon was charmed by what he saw. Lining the walls of the airy and well-lit room were shelves of manuscripts ready for perusal and purchase. In the center of the room sat a spinet piano, where a shop assistant was performing a lively piece of music for two young ladies and their mother, who apparently approved since the matronly woman removed a coin from her reticule. The assistant, whose name was Mr. Tree, and whose tall, spindly body mirrored his name, placed the music in the woman's hands, took the coin and walked to the back of the room, where an elderly gentleman sat at a massive desk whose top was stacked high with mounds of manuscripts.

When the assistant bent down to speak to his employer, Mr. Herman Kimml raised an ear trumpet to his left ear. "Well, Mr. Tree? What is it?"

"Haydn. Sonata. G Major," Mr. Tree shouted into the horn.

Mr. Herman Kimml glanced down at the coin that Mr. Tree had placed on the desk, shoved it into a drawer, and waved an expression of thanks to the ladies. "*Con brio*! Please to remember that the Allegro must be lively, my lady, and both your daughters will be married by the end of the season!"

The two girls giggled and the mother smiled. While they made their departure, Mr. Salomon took the opportunity to ask his companion, "Your brother is deaf?"

"A tragedy for a man who loves music as much as he does. But in life we must accept the good with the bad, Mr. Salomon. You may still be too young to accept the truth of such a statement, yet it is true just the same."

"I suppose, then, there was no need for me to bring my violin."

"No, only your music."

Mr. Salomon removed a small roll of paper from his coat pocket. "I brought only one composition, a trio. I had hoped to play my other composition for Mr. Kimml."

"Well, let us show my brother the one that you have brought."

Mr. Salomon looked doubtful. The elder Mr. Kimml had hair that had turned white, but in every other way he closely resembled his younger brother, including the foolish-looking gaze, which, when coupled with the man's deafness, did not inspire confidence.

Mr. Herbert Kimml, seeing the young man's hesitation, reassured him, saying, "My brother is quick to understand a piece of music, sir. His eyes *hear* more than the ears of most people."

Mr. Salomon glanced about the music shop a second time. The furnishings were not extravagant, but they were certainly comfortable and gave an air of congenial prosperity. The manuscripts piled high upon the desk suggested that many other composers were seeking Mr. Kimml's patronage. And there was Mr. Tree, who was now flitting about the room like a driven leaf, putting musical scores back into their proper places, straightening chairs, and doing other little chores to make the room presentable for the next wave of customers. Yes, it seemed to be a prosperous place of business, and therefore worth a few minutes of Mr. Salomon's time.

After the introductions had been made, Mr. Herman Kimml perused the manuscript for a full quarter of an hour, tapping out the tempo with his left foot, while running his right hand along the surface of his desk, as if the table's edge was a pianoforte's keyboard. At certain points he nodded his approval, at others he shook his head and frowned — and Mr. Salomon watched it all with a mixture of apprehension and admiration.

At the end of the "recital," Mr. Kimml sat in thought for several minutes. Then he said, shouting slightly, "My compliments, sir. It is a very impressive sonata, for a young gentleman."

"Thank you," said Mr. Salomon with his normal tone of voice. Remembering the other man's deafness, he said again, this time more loudly, "Thank you!"

Mr. Herman Kimml waved his hand in response. He then returned his attention to a section of the sonata and began to shake his head. He lifted a pen as though wishing to write in a correction, but, changing his mind, he shook his head again and set down the pen.

"Yes, for a young man it is very impressive," the music publisher finally said. "But, and I beg your pardon for having to say so, there are many young gentlemen composing music at the present time. London is awash with music at the moment, and good music, too. Isn't that true, Mr. Tree?"

Mr. Tree shouted into the ear trumpet, "Very true, Mr. Kimml!"

"Does this mean you are not interested in publishing my music, sir?"

Mr. Kimml glanced enquiringly at Mr. Tree, who hurriedly wrote down what Mr. Salomon had said.

"I did not say that, Mr. Salomon," said Mr. Kimml, after he had read the note. "Before I can make a decision as to whether or not to invest in your career and offer my patronage, I must see more of your work. That is fair, I believe."

"Of course," replied Mr. Salomon, rousing himself from his initial disappointment. "I could bring round the other piece tomorrow."

Mr. Kimml waved his trumpet in Mr. Salomon's direction, to show he had not understood. Mr. Salomon replied by displaying one finger of his hand. "One! Tomorrow!"

Mr. Herman Kimml shook his head and raised six fingers. "Six!"

"Six?"

Mr. Tree turned to the young composer and said, "Mr. Kimml's policy is to request six compositions, before he makes a decision."

"He will not consider publishing just two compositions?"

Mr. Tree shrugged. "At Kimml Music we do not just present a composer's notes, we present composers of note."

Mr. Herman Kimml pounded his fist on the table to get the attention of the others. When he had it, he shouted, "Three pianoforte solos, one string quartet and something for the harp. This," he added, waving Mr. Salomon's composition for piano, violin and cello, "will serve as the sixth."

Mr. Tree retrieved the manuscript and returned it to Mr. Salomon's hands. "When can we expect to receive the others, sir?"

"I do not know, Mr. Tree. I am not a machine. Inspiration may come tomorrow, or it may wait until next year."

"Whenever you are ready, sir, we will be pleased to receive you. Now, if you will excuse me." Mr. Tree glanced toward the door, where a quartet of young men had just entered.

"Of course."

Mr. Salomon followed Mr. Tree with his eyes. It was apparent that Mr. Tree was acquainted with the group, since it only took him a moment to suggest a few compositions and take his seat at the piano. In Mr. Salomon's opinion, the piece the assistant was playing was much inferior to his own composition, but at the moment there was nothing he could say or do.

"I do not understand your hesitation, Mr. Salomon," said Mr. Herbert Kimml of the curio shop, also watching the men gathered around the piano. "Opportunity is staring you in the face. Did you not say you have another composition waiting at your home?"

"Yes, I do have a sonata for the violin that could be adapted for the piano, I suppose."

"Then you are already on your way. Can you not burn the midnight oil for a few weeks and make an effort to compose those other pieces?"

When Mr. Salomon did not reply, Mr. Kimml filled in the silence for him. "I know what you are thinking, sir. You are thinking that you are much obliged to Mr. Herbert and Mr. Herman Kimml, but there are other music publishers in London."

Mr. Salomon smiled. "Well, there are, are there not?"

"Yes, for instance there is the establishment founded by Mr. Muzio Clementi. Perhaps it is there you are thinking of approaching next?"

"It is a possibility," Mr. Salomon conceded.

"By all means, go to Mr. Clementi. But remember, sir, and I say this as a friend, at the establishment of Mr. Muzio Clementi the first thought is to sell the music of Mr. Muzio Clementi."

"You mean that when a customer comes in, the shop assistant will select one of Mr. Clementi's compositions to play, before one by another composer, such as myself?"

"We understand each other. Now, if you are able to make a name for yourself in the concert hall, if people are clamoring to hear the music of Mr. David Salomon, it will not matter. When customers walk into Mr. Clementi's establishment, they will demand to hear the newest work by Mr. David Salomon and nothing else."

"But until that happy day, I am better off elsewhere? Is that your meaning, Mr. Kimml?"

Mr. Kimml bowed. "It is your decision, Mr. Salomon. I only offer my opinion."

"And I appreciate that opinion, sir. But I need a piano to compose, and my mother and I are so newly arrived in London that we have not yet found the time to acquire one." He then added, "I know that most composers can hear their music in their head and write it down without playing it on an instrument. For me, though, music is also a tactile experience. I need to feel the keys under my fingers to release the musical notes swirling around in my head."

"You cannot achieve the same thing with your violin?"

Mr. Salomon shook his head. "It is perhaps a perversity that is unique to my personality. My violin is my breath, the passion of my life, the voice of my soul. When I try to compose on the violin I soon become transported by my emotions to some magical place where perhaps I am composing works of genius—I certainly feel so at the time—but when I return to our ordinary, workaday world I cannot remember more than a few solitary notes. Therefore, when I wish to give form and content to my thoughts and feelings, to preserve them within the confines of a formal composition, I turn to the piano, which does not evoke within me the same intensity of emotion as the violin."

"Well, then, Mr. Salomon, if you must have a piano to compose, we must find you one. London is not the end of the world, and Cornhill Street is not a desert island. I mentioned earlier that my younger brother, Mr. Harold Kimml, manufactures pianos. Let us pay him a visit."

Mr. Herbert Kimml was already moving toward the door when Mr. Salomon stopped him and said, "There is yet another obstacle, Mr. Kimml."

Mr. Salomon paused and a rosy blush began to creep up onto his cheeks.

"I understand," said Mr. Kimml, "and I beg you to believe that you may be perfectly frank with me. Once, many years ago, my brothers and I were strangers to this great city, too. We know what it is to have more talent than money and subsist on bread and cheese. My brother sometimes has a spare piano in his workshop. Let us see if he can lend you one for a few weeks."

Mr. Salomon was not surprised by the wide-eyed expression of Mr. Harold Kimml, the piano manufacturer, who closely resembled his other brothers in all things, except that the color of his hair was red just beginning to be streaked with grey. Mr. Salomon was already accustomed to the facial features the three brothers had received from their ancestors. Besides, his attention was partly engaged by the sight of a variety of pianofortes in various stages of construction.

The piano manufacturer listened with great sympathy to Mr. Herbert Kimml's reprisal of what had occurred in the establishment of Mr. Herman Kimml, yet had to beg the young gentleman's pardon. "At the moment, sir," he explained, "I have nothing I can lend you."

"But, Harold, what about that old piano above Herman's shop?" asked Mr. Herbert Kimml. "Could he not use that?"

Mr. Harold Kimml looked doubtfully at Mr. Salomon. "You are a serious musician, sir?"

"I like to think so."

"Then I do not know if that piano would suit you. I do not know if it is even in tune, it has been so long since anyone has used it."

"We can at least go there and find out," said the other brother.

Mr. Salomon, sensing that perhaps the piano manufacturer had more important business to attend to, shook his head. "I've already taken up too much of your valuable time. I cannot impose on you further, Mr. Kimml, or your brothers."

"Nonsense," said Mr. Herbert Kimml. "If you will not take offense at the familiarity, Mr. Salomon, I have taken a liking to you and I would like to help you." He then turned to his brother and said, "Will you come with us?"

"With pleasure. I had entirely forgotten about that piano. I am curious to see what condition it is in."

The three returned to Mr. Herman Kimml's establishment. Mr. Harold Kimml and Mr. Salomon waited on the landing, while Mr. Herbert Kimml went inside the shop to speak with his brother, who was the possessor of the key to the upstairs room.

When he returned, the key was in his hand and a smile was on his face. "Success!" he said, as he headed up the stairs. The two other gentlemen followed his lead.

"It is hardly the palace at Versailles," said Mr. Harold Kimml, when they were all inside the room, which was bare of all furniture except the piano, an old bench, a small table and two chairs. One small window let in a little light.

"I only need this," said Mr. Salomon walking over to the piano. He softly ran a few scales. To his surprise, the instrument was in tune and had a passable sound. The only drawback was that the piano sat in a dark corner, far away from the window. "Would anyone mind if I moved the piano closer to the light?" he asked.

Since neither Mr. Kimml minded, he tried to move the piano. It would not budge from its gloomy place. "That is odd," he said, stooping down to examine the bottom of the piano. "It looks like someone has nailed it into place."

Mr. Harold Kimml shrugged. "People do odd things."

"Surely, sir, you have a spare candelabrum at home," said Mr. Herbert Kimml. "Bring it here and light the room in that way."

"Yes, I could do that. Are you certain I will not be disturbing anyone? I sometimes get carried away when I am composing and make a great deal of noise."

"Who is there to disturb? You saw for yourself that our brother Herman is practically deaf. Mr. Tree does not matter. Besides, most of the day he is playing the piano himself, demonstrating new pieces for the customers—and making a noise, too, if I may say so."

"You shall be as alone here as if ... as if you were Adam in the Garden of Eden," added Mr. Harold Kimml.

"It is settled then," said Mr. Herbert Kimml. "If you do not object to doing your composing in this rather dreary room, and you are willing to let our brother Herman be the first to see your work—and have sole rights to publish it, should he like what he sees — you may consider this room and the piano as being temporarily your own." He then placed the key in Mr. Salomon's hand. "Well, what do you say?"

Mr. Salomon stared down at the key. "I say I do not know how to thank you."

"Write something brilliant," replied Mr. Herbert Kimml, "and dedicate it to me! That is how you can thank me."

"And what about me?" added Mr. Harold Kimml, laughing. "I want a dedication, too."

"I will try to satisfy you both, gladly!"

They all shook hands. Then the two brothers left the room. Mr. Salomon sat down at the piano and began to play.

On the other side of the closed door the two Mr. Kimmls stopped to listen.

"He is good," said Mr. Harold Kimml. "How did you know?"

"I heard him play in Leeds. I recognized him the minute he walked into my shop."

CHAPTER X

IT WAS LATE by the time that Mr. Salomon returned home. His mother, who had entertained guests in the drawing room that afternoon, was sitting on the sofa with a pleased look on her face.

"Normally, I would scold you for not returning in time for tea, David. Today, Lady Windsbury called and she was most disappointed to have missed you."

"Do we know Lady Windsbury?"

"Now we do. She heard about you from her sister, Lady Bickleton, who has a home near Leeds. But your absence has worked to our advantage. Apparently, Lady Bickleton was one of the ladies who fainted during your performance. Now Lady Windsbury is so curious to see you that she insists we accept her invitation for next week—a little supper party, which anyone who matters in London is sure to attend. She also asked if you would be willing to play, after supper. I assured her that you would be honored to perform for her and her distinguished guests."

"I don't mind playing. But will there be kosher food at Lady Windsbury's supper party, Mother?"

"Don't be ridiculous."

"I wish you would have found a way to have us join her guests after supper."

"Push the food around on your plate and pretend to eat, if you must be so stubborn," Mrs. Salomon replied, the soft smile on her face hardening into a thin line of determination. "But don't be a fool, as well. These people can help you. With Lady Windsbury as your patron, the doors of every fashionable home in London will be open to you. One of her guests might decide to finance your first public concert in London, if she doesn't offer to do it herself."

David took a seat beside his mother. He had no wish to reopen the arguments they had had in New York about his mother's declining level of religious observance. It had pained him to watch the lives of his parents disintegrate, each in their own way.

His father rarely spoke about what had caused his previously flourishing business to flounder. When he did speak, he usually said that he was being squeezed out of business by a competitor, John Jacob Astor, who was trying to create a monopoly with his American Fur Company and had powerful friends in the United States government. Once war broke out between the United States and England in June of 1812, the war supplanted Mr. Astor as being the prime reason for the business's diminishing fortunes.

There were rumors that the real cause was the elder Mr. Salomon's fascination with the race track. Whether he turned to betting on horses as a way to make back some of the money he was losing in the fur trade, or his gambling addiction was the source of the firm's financial problems, would perhaps never be known.

It was during the time that the father's fortunes began to fade that the son's star began its ascent. David Salomon was invited to perform at both public and private concerts, where his playing was enthusiastically received by critics and the public

alike. It was considered a prize to have him as a
music teacher for a family's daughters, since the
requests were so numerous that he could pick and
choose among the offers. Mrs. Salomon began to
harbor ambitions that her talented son might marry
into one of New York's finest and richest families.
The religion of the young lady was not important.

It did matter to Mr. David Salomon, though.
Whereas it might be supposed that since he belonged
to the younger generation, he would be the one to
want to cast off the yoke of the Torah's
commandments, this was not the case. At heart, he
had a love for tradition — whether it was the musical
tradition that originated with the great composers of
Europe, or the tradition of his spiritual fathers, the
great rabbis of Europe. Even his performance of the
Clementi Sonatina in Leeds, which some might have
interpreted as a smashing of certain music idols, was
not seen in this light by him. His purpose had been to
dig deeper into the established tradition and see what
treasures could be discovered underneath a surface
that was becoming superficial and trite, rather than
throw away the edifice and offer as a substitute
something new that was created entirely in his own
image.

In New York, while his name was becoming
known, he had fought with his mother about whether
or not to perform on the Jewish Sabbath, or attend
supper parties where food that was not kosher would
be served. If the old argument was going to be
revived in their new home, it was just another worry
to add to what seemed to be a growing list — a list that
was topped by worries about their financial situation.

"I wish you would tell me exactly how things stand with our finances," he said, ignoring, for the moment, the complications of being a Jewish musician and composer in a world where one was expected to bow to the dictates of society and cast personal scruples to the wind in the pursuit of a successful career. "Have we at least money enough to last us for a year?"

On another day, Mrs. Salomon might have brushed aside the question with a wave of her bejeweled hand and her melodious laugh. Today, though, Lady Windsbury's supper party was at stake. She therefore sat on the sofa as stubbornly silent as a glum mummy.

"If not a year, will our money last for six months?" Mr. Salomon asked.

Still, she did not answer.

He took his mother's hand and placed it in his own. "When do we find ourselves on the street, Mother?"

"We have three months, if we economize. I did not want you to feel the pressure of our circumstances, but you have forced me. Either you must find a patron or I must find a wealthy husband very soon. Otherwise, we will be ruined."

"At least we were able to pay off all of Father's debts before we left New York. And anything can happen in three months," he said, in an effort to be cheerful and mask his true thoughts. Inwardly, though, he was chiding himself for not having taken a more active role in their financial affairs. They could have rented a smaller house, not filled the rooms with so much rented furniture. He had no quarrel with the money his mother had spent; he knew how important appearances were. But three months! It would be over in the blink of an eye.

"In fact, I already have some good news," he continued, still trying to sound optimistic. "I think Mr. Kimml is very interested in publishing my music."

"That is wonderful, David. Just be sure to read over the contract carefully before you sign. Don't let him cheat you."

"We are not at that stage yet. He wants to see more of my work before he makes a decision. But he and his brothers have offered to let me use one of their pianos to do my composing, and that must mean something. It's in a room above Mr. Kimml's place of business, so I shall have to be away from here most of the day — and most of the night, as well, if we will be in the poorhouse otherwise. You don't object to my being away, do you, Mother?"

"How can I? But how did they know that you needed a piano? You didn't mention anything about our financial state, did you?"

"I did mention something, to Mr. Kimml's brother. They are very nice people, Mother. I think ..."

She raised her fingers to his lips to stop him. "Be more careful next time, dearest. When people like Lady Windsbury find out that a person is poor, they run from him like the plague."

"I know. I'm sorry."

"As far as London society is concerned, I am the well-off widow of a successful fur merchant, and you are the talented only heir to your father's fortune."

Mr. Salomon went over to the tea table and wrapped in a napkin the sandwiches that remained on a platter. "I'm going back to Cornhill Street, to work for a few more hours."

"Do you think you can finish one of your new compositions in time to play it for Lady Windsbury's guests?" she asked, following him.

"I think I shall have to."

"Try not to worry too much," said Mrs. Salomon, lightly kissing her son's brow. "We may have lost one fortune, but we shall find another. I know it."

When Martin Roth returned to London, it was with the intention of losing himself in that great city so completely that his elder brother would never again be able to find him. He immediately began to search for some honest employment, but could find nothing other than odd jobs that lasted for only a day or two. On a bad day, he found nothing at all. This was such a day, and by the time he stumbled down Cornhill Street and into Mr. Salomon he was dizzy from hunger.

"I beg your pardon, sir," said Mr. Salomon, extricating himself from the other man.

For a moment Martin could not reply. His nose had caught the tantalizing whiff of the sandwiches that sat in Mr. Salomon's pocket, and his eyes were fixed upon the top of the napkin, which could just be seen.

Mr. Salomon followed the direction of the young man's gaze and immediately removed one of the sandwiches, which he handed to the stranger. When he saw that the young man merely looked at the sandwich with ravenous eyes, Mr. Salomon inquired if there was anything else the young man needed.

"Water, sir, to wash my hands, if you please."

"You know, then, that the food is kosher?" asked Mr. Salomon, correctly assuming that the stranger must be Jewish and therefore wished to perform the traditional washing of the hands before eating bread.

"I know you are Mr. David Salomon, sir, and that you ate kosher food in the home of my former employer, Mr. Deare."

"Come with me. There is water upstairs."

Mr. Salomon asked no more questions until Martin had eaten his sandwich. When Mr. Salomon tried to convince the young man to eat the other sandwich, Martin replied, "The Torah forbids it, sir. A guest may not eat all of his host's food."

"I have food at home and you, from the looks of you, do not. Eat."

Martin did not have to be further persuaded. While Martin ate, Mr. Salomon prepared some coffee—the Kimml brothers had done what they could to make the shabby room comfortable—and thought about what he should do with the young man.

"I am not in a position to find you work," he said, when he had brought the coffee to the table. "But if you are Jewish, why do you not turn to Mr. Melamed? I understand he has both the means and the desire to help newcomers to the London Jewish community."

Martin shook his head. "I must make my way on my own."

Their conversation was interrupted by a knock on the door, which was followed by the entrance of Mr. Tree.

"I am sorry to disturb you, Mr. Salomon, but I heard voices. As I thought I saw you leave, earlier, I thought it best to discover whose voices they were."

"Thank you, Mr. Tree. I am quite all right, and I shall be working late for the next several nights. By the way, Lady Windsbury has invited me to perform at a supper party she will be giving next week. Could you ask Mr. Kimml if he would mind my playing my new sonata at this party?"

"I shall ask him, sir."

Mr. Tree made his bow and left the room. Mr. Salomon noticed that his visitor's eyes remained fixed on the now closed door. "Is something wrong?"

Martin roused himself and said, "No, Mr. Salomon. For a moment I thought the man looked familiar. I am most likely mistaken."

"What sort of work are you looking for, Mr. ...?"

"Martin Roth, sir."

"You say you were employed by Mr. Deare?"

"Yes, sir."

"You were not happy in Leeds?"

Martin took a swallow of coffee before he replied. "I have an elderly father in London."

Mr. Salomon did not press the young man further. Although he did still wonder why the young man did not ask Mr. Melamed for assistance, it was not his nature to pry into the personal affairs of others. He therefore turned the conversation to a less delicate topic and asked, "Are you looking for similar employment?"

"I am, if similar employment can be found. If it cannot, I am willing to work at almost anything."

Once again their conversation was interrupted by a knock at the door, followed by the entrance of Mr. Tree.

"Mr. Kimml sends his compliments, sir. Normally, he would not allow your request to perform in public a piece he might wish to commission, before a contract has been signed. But he is willing to make an exception, in your case, Mr. Salomon, and rely upon your honor as a gentleman that if the piece is well received at Lady Windsbury's supper party, and if you are approached afterward by a competing music publisher, that you will not sell the composition to this competitor before speaking with Mr. Kimml."

"Please tell Mr. Kimml that he has my word."

Mr. Tree was about to bow himself out of the room when Mr. Salomon said, "Mr. Tree, my friend here is newly arrived in London and looking for work. Do you think something could be found for him at one of the Kimml places of business? He can do carpentry work."

Mr. Tree glanced over at Martin. "The Mr. Kimmls sometimes are in need of a skilled carpenter. If you would care to come downstairs, sir, we can discuss the matter without taking Mr. Salomon from his work."

After Martin said the Grace After Meals prayer, he said goodbye to his host and went downstairs. Mr. Tree was waiting for him on the landing.

"Newly arrived in London?" said Mr. Tree. "I thought I should burst out laughing and spoil the joke when the American said that!"

"And how do you think I felt when I saw *you*?"

They laughed and then Mr. Tree grew silent. "What's the game this time, Master Martin? You know as well as I do that I was employed in your father's London house as a serving boy when you entered this world. I was also there when you and your brother snitched gooseberry pies from the kitchen. I hope you have not followed your youthful exploits with crimes that are more serious."

"Never mind me, John. What are you doing employed in a musical establishment?"

"After I left your father's service, I joined an orchestra in Brighton."

"Yes, I recall that you were better at playing the pianoforte than polishing the silver."

The two laughed again, savoring the memories of times long past. Then Mr. Tree once again grew serious. "While I was in Brighton, I made the acquaintance of Mr. Kimml, who offered me a position as sales assistant. London suits me better, I have discovered, as does steady employment. But what about you, Master Martin? It was all I could do to conceal my surprise when I saw you upstairs with Mr. Salomon, looking like a forlorn orphan who hasn't had a good meal in days. Or are you too high in the instep to talk about your troubles with a former servant?"

"Not at all, John, only there is not much to tell. I have had a falling out with my father, and I am looking for employment. If Mr. Kimml could use my services, I would be very much obliged."

"Are you still as clever with your hands as you used to be?"

"I think so."

"Would you mind working, instead, for a man who is a former servant?"

"You?"

Mr. Tree nodded his head. "Mind, I cannot afford to pay you high wages. Indeed, if you accept my offer you will probably have to lodge in my rooms — we could set up a curtain so you can have a private corner to yourself."

"Never mind the wages for the moment. What is the work?"

"I have something in mind, Master Martin, that if I could only see my way to doing it, my invention would turn the entire music world upside down. It would make my fortune, and yours, if with my idea and your golden hands we can build the thing and make it work."

"Details, John, tell me details. I am burning with curiosity."

Mr. Tree looked around the empty staircase. "Not here. Go to my rooms and make yourself at home. We will discuss it later tonight. Now I must return to work."

Mr. Tree took out his notebook and pencil and quickly wrote down his address. Martin saw that it was located in one of the poorer parts of town, but it was better than spending another night out on the street.

"Here is the key," said Mr. Tree. "And, Martin, I think it best you do not return to Cornhill Street, at least not while we are working on our invention. You might let something slip, during your conversations with Mr. Salomon, and we don't want the secret to get out."

"From now on I have never heard of Cornhill Street, or Mr. Salomon."

Martin left and Mr. Tree returned to the music shop. Mr. Kimml looked up when he entered.

"Anything wrong, Mr. Tree?" he shouted.

"Not now," Mr. Tree shouted back.

CHAPTER XI

MR. GRIMM BRUSHED off the dust that had accumulated on his hat and ran his fingers through his tangled hair before placing the hat back upon his head. Having thus finished his toilette he ascended the stairs that led to Mr. Herman Kimml's music publishing establishment. He paused when he reached the top of the landing, to catch his breath. Once, he noted bitterly, he could have flown up many more flights of steps and not felt the least bit tired, buoyed by nothing more than youthful hope and dreams of glory. Those days were long gone. Instead, he was a man of middle age and middling health and vigor—and still standing on the wrong side of a closed door.

That door suddenly opened and a man of mature years and not quite fashionable clothes stepped out, a roll of music in his clenched hand. By unspoken agreement, neither man looked at the other. They did not need words to communicate that they were both musicians that fame and fortune had passed by. Even crumbs from the banquet of life eluded them more often than not.

Mr. Grimm waited until the other man had departed and slammed the front door behind him. Then he summoned up what remained of his tattered dignity and strode into the room.

"Good afternoon, Mr. Tree," he said. "I sent some music to Mr. Kimml a month ago."

"Your name, sir?"

Mr. Grimm stared at the man with his haughtiest look. "Grimm, sir. Mr. Karl Grimm. It is a name that is well known in Europe."

Mr. Tree bowed and went to the back of the room, where Mr. Kimml was sitting. "Mr. Grimm, sir," he shouted into the ear trumpet. "He sent some music a month ago."

Mr. Kimml nodded and began to rummage about the desk. After retrieving the manuscript from the bottom of a pile, Mr. Kimml looked over Mr. Grimm's musical scores one last time. He then handed the papers to Mr. Tree with a slight shake of the head.

Mr. Tree, in turn, brought the music to the waiting composer. "Mr. Kimml conveys his compliments to Mr. Grimm, and regrets that he is unable to act as Mr. Grimm's publisher."

"Does Mr. Kimml say why?" asked Mr. Grimm, taking back the manuscript.

Mr. Tree shrugged. "Mr. Kimml never says why. Good day, sir."

The shop assistant turned toward the piano and Mr. Grimm turned toward the door.

"Mr. Tree!" shouted Mr. Kimml.

"Yes, Mr. Kimml?" the assistant shouted back.

"What have we heard from Mr. Salomon?"

"Nothing yet, sir!"

"Ask him if he has a sonata for the piano ready. We need something to complete this collection." Mr. Kimml waved a sheaf of papers in the direction of his assistant.

"Yes, Mr. Kimml!"

Mr. Grimm's hand gripped the doorknob as though the object were the only thing saving him from tumbling off a high cliff and falling into an abyss. The mention of Mr. Salomon's name not only reminded him of the concert in Leeds, but also of the fact that soon afterward he had been relieved of his position with the Leeds Musical Society, which was why he had come to London to find new work. When he left the room, he descended the stairs with twice the speed that he had ascended them; anger always gave him new strength. But after a few minutes of strenuous walking down Cornhill Street the breathless feeling recurred and he was forced to slow his pace.

What he needed, he decided, after the morning's disappointments was a place where he could sit and drink his gin undisturbed. Turning down various streets until he was quite lost in the maze that comprises the City, he came at last to Sweeting's Alley and an establishment that he thought could provide him with the refreshments he required. He made his way to the serving counter and called out to the person standing there, "Gin, sir!"

"This is a coffee house, sir," said Mr. Baer, for, indeed, the pianoforte player from Leeds had stumbled into the kosher establishment by mistake. "We serve coffee here, and food."

Mr. Grimm looked about the place with disgust. He could not see the point of an eating establishment that did not serve alcoholic refreshments. His disgust increased tenfold when he saw Mr. Salomon sitting at one of the tables. "You serve violinists, too, I see."

"I hope you do not intend to be quarrelsome, sir," said Mr. Baer, who had come out from behind the counter to stand between Mr. Grimm and his other customers.

Mr. Grimm sized up the coffee house's proprietor, who was a burly man, and if he had thought to be quarrelsome a moment before he now quickly changed his mind.

"I have no quarrel with you," he said, bowing and then making for the door.

Once back outside, he dashed across the street, his anger having returned at the sight of Mr. Salomon, and promptly ran into a man who was standing by the stall of a vendor selling fruit.

"Watch where you're going," Mr. Grimm said, before stooping to pick up the sheets of music that had fallen to the ground.

"I wasn't the one who was going," Jonas Street snapped back, placing a muddy boot on one of the pages. "I was standing here."

Mr. Grimm grabbed the page and stood up. "Next time, stand elsewhere."

Jonas was about to reply in kind, when he recognized the other man's face. "Aren't you the piano player? Didn't I see you in Leeds?"

"You may have, sir," replied Mr. Grimm, straightening up to his full height. "My name is Karl Grimm. It is a name that is well known in Europe. I was in Leeds only temporarily, as a favor to the King of Bohemia."

"That's right. And I'm here in London as a favor to the Emperor Napoleon."

Mr. Grimm glared at Jonas before storming down the street.

Mr. Salomon, who had noticed the arrival of Mr. Grimm with trepidation, was relieved by the man's hasty departure. He had taken to eating his meals at the coffee house after he was offered use of the room on Cornhill Street, since it was more convenient to eat there than return home. Now he was anxious to pay his bill and return to work. Inspiration had come, to his relief, and he was in the midst of working on his new sonata. What's more, he was certain that the new piece was good—very good.

"I hope everything was satisfactory, Mr. Salomon," said Mr. Baer, taking the money.

"Yes, my compliments to your wife. She is an excellent cook."

Mr. Baer watched the young musician depart. Since Mrs. Baer was busy with marrying off the mother, Mr. Salomon had so far escaped from Mrs. Baer's matchmaking attentions. But the day would come when it would be the turn of the musician, Mr. Baer thought with a smile, before returning to his own work.

Mr. Salomon had not gone far before he was joined by Jonas Street.

"Enjoyed your food, Davey?" asked the former trapper.

Mr. Salomon reached into his pocket and took out a coin. "Buy yourself some supper."

"You can't buy me off so easily."

"And you cannot frighten me, Jonas. I spoke to my mother. She says Father's lawyer assured her that he paid you, along with the others, everything you were owed."

"Then one of them is a liar."

Mr. Salomon stopped. "You dare to speak like that about Mrs. Salomon? And to me, her son?"

"Would I be here, Davey, if I had been paid? Would I have thrown away good money on a ship and lodgings here in London just to hound you?"

Mr. Salomon was silent.

"If it had just been me, Davey, I wouldn't have wasted my money on coming over here. But Roger — that was the other trapper, the one who got killed by those Indians — he was married to my sister, and now she don't have anything to live on. How is she supposed to feed her little ones, Davey?"

"All of my Father's debts have been paid. Good day."

Mr. Salomon turned to walk away, but Jonas gripped his arm tightly and stopped him. "Write to the lawyer, Davey. Ask him if what I'm telling you is true, or not. When one of those lawyers gives a man like me some money, he writes it down in a big book. You ask him to check his book and see if there's in it an entry for me and Roger Paul, my sister's dead husband."

"If you are certain those entries will not be found, why did you not bring a letter from the lawyer with you? It would have saved you time and trouble."

"Do you think I didn't try? Your lawyer wouldn't talk to me. Probably your mother paid him to keep silent. But he'll answer you, Davey. He'll have to."

"There is a war going on, Jonas. I will write to the lawyer, but I cannot guarantee that the letter will ever reach its destination."

"So that's how it is. I thought you would be different, being an artist and all that."

Mr. Salomon felt the color rising to his cheeks. "Different from what?"

"You know as well as me that your father didn't get a knife stuck in his back at that race track because he was a fine, upstanding citizen who honored his financial obligations."

Mr. Salomon angrily removed his arm from the other man's grip and hurried down the street.

"My sister is counting on me to get that money," Jonas called after him. "And I'm going to do it!"

Jonas watched while Mr. Salomon disappeared into the crowd. Mr. Grimm, who had observed the encounter with interest from his seat by the open window of a gin house, now exited that establishment and joined Mr. Street.

"I see we have something in common, sir," said Mr. Grimm, "besides our respective royal commissions."

Mr. Street regarded the pianoforte player with a wary eye. "And what might that be?"

"A mutual dislike of Mr. David Salomon."

"What if we do?"

"Perhaps we can be of service to one another."

"The King of Bohemia won't mind your dabbling in American affairs?"

Mr. Grimm made a face that was for him a smile. "I think he can spare me, for a little while."

Mr. Powell was at breakfast when the invitation to attend Lady Windsbury's supper party was carried into the morning room on a silver salver by Mr. Powell's butler, along with the other morning's correspondence. Usually, upon the receipt of these invitations, Mr. Powell would wrack his brain to think of some excuse why he could not possibly go and then, when the inevitable must be faced, enter the event into his calendar, along with a reminder to reply to the hostess that he would be delighted to attend. Such were the responsibilities of a man of fashion. He was not allowed to work at a common trade and still retain the title of gentleman, yet that did not mean he did not toil. His labor was to be present at one dreary supper party after another and pretend that an evening spent in insipid conversation, followed by cards or a concert or a ball, was a glorious way to spend the preciously short amount of time that a person has on this earth.

Before he tossed the invitation to the side, a line caught his eye — an announcement that after supper there would be a concert given by the well-known American violinist and composer, Mr. David Salomon. His fingers began to drum upon the table, something they often did when he was thinking. And what were his thoughts? First, wonder that he seemed to have caught from Mrs. Baer a severe case of matchmaking fever. Second, that he had discovered a way to avoid the supper party and attend only the concert.

Mr. Powell had been at his friend's side during the first few months of Mr. Melamed's widowhood, offering quiet company so that the widower would not sink totally into depression. Afterward, he had coaxed Mr. Melamed to again take an interest in their mutual business concerns, since they often worked as partners in the buying and selling of property in London and elsewhere in England. They were both widowers, and so they had sometimes discussed the idea of remarrying; Mr. Powell was therefore aware that London's Jewish community was too small to offer a man of Mr. Melamed's age and sensibilities a variety of eligible women to choose from. In addition, the war with Napoleon had severely curtailed not only the entry of food and fashions from the European Continent, but also private travel between Europe and England. Therefore, Mr. Melamed could not go to Europe to look for a Jewish wife and a Jewish widow could not come to England to find a Jewish husband. The appearance of Mrs. Salomon, who had somehow managed to evade the British warships and arrive safely in England from the United States, therefore seemed more and more provident the longer Mr. Powell considered it. But after he had been the one to warn his friend to be cautious, how could he now urge Mr. Melamed to charge forward?

This concert seemed to offer a solution. Mrs. Salomon would most likely attend her son's London debut, and a concert offered more leeway than a formal supper party, where one was a captive party for several hours, forced to keep up polite conversation whether one's dinner companions were of interest or not. At a concert, if one party decided they had no desire to further their acquaintanceship with the other, they could choose not to speak, since the excellence of the music would explain their silence. However, if both parties were interested and did choose to converse, they could repair to the refreshments room with the excuse that the music was not to their taste, and thereby deepen their acquaintance in a socially acceptable way.

Mr. Powell's drumming fingers came to a halt, having run into something of a wall. Mr. Melamed could hardly say that Mr. Salomon's playing was not to his taste and expect to garner the approval of the young man's mother. Therefore, there could be little hope of conversation between the two while the concert was going on. Yet at least the introduction would have been made. It would then be up to Mr. Melamed to choose how to proceed.

Mr. Powell rose from the table and repaired to his library, where pen and paper awaited him. A half hour later a note outlining his plan was already on its way to Bury Street and Mr. Melamed.

Mr. Melamed was less pleased with what the morning's post had brought him. A letter from Leeds, which had gone astray in the mail, so that it had only just now reached him, sat upon his breakfast table. First, he read the short letter from Mr. Deare. Next he glanced at the promissory note and glanced at the date. It was strange that he had seen nothing of Martin Roth in London—strange that the young man had not made an appearance at the Great Synagogue for the daily prayers and strange that Martin had not made an appearance at Mr. Melamed's home to at least offer an explanation as to why Mr. Melamed's attempt to help had been repaid with a theft.

He was still pondering that question when his butler announced that Mr. Nathan Roth wished to speak with him.

"Send him in," said Mr. Melamed, and a few minutes later Mr. Roth was seated at the table, helping himself to a breakfast of eggs, rolls and coffee.

"I am worried about my brother," said Nathan, who had not given up hope that he might yet convince his younger brother to help him in the matter of their father's will. "I hear he has left Leeds. I would assume that he would come to London, yet I have not heard a word from him."

"Do you know why he left Leeds?"

Nathan assumed an attitude of interest. "No, Mr. Melamed. Do you?"

Mr. Melamed evaded the question. He did not like Nathan Roth. "Perhaps your brother received a better position elsewhere," he said.

"That would be a happy end to my worries. Still, I hate to think of him in trouble somewhere, perhaps ill and too feverish to write, and all alone. Is there no way you can help me find him?"

Mr. Melamed considered the promissory note, which he had placed in the desk drawer before Nathan Roth entered the room. He had not considered the possibility that Martin might try something rash—either out of despair or out of hope that he might recover the money quickly—and gotten himself into serious trouble. Yet at the same time he wondered what was really behind Nathan Roth's brotherly concern.

"I shall keep my ears open," said Mr. Melamed. "If I hear anything that will be of interest to you, I will let you know."

Mr. Roth's exit was swiftly followed by the entrance of the note from Mr. Powell. Mr. Melamed read the message and then placed it in the desk drawer, on top of the promissory note. He would decide what to do with both of them later.

The Earl of Gravel Lane, who was not an early riser, had only just begun his breakfast of day-old rolls and ale when Mr. Melamed was announced.

"Show him in," the Earl said to General Well'ngone. When the visitor had been seated at the breakfast table, the Earl graciously moved a chipped mug in Mr. Melamed's direction.

"Thank you, I have already breakfasted," said Mr. Melamed, trying to hide the discomfort he felt whenever he entered the damp-infested, crumbling quarters that the Earl called home.

The Earl was not surprised by the sight of one of Jewish London's wealthiest men sitting in his dilapidated drawing room. He knew that Mr. Melamed despised everything that the Earl stood for — the contempt for honest work, the corruption of poor orphans who fell into the Earl's disarming trap because they had nowhere else to go. Yet more than once Mr. Melamed had needed the Earl's services to help solve a crime, since the young criminal was all too familiar with the dark labyrinth of narrow alleyways that comprised the poorest parts of London, as well as the poverty-stricken denizens who flitted through those alleyways like dark moths led onward to their destruction by the refracted light of broken dreams and weary despair.

The Earl therefore leisurely finished buttering his roll, before he said, "To what do I owe this pleasure, Mr. Melamed?"

"I would like to know if a certain person has arrived in London. His name is Martin Roth."

The Earl raised his eyebrows. "Is Mr. Roth in trouble with the law?"

"I do not know."

"Does he owe you money?"

Now it was the turn of Mr. Melamed to look surprised. "Have you turned prophet, Earl?"

"I could tell you something that would astonish you even more. But although I have my faults, being a common gossip is not one of them." The Earl took a bite from his roll, daintily wiping the crumbs from his lips with a filthy handkerchief afterward.

"Can you help me find Martin Roth? I only wish to know if he is in London, and if he is safe."

The Earl glanced over at General Well'ngone, who was also seated at the table. "Can we spare any of our men, General?"

"Saulty is at your service, Earl. His hand is still healing after it got caught in that gentleman's pocket."

"A nasty affair," said the Earl, shaking his head. "That so-called gentleman nearly broke Saulty's thumb. The world has become so violent."

"Shall I pay you now?" asked Mr. Melamed, wishing to be already on his way, now that he had stated his business.

The Earl made a gesture to wave away the question. "I trust you, sir. Your credit is good with me."

"Speaking of credit, Earl," said General Well'ngone, going over to the mantelpiece, where the musical sewing box was sitting, "perhaps Mr. Melamed would be interested in purchasing your sewing box."

The General gave the key a few turns and the music began to play. "Mrs. Salomon is a musical lady, from what I hear."

Mr. Melamed ignored the General's impish grin, though he would have sorely liked to wipe it from the young man's face, and rose from the table. "Let me know when you have found Martin Roth. Good day."

The Earl and the General waited until they were sure their guest was out of hearing. Then the General said, "Do you think he knows that Mr. Roth, senior, is getting into Queer Street?"

"I don't know," replied the Earl. "But the name of Roth is on too many lips at the moment, and we must find out why. And while you're hunting down Martin Roth, find out what you can about Mrs. Salomon."

"Do you think she's in Queer Street, too?"

"I have no idea," replied the Earl, testing the dull blade of his knife with his finger. "But I have heard a rumor that Mr. Salomon, senior, was not scalped by Indians."

The General looked disappointed. The exciting tale had been enjoyed in their little corner of the world. Then he cast a knowing eye at the Earl. "Do we care if the lady is a liar?"

"We might. Let us say, for instance, that a marriage between Mrs. Salomon and Mr. Melamed might not be in the best interests of the gentleman. If we are the ones to save Mr. Melamed from an embarrassing attachment, he will not forget it."

"Which will come in handy should we ever be invited to call upon the King's hangman."

The Earl smiled. "Thank heavens we live in a civilized country. I should hate to lose my life and my wig to one of those heathen Indians."

CHAPTER XII

THE PROBLEM OF Martin Roth's disappearance had not yet been solved when Mr. Melamed entered Lady Windsbury's drawing room with Mr. Powell. Mr. Melamed was no stranger to luxurious apartments, but the display of wealth in the room — which was large enough to serve as a ballroom in another, less impressive London townhouse, and was filled with London's most glittering society — made him pause.

"Lady Windsbury has her own idea of what an intimate evening at home means," Mr. Powell whispered to his friend. "She rarely has less than forty at table. Then the rest of the world is invited for the after-supper entertainment."

For a moment, Mr. Melamed considered that in such a crush of people he might escape from making the acquaintance of Mrs. Salomon. Then he chided himself for even thinking such a thought. He was not a young man being introduced to a young lady for the first time in his life, and so it was ridiculous to feel awkward and shy. He was also conscious of Mr. Powell's eyes upon him, and the desire to not look foolish before his friend further steeled his resolve to at least appear like a confident man of the world, no matter what he might be feeling.

This crowd, though, brought back to him that sense of isolation he still felt so intensely whenever he was in society, even though a few years had passed since his wife had died. He might gaze into every face in that cavernous, crowded room and yet he knew that he would not see the one face that meant the world to him.

However, he also knew that a Jew could not rebel against the decrees of the Almighty. He might have chosen to have gone through life with his beloved wife at his side, but since the Almighty had had other plans he had no choice except to accept them. And, if truth be told, there were now times when he could go through an entire day without falling into a depressed state. Therefore, perhaps Mrs. Baer was right; perhaps it was time to give serious thought to the idea of remarrying.

"That must be her," Mr. Powell whispered in his ear, "the lady standing next to Mr. Salomon."

Mr. Melamed looked in the direction of the pianoforte, which sat at the head of the room. He recognized Mr. Salomon, since he had met the gentleman before. And, of course, Mr. Salomon was the only one in the room holding a violin.

His gaze turned to the woman standing beside Mr. Salomon, and he had to admit that she possessed a commanding presence even in that room filled with imposing people. Unlike some women who were no longer in the first blush of youth, she had not tried to divert attention from her more mature looks by wearing an abundance of jewels or an elaborate millinery concoction of feathers and beaded cloth on her head. Instead, she was attired in an elegant gown of lavender, a color that suited her well, which was adorned by nothing more than fine lace. The few diamonds that she did wear gave off just the right amount of sparkle and flash—enough to signify that she was a woman of means, but not enough to convey the impression that she was a member of the despised newly arrived, vulgar commercial class.

Mrs. Salomon was speaking with Lady Windsbury, who happened to look in the direction of Mr. Powell and catch his eye.

"That is our cue, Melamed."

Mr. Powell set off, followed by Mr. Melamed. Lady Windsbury made the introductions. Then she left them, to attend to her other guests.

"At last we meet, Mr. Melamed, and I can thank you in person for all that you have done for David," enthused Mrs. Salomon, looking over to where her son was speaking with the pianoforte player.

"I have done very little, as I recall."

"You introduced him to Mr. Kimml," she said, returning her gaze and her smile to the gentleman standing beside her. "Mr. Kimml commissioned the sonata we shall hear tonight. I should say that your 'little' has accomplished a great deal."

"That is the way of all great men," Mr. Powell said, and then, having said his piece on his friend's behalf, he took his seat.

Mrs. Salomon took her seat, as well, and returned her attention to the impromptu stage. She knew the rules, that not too much should be said during the first meeting. But she felt confident that she had seen an interest in Mr. Melamed's eye.

And she had not been mistaken. Mr. Melamed did feel an interest in Mrs. Salomon, but not for the reason that she suspected. There was no doubt that her outer appearance was pleasing—although on closer examination, Mr. Melamed, who was something of an expert of fine jewels, saw that the lady's diamonds were not the real thing. And her mistake in believing that he had been the one to mention Mr. Kimml could be easily attributed to the overzealousness of Mrs. Baer. But in Mrs. Salomon's eye he had seen something surprising, a momentary glance of cold calculation, which the lady had quickly masked with her smiles and honeyed voice. Of course, a lady of Mrs. Salomon's age would be guided by practical considerations when choosing a new husband and Mr. Melamed had no objection to that. Yet there was something else in that swift glance that, when coupled with the "diamonds," troubled him. He was therefore thankful when the music began and there was no more need for conversation.

Mr. Salomon began the evening with a duet for violin and piano by the composer Ignaz Pleyel, a popular and undemanding composer who would not try the patience of an audience that might prefer their own whispered *bon mots* to the good notes of a more serious composer. After the duet was done, this portion of the audience drifted toward the rooms where card tables were set up, as well as tables for refreshments, satisfied that they had done their duty to the arts.

The next piece was one by Bach, which had the virtue of being both familiar and technically challenging. This was warmly received, and Lady Windsbury smiled as she walked toward the stage and received the compliments of her guests, for as hostess an evening's success belonged as much to her as to the artists.

She motioned for the audience to cease their applause. "Now, my dear friends, we are about to enjoy a very special delight. Mr. Salomon has agreed to perform for us his new sonata for violin, which has never before been performed in public. Indeed, he has told me that until this evening no ears have heard a note of it, except for his own. Mr. Salomon, if you please."

Mr. Salomon waited until Lady Windsbury retook her seat. Meanwhile, the crowd that had remained in the room reacted with eager excitement. In their world, where weariness with life was the norm, the word "new" was like an electric spark that brought them back to life.

The musician at the pianoforte began to play. Mr. Salomon listened intently as the opening theme was developed, pleased with what he was hearing. Then he lifted his violin and began to play, in answer, the melody that had come to him in a moment of inspiration, the like of which he had never experienced before—the melody that he was sure would make his reputation, as well as his fortune, and would be remembered whenever his name was recalled.

At first, he was too wrapped up in his own playing to notice that something was wrong. It was only when the whispers had turned to outright laughter that he awoke from his dream and looked about him with bewilderment. Even then it took several moments for it to dawn upon him that he had fallen into what could only be described as a musician's hell.

Lady Windsbury, who was not one to be easily flustered, having been one of the queens of London society for many years, uncertainly rose from her seat and approached the stage. Motioning for the laughing ladies and gentlemen to be silent, she turned to the violinist and said, "I beg your pardon, Mr. Salomon. I thought you said this sonata was your composition. Please forgive my mistake."

"There was no mistake, my lady," replied Mr. Salomon. "I am the composer."

The crowd again began to laugh. Mr. Salomon cast a bewildered glance about the room.

"But Mr. Salomon, this sonata was introduced two nights ago, at Lady Mercer's birthday celebration. Everyone has gone wild for it and rushed to purchase the music. See, I have it here."

Lady Windsbury went over to the pianoforte and looked through the small stack of music that sat upon the instrument. When she returned, she showed the sonata, which was written for the pianoforte, to Mr. Salomon.

The young man quickly looked over the score. It was not exactly what he had written—the accompaniment differed in certain places. But the melody—his melody! his gift of sacred inspiration!—was exactly the same. His bewildered eye quickly traveled to the top of the page to seek out the name of the composer.

"S. Romberg?" he said to Lady Windsbury. "Who is S. Romberg?"

"No one knows, although everyone would love to know who this new genius is. However, since we know it is not you, Mr. Salomon, would you like to play something else, or would you like to have some tea?"

Mr. Salomon looked about the room, which was by then more empty than full. From the room where crowds of people had gathered to drink tea and sip lemonade he heard cascades of laughter rippling through the air. His face glowed warm with embarrassment at the sound, each new burst of laughter cutting through him like the blade of one of Boney's bayonets.

"Mr. Salomon?" said Lady Windsbury.

"I apologize for spoiling your evening, my lady," he replied, bowing.

"Not at all. I can't remember when we all had such a good laugh."

She drifted toward her other guests, leaving Mr. Salomon standing alone on what a few minutes before had been a stage.

Mrs. Salomon, who had been struck immobile by the scene, now rose from her seat and approached her son. "David?"

"Yes, Mother?"

"I do not understand."

"Neither do I."

CHAPTER XIII

WHEN MR. SALOMON entered the music publishing establishment on Cornhill Street the next morning, the dark circles under his eyes were witnesses to the sleepless night he had endured, for how could he sleep when the scene of his disgrace refused to release its humiliating grip upon his troubled mind? But if the morning did not bring with it the calming peace of forgetfulness, at least the new day returned to him a sense that life could go on. One defeat did not mean the war was lost. He would start anew and write an even better sonata, with the help of the Almighty.

"Mr. Salomon? Mr. Kimml would like to speak with you."

Mr. Salomon's momentary victory over despair vanished and he wearily followed Mr. Tree into the music publisher's showroom. He was not totally unprepared for a request for an interview. News traveled fast in London. It was very likely that Mr. Kimml had read one of the satirical accounts of Lady Windsbury's party that had appeared in the morning's scandal sheets.

Indeed, when Mr. Kimml saw Mr. Salomon, the music publisher began to wave a newspaper in his direction. "What is the meaning of this, sir?" he shouted, jabbing a finger into the offending newsprint. "Never in the history of Kimml Music has one of my protégés been accused of stealing the work of another composer! Is this how you repay my thanks? By disgracing my establishment? By sullying my good name? Well, is it? Is it? What's wrong with you, man? Why don't you speak? Speak!"

Mr. Herbert Kimml, who was also in the room, placed a hand on his brother's arm and shouted, "Brother Herman! Calm yourself. Give him a chance to explain."

Mr. Herman Kimml settled back into his chair with a scowl and angrily raised his ear trumpet to his left ear. "Well?"

Mr. Salomon looked from one brother to the other. "I have no explanation."

"What? Speak up, Mr. Salomon! Speak up so a man can hear you!"

Mr. Salomon removed the key to the upstairs room from his pocket and waved it at the music publisher, before dropping it on the desk. "I have nothing to say."

Mr. Herbert Kimml snatched up the key and, taking Mr. Salomon by the arm, directed the young man toward the door. "We shall discuss this in private," he shouted back to his brother.

When they reached the upstairs room, Mr. Kimml sat down at the pianoforte and began to play the melody that had caused the uproar the night before. Mr. Salomon cringed at the sound of every note.

"The street musicians are playing it on practically every street corner," said Mr. Kimml, explaining his familiarity with the tune. "It is excellent publicity for Mr. Romberg, whoever he is, and his publisher, Mr. Schumetti. After the newspaper accounts, the story will make the rounds of all the coffee houses. It will be talked about in all the drawing rooms."

Mr. Kimml stopped playing and stared gloomily down at the piano's keys. "Ach, a person cannot buy such publicity! I am sure it will have a wonderful effect on his sales. You are not in league with Mr. Romberg, are you?"

The question roused Mr. Salomon from his depressed inertia, and he looked up to face his interrogator. "I? Of course not! Before last night, I had never heard of Mr. Romberg."

"That's what I thought. You must excuse my brother, Mr. Salomon, for being suspicious. To the public, the world of music may seem like a gracious realm of many-splendored charm. But for those of us who have made music our business, we know just how cutthroat the enterprise can be."

"You have encountered Mr. Romberg's publisher before?"

"No. Mr. Schumetti is as unknown to us as the composer. That is what makes this whole episode so strange. How did you get hold of that sonata, if you are not acquainted with Mr. Romberg?"

"I have no idea. Until last night, I was convinced that it was my own work."

"Perhaps you heard it being played by one of the street musicians?"

"Impossible. I first got the idea for the melody over a week ago. It debuted at that birthday celebration just a few nights ago."

"Well, you must have heard it somewhere." Mr. Kimml played a few more bars of the music, before ending with a crash of discordant notes. Then he went over to where Mr. Salomon was standing and looked into the young composer's eyes. "Mr. Salomon, I am a simple man. I love music, and I like to help those who love it as I do. If you tell me that you copied another man's work unknowingly, that you are innocent of this heinous crime, I will believe you and find a way to appease my brother so that you can continue to work with us. But if, for whatever reason, you have deceived us, I beg you to have pity on a simple man and take your deceitful ways elsewhere."

"I can only repeat what I said before, Mr. Kimml. I thought, I truly thought, the sonata was mine."

"Very well, then, what are we wasting time for with talking? You must get to work."

Mr. Kimml directed the composer over to the pianoforte and sat the young man down upon the seat. "If you need anything, do not bother calling for Mr. Tree. I am giving orders down below that no one is to disturb you until you have composed a work that is so magnificent, so brilliant, so perfect that when people hear it they will forget all about Mr. S. Romberg and his sonata!"

Mr. Kimml left the room on that flourish and closed the door behind him.

Mr. Salomon watched the man go, relieved that there was at least one person in London who believed him. Although the melancholy lingered, that knowledge made him feel less alone.

He placed a hand upon the piano's keys and aimlessly began to play a few notes. The notes became less aimless, and he closed his eyes. The ache in his heart slowly began to take the shape of sound. He could see the notes rising and falling, sometimes in a rush and sometimes startlingly alone. Then from somewhere, from someplace, came a call, an answer to his anguished cry.

He reached out to grasp it.

By the time Mr. Salomon snuffed out the nearly finished candle and locked the door to his room, the hour was late and the streets of London were quiet. He looked in vain for a carriage, but there was none to be found. Yet despite his weariness, he didn't really mind the thought of the long walk home. Sitting in his coat pocket was the preliminary sketch of his new sonata, which he began to hum.

The Lyon family was having their breakfast the next morning, when a street musician appeared in Devonshire Square. The strains of the violin came in clearly through the open window, and the charm of the melody attracted the attention of Miss Rebecca Lyon. She rose from her chair and went to the window to observe the musician, for her love of good music had not been dampened by her experience with Mr. Salomon and his mother in Leeds. It was then that she noticed that the violinist was not alone. Standing beside him was a little girl, who held pages of music in her tiny hand.

"Papa, they are selling the music to that lovely song," Rebecca said to her father. "May I please buy a copy?"

"We have an entire drawer full of music that you do not play," Mr. Lyon replied.

"I shall play this song, if you will let me buy it. And I will practice the others, at least some of them."

Mr. Lyon was sorry he had spoken. He loved his daughter and admired her many good qualities. Yet the thought of her spending long hours at the pianoforte was not a pleasing one, since music was not one of her talents.

"Please."

Mr. Lyon relented, and Rebecca raced down to the square, to catch the violinist before he and his daughter went on their way. The little girl gave a pretty curtsy when Rebecca handed her the money, which made Miss Lyon feel like quite the munificent patroness of good works. But once the music was in her hands, she returned to her usual self and raced back up the stairs and into the hallway, almost knocking over Perl, who was bringing the coffee tray into the breakfast room.

"I am so sorry, Perl," said Miss Lyon. "I shall play you my new song later, to make amends."

"Thank you, miss," replied Perl, already considering how she might escape from the promised treat, since Rebecca's playing skills were as famous in the kitchen as they were in the drawing room.

When Rebecca returned to the breakfast table, she showed her father the music. He recognized the name of the composer at once, having heard all about the scandal concerning Mr. Salomon and Mr. Romberg at Baer's Coffee House the previous day.

Mrs. Lyon asked to see the music, as well. She too recognized the name of Mr. S. Romberg, since the news had come to her drawing room through two friends who had come for tea.

"So this is the sonata that everyone is talking about!" Mrs. Lyon exclaimed, with gossipy delight.

Before his helpmeet could say more, Mr. Lyon took the music and gave it back to his daughter. "Rebecca, I should like to hear you play this before I leave."

Miss Lyon rushed to obey her father's command—it was not often that the obligation to honor one's parents corresponded exactly with one's own wishes! The other children followed her into the drawing room, and soon the happy home was filled with a melody that sounded almost like the song that they had heard played in the square.

Mrs. Lyon, who was not particularly musical, listened to her daughter's playing for a moment and then said, "I do not understand what all the fuss is about. The song sounds quite ordinary to me."

"I suppose it sounds different when played by a professional musician," said Mr. Lyon, wincing slightly as a not quite right note was played in the other room. "But I would prefer that Rebecca and the other children do not know what happened to Mr. Salomon. After all, he and his mother are members of our community. We should not contribute to their shame by needlessly talking about what occurred."

"I do not like to gloat, Mr. Lyon, but I cannot help but think that the Almighty has repaid them for the way they treated you in Leeds."

"If that is so, then I consider their account paid in full—and we must invite them for a meal on Shabbos."

"Why should we do that?"

"To show them that there are some people who believe that whatever happened at Lady Windsbury's party was an honest mistake."

Mrs. Lyon was not happy. "If you feel it is the right thing to do, I shall send an invitation today. However, I shall not invite Mr. Melamed. I draw the line there, Mr. Lyon. I do not wish to encourage an alliance between Mrs. Salomon and Mr. Melamed until we are sure of the truth."

"I was actually thinking it would be a good thing to invite someone else."

"Who?"

"Samson Roth."

"Mr. Roth?"

"Yes, Mr. Roth. He is also a widower."

"Mr. Roth and Mrs. Salomon?"

Mrs. Lyon considered the suggestion. She was not overly fond of Mr. Samson Roth, who had treated his late wife abominably, in her opinion. She also did not like Mr. Roth's sons, at least not the older one. Despite that young man's highly polished manners, she always felt like one must count the silver afterward, on those rare occasions when he attended a synagogue affair.

"What an excellent suggestion, Mr. Lyon. How ever did you come to think of it?"

"It just came into my mind this morning, at the Great Synagogue," he replied, keeping to himself the real reason for the suggestion.

What had actually happened at the synagogue was that Mr. Melamed, tired of the winks and stares, had muttered angrily to Mr. Lyon, "Am I the only widower in London? Why should Mr. Roth not receive the same treatment?"

However, Mr. Lyon could hardly tell his wife all this. That good woman already heartily disliked Mrs. Salomon. To give Mrs. Lyon even more ammunition would be like placing a stumbling block before the blind. Mr. Melamed's words would be all over London by supper time, despite the Torah's wise prohibition not to be a gossip.

Mrs. Salomon was pacing up and down the beautiful but rented Turkey carpet that adorned her drawing room floor when the front bell rang. She stopped her nervous pacing and smoothed down the folds of her dress. However, it was only the second housemaid, bearing a salver, who entered the room.

Mrs. Salomon took up the letter from the salver and waved the housemaid away. When she saw that the letter was only an invitation from Mrs. Lyon for a meal on Shabbos, she waved that away as well and resumed her pacing.

The door's bell clanged a second time. Once again she smoothed the folds of her dress and tried to calm her frayed nerves, too. Then she forced herself to smile and turned to the open door.

"Mrs. Baer! How very kind of you to answer my plea for advice. I hope I am not inconveniencing you too much. Please, sit down."

The two ladies arranged themselves for a comfortable chat. After the tea had been brought in and two cups had been poured, they put aside their idle conversation about Mrs. Baer's health and the elegance of Mrs. Salomon's cap and turned to the pressing matter that most interested them both.

"I fear I have not made a favorable impression upon Mr. Melamed," said Mrs. Salomon. "First there was that unfortunate incident in Leeds, and now ... After what happened at Lady Windsbury's party, I cannot imagine what he must think of my son or me."

"I am so relieved to hear you say that you and Mr. Melamed are not suited," replied Mrs. Baer, ignoring both the fact that Mrs. Salomon had said nothing of the kind and the astonished look on Mrs. Salomon's face. "I spoke to Mr. Melamed this morning and, poor gentleman, he says he does not yet feel ready to marry again. Some men are like that, it takes years until they are able to give their heart to another. And some men never remarry, which in my opinion is a terrible shame. But what can we do, Mrs. Salomon, except go forward? It would also be a terrible shame for someone like you to waste these precious years when you are still young enough to enjoy life, which is why I have another suggestion."

Mrs. Baer stopped to take a breath. What she had said was not exactly the truth. She had spoken to Mr. Melamed. That much was true. But the gentleman had told her that he had no wish to further discuss the matter of Mrs. Salomon. He was not interested.

With another gentleman, Mrs. Baer might have used her considerable powers of persuasion to convince the person to wait a little and give the matter more thought, before closing the door entirely. But she had known Mr. Melamed for many years, and she knew him to be a man who thought before he spoke. Therefore, there was nothing to do except find someone else for Mrs. Salomon, and she now waited to see how the woman would respond to this new twist in the road to matrimony.

Mrs. Salomon, for her part, had enough experience with society to know that she must not openly express the depressed emotion she was presently feeling. She had no personal feelings for Mr. Melamed, since she had not had the opportunity to have more than one conversation with him. Yet that one meeting had been enough for her to form a favorable opinion. His appearance and manners were acceptable and, of course, there was his fortune, which was outstanding. She could have no objection to marrying Mr. Melamed. But if the opportunity had passed, she must accept it and formulate a new plan. The days were passing and the bills were piling up. This was no time to act like a schoolroom miss and throw a fit because her plans had been thwarted.

Still, she did need to make it clear that she could not marry just anyone, and so she said, "I had not realized there was another gentleman in the community who was of Mr. Melamed's caliber."

"I cannot pretend that Mr. Samson Roth is as wealthy as Mr. Melamed. Few men in our community are. Yet he lives quite comfortably, Mrs. Salomon."

Mrs. Baer was about to continue to sing Mr. Roth's praises when pangs of conscience stopped her. It was one thing to tell a lie to save the dignity of Mrs. Salomon; no woman likes to hear that she has been adamantly rejected by a prospective suitor. But Mrs.

Baer was not as enthusiastic about Mr. Roth as she would have liked to be. She knew that his first marriage had not been a happy one. Although she also knew, from her vast experience with marital matters, that no one except the husband and wife could know the truth of what went on inside the home, there were too many rumors that Mr. Roth had not been an amiable companion to his first wife.

However, the gentleman had come to the coffee house to engage her services as a matchmaker and had assured her that age, and the maturity that comes with advanced years, had shown him the error of his younger days. He had seen Mrs. Salomon from afar and had been enchanted by what he saw. (He of course did not mention that, as a silk merchant whose business was ladies' fashions, he had summed up the value of her gown, furs, and jewels with an experienced eye and decided that she possessed great wealth.) Now he wished to renew her acquaintance — he had been acquainted with the late Mr. Salomon when they were both young men starting out in life in England — if the lady was agreeable. Since the objective was holy matrimony, Mrs. Baer agreed to broach the idea with the lady in question. From there it was up to the One Above, who would either arrange things so that the two walked to the marriage canopy, or not.

While Mrs. Baer was thinking her thoughts, Mrs. Salomon was analyzing the word that the matchmaker had used to describe Mr. Roth's financial position. She vaguely recalled Mr. Roth from her youth. In those days he had not been at all well off. That meant very little, though. There was many a man who began life poor and ended it in wealth. He could be one of them.

Still, "comfortably" could mean so many things — anything from a truly luxurious set of rooms located on a fashionable square to a merely adequate way of life. Yet Mrs. Baer had seen her, seen the rooms that Mrs. Salomon had taken pains to furnish with elegance. The matchmaker must know that any suitor she proposed must be a man of suitable means. Mrs. Salomon therefore made a decision to go forward, and asked, "Is Mr. Roth ready to remarry, soon? Have you asked him?"

"He assures me that he has only to find the right lady."

"And his children — I assume that he does have children — will they mind?"

Mrs. Baer had anticipated that this question would be asked and considered how to answer. Deciding that in this instance honesty was the best tactic, since the news had become common knowledge, anyway, she said, "I am afraid that Mr. Roth's children have disappointed him. He intends to disinherit them."

"How terrible," replied Mrs. Salomon, raising her linen napkin to her lips to conceal a smile.

CHAPTER XIV

WHEN HE WAS in an intensely creative state, Mr. Salomon almost did not realize when it was night and when it was day. He felt he could work forever, without sleeping or eating — until, of course, he nearly fainted from hunger and exhaustion. Yet he needed only a morsel of food and a few hours of sleep to feel sufficiently revived to continue his work.

Others, those who had never drunk from the elixir of inspired imagination, might view his frenzied, feverish existence with censure and disdain. For him, the toll his composing took upon his health was as nothing in comparison to what his toil had accomplished: a new sonata, a new song wrested from the holy Chamber of Music. Heavenly music to be enjoyed in this weary, worry-filled world. Music that would gladden the heart of the sorrowful and uplift the spirits of the downtrodden. Music that would awaken the spirit of life-giving love in hearts grown bitter with grief and disappointment. Music that would ...

Mr. Salomon realized, with embarrassment, that he had been dancing about the room with his completed manuscript. He further realized that Mr. Tree was standing in the doorway, watching him.

"I've brought you some tea," said Mr. Tree. "Compliments of Mr. Kimml."

The shop assistant placed the tray on a table. He then glanced over at Mr. Salomon and smiled. "Is it that good?"

"Can a parent be objective about his child?"

"May I hear it? I can play it while you drink your tea."

Mr. Tree reached out his hand, but Mr. Salomon was not yet ready to part with his precious manuscript.

"I shall play it for you."

They went over to the pianoforte. Mr. Salomon kept his eyes on the keys. He was always anxious the first time he played one of his compositions for someone. But even without looking, he could sense that Mr. Tree was pleased.

When the final note had been played, Mr. Tree said, with feeling, "If I had even half your talent, Mr. Salomon, I should consider myself a fortunate man."

Before Mr. Salomon could reply there was the familiar shout of Mr. Kimml coming from below.

"Mr. Tree! Mr. Tree!"

"Shall I bring the sonata to Mr. Kimml? Perhaps I can convince him to make an exception and publish it now, even without the other compositions."

Mr. Salomon was tempted to accept Mr. Tree's offer, but he knew it was best to wait for a few days. He was a perfectionist, and he wanted to be sure that before the sonata was published it would need no further corrections. "Perhaps later this week," he therefore said.

"Mr. Tree!"

The shop assistant hurried out of the room.

Mrs. Salomon was going through the contents of her armoire when there was a knock on her bedroom door. She quickly closed the bureau's doors before she called out, "David, is that you?"

"Yes, Mother," he said, entering the room.

"You are home early. Are you not feeling well?"

"I am feeling wonderfully well. I finished my sonata today. I thought I would come home and keep you company tonight, before I start the string quartet tomorrow."

Mrs. Salomon frowned. "If I had known, I would not have accepted Lady Allyn's invitation for supper and cards. But it is wonderful news about your sonata. Will you play it for me?"

"Can you not cancel your engagement?"

"If it were a large party, I would. I cannot, though, since there is only going to be Lady Allyn, her mother, her daughter and me. If I do not go, her mother will not have her game of whist, and the Dowager Duchess must have her nightly game of whist."

"I understand."

"I am only doing it for you, David. When you are ready to perform in public again, Lady Allyn will be willing to help you, I am certain."

Mr. Salomon nodded and turned to go.

"Oh, and David, we have an invitation for Shabbos. Mr. and Mrs. Lyon have invited us to join them for the evening meal."

"You have accepted?"

"Yes, I hope you do not mind. I thought you would be pleased."

"I am. It will be a pleasure to sit at a dinner table where we expect nothing from our hosts except good food, good spirits and good conversation—and they expect only the same from us. Will there be any other guests?"

"Yes, a Mr. Samson Roth. Do you know him?"

"I have seen him at synagogue. I have not spoken to him."

"Yet one can form an opinion of a person without speaking to him. Have you formed an opinion of Mr. Roth?"

Mr. Salomon gave his mother a knowing look. "What happened to Mr. Melamed?"

"Apparently, he is not interested in remarrying."

"Are you disappointed?"

"Does it matter?"

Mr. Salomon walked over to his mother's full-length mirror and gazed at his reflection. "My opinion is that if one of us must sell ourselves for money, it should be me. Frankly, I am better looking, and when life becomes too depressing I at least have my violin."

"Be serious, David," she said, pulling him away from the mirror. "The matchmaker made the suggestion, and I consider it the polite thing to at least meet the man. Mr. Roth cannot be so terrible."

"True, he could be one of those individuals hiding a heart of gold beneath his coarse and vulgar exterior. I would be certain, though, that there is gold in his bank account as well, before you agree to marry the man."

"That is obvious. Now, please leave. I must finish dressing."

Mr. Salomon was at the door when he stopped and turned. "Does Mr. Roth have a son named Martin?"

"I don't know their names, but I understand that Mr. Roth has two sons, though we needn't worry about them. Mr. Roth intends to disinherit them both. Now you really must go, or I shall be late for Lady Allyn's party—and the Dowager Duchess does not like people to be late."

Mr. Salomon went down to the drawing room, which now seemed more than usually empty. They had sold all their own furniture before they left New York, and the rented furniture in the room held no memories for him. He glanced through the stack of calling cards sitting on the mantelpiece. They were all for his mother. He supposed he was also included in most of the invitations to supper and breakfast and tea, if he chose to go. But the invitations offered no real prospect of friendship, of congenial company to fill a lonely night, such as this one promised to be.

He therefore did what he had always done back in New York whenever he felt lonely or sad. He took his violin over to the window seat and, after opening the window wide, so that the cool evening breeze brushed against his cheek, began to play.

General Well'ngone and Saulty of the wrenched thumb were returning to Gravel Lane after yet another fruitless day of searching for Martin Roth. It was a matter of pride to the General that he could find anyone in London within a few days, and he was not happy that he had so far met with nothing but failure.

"Come on, Saulty, don't dawdle," he grumbled.

"I'm so hungry I'm ready to perish," the boy replied, before coming to a sudden stop. "Giblets, I am going to perish. Do you hear it?"

"Hear what?"

"The music. Some angel is playing his harp."

General Well'ngone stuck his hands in his coat pockets and cocked his head to one side. "That's not a harp. It's a violin."

"Do angels play the violin?"

"How should I know?"

"Do you think it's the Angel of Death, General, coming for someone?"

Despite himself, General Well'ngone shivered. "Don't talk nonsense," he growled, trying to shake off the unpleasant sensation. "This is London. There aren't any angels in London."

Martin Roth watched from his perch on a low wall as General Well'ngone and Saulty continued on their way. He knew them, since he had grown up in London, too. But he did not greet them, since he had no idea that anyone was looking for him.

He had been out for a walk, and now he was on his way back to Mr. Tree's rooms. Those rooms were far from luxurious, as the shop assistant had warned him, but Martin barely noticed. The work fascinated him, although finding a solution to the problem of Mr. Tree's invention had proven to be harder than he had anticipated. Yet the difficulty only spurred Martin to work even harder. He was certain that one day the solution would come to him.

Martin hadn't told Mr. Tree that sometimes he left the rooms to walk outside in the fresh air. There was no reason why the shop assistant should mind, Martin told himself, since he never spoke to anyone during his rambles. And walking helped to clear his mind.

Music did, too, which is why he had stopped to listen to the sounds of the violin. He wasn't a connoisseur, yet he sensed that the musician was no ordinary player. What was more, the longer he listened, the more certain he became that the piece the violinist was playing was no ordinary song.

"Strange," he murmured, when the music came to an end. "Very strange."

Mrs. Lyon wondered for how much longer she would be required to keep her smile plastered upon her face. The first two courses of the Shabbos meal had gone better than she had expected, but there was still the chicken and the beef dishes to hand round, along with the vegetables. And then her guests might expect tea afterward.

One of the wicks of the Shabbos lamp above them sputtered and the flame went out. She hoped the others might take that as a signal that the hour was getting late. But, no, her husband was encouraging Mr. Roth to tell yet another story.

She had never thought of Mr. Roth as being a particularly droll man, yet there he was entertaining her guests as though he were the most jovial man in London. Only Mr. Salomon appeared to be a little bored.

To tell the truth, Mrs. Lyon was surprised that Mrs. Salomon seemed to find Mr. Roth fascinating. The lady was not openly flirting, of course. This was a respectable home. And it was Shabbos! But Mrs. Salomon was always ready to laugh when the story was humorous, and offer her sympathy when the story was not.

Mrs. Lyon shook her head, in silent conversation with herself. Perhaps there was something to the old adage that it was the woman who made the man. She did not fault the first Mrs. Roth, of course. Yet perhaps that first marriage would have been more successful if Mrs. Roth had laughed more often at her husband's stories.

"What do you say, Mrs. Lyon? Should a woman be able to hold on to her own property, or is the law right to say that everything she owns belongs to her husband after they are married?"

Having asked her question, Mrs. Salomon beamed a smile in Mrs. Lyon's direction.

Mrs. Lyon look flustered for a moment, having been thrust from her inner thoughts and into her guests' conversation so unexpectedly. "Thank God, Mr. Lyon and I are happily married," she finally said. "The money may belong to him by law, but he has never denied my right to spend what is needed to maintain a comfortable home for our family."

Mr. Lyon saluted his wife from the other end of the table, while Mr. Roth commented, "Well said, Mrs. Lyon, well said." Mr. Roth then added, casting a glance in the direction of Mrs. Salomon, "And I should expect my wife to express a similar sentiment."

Mrs. Salomon smiled, by way of acknowledging the hint, and then turned her gaze to her son, Mr. Salomon. "What if that lady has a son whom she loves very dearly? Should she not be able to see to it that he will always be comfortably provided for?"

Mr. Roth turned red. Addressing Mr. Salomon, he said, "I beg your pardon, sir. I hope you do not interpret my words as an attempt to steal your patrimony."

Bowing his head in the direction of the other man, Mr. Salomon replied, "Rest assured, Mr. Roth, there is no danger of that. My inheritance is locked away in a place so secure that no man alive can touch it."

Afterward, Mrs. Salomon soundly berated her son for that comment. Fortunately, no one at the table had seemed to understand the meaning—that there was no inheritance, since their fortune had been squandered by Mr. Salomon's deceased father. At least she didn't think so, although she did notice that Mr. Lyon had raised an eyebrow.

"It's no good, Mother. I cannot let you marry a man like Mr. Roth."

"What then are we to do?"

"I shall give my new sonata to Mr. Kimml on Monday. Mr. Tree has hinted that Mr. Kimml might be willing to publish it immediately. If it is a success, it will give us enough to live on for a little while longer."

"Do you dislike Mr. Roth so much?"

"Do you like Mr. Roth so much?"

Mrs. Salomon smiled. "I am a very lucky woman. You are worth ten husbands to me, David."

CHAPTER XV

MR. HAROLD KIMML was coming out of his brother's music publishing shop when Mr. Salomon arrived.

"You are just the person I wish to see, Mr. Salomon," the maker of fine pianos said, by way of greeting. "Have you a few minutes to spare? I hate to take you away from your composing, but Mr. Tree is with a customer and my brother Herman, unfortunately, can be of no use."

"How may I be of service?"

Mr. Harold Kimml led the young man back out onto the street and towards his shop. "It's the new piano. My assistant, whose judgment I would usually trust, insists the sound is fine. But to my ear, something is slightly off. I was hoping to get the opinion of Mr. Tree. If you could listen to the instrument instead, I would be much obliged."

"With pleasure, sir."

By then they had reached the shop. Mr. Salomon looked with envy at the just finished piano. If it sounded as wonderful as it looked, some wealthy family was going to receive a treasure.

"Shall I just listen, or would you like me to also play?"

"If you don't mind." Mr. Kimml gestured toward the seat.

Mr. Salomon did not announce the name of the piece he was about to play, since he wanted to try out his new sonata on an impartial audience. He was delighted when Mr. Kimml reacted with pleasure soon after the main theme of the exposition was introduced. That initial delight faded, though, when Mr. Kimml began to sing along, using his hand to mark out the beat. At the end of the coda, Mr. Salomon stopped playing and looked inquiringly at the piano maker.

"Your playing is delightful, Mr. Salomon. When you play, the piano sounds wonderful! And I am happy to see that you have recovered from that unfortunate incident at Lady Windsbury's and can now make light of what happened. But tell me, where did you hear Mr. Romberg's new sonata? Were you in the audience when it received its debut on Saturday night? I did not see you there."

Mr. Salomon stared at the piano maker. "You heard this sonata on Saturday night?"

"It was very well received." Mr. Kimml hummed a few bars. "A triumph!"

"Did Mr. Romberg perform the sonata himself?"

"No. For the moment, Mr. Romberg is a man of mystery. Some people say he does not like to perform — that he is of noble birth and cannot disgrace his family by performing in public like a common musician. Others say he is the younger brother of Andreas Romberg, or his cousin Bernhard, and he is living on the Continent and his music has to be smuggled into England along with fine French lace and wine. There are others, cynics, who say that it is his publisher who is the one who has concocted the whole mystery; that when the truth is discovered we will find out that Mr. Romberg is the son of a fishmonger and lives in two shabby rooms near Petticoat Lane. Whatever the truth is, Mr. Romberg is a very lucky man. All of London is talking about him — and rightfully so. He has real talent. I would go so far as to say that he has genius."

Mr. Kimml paused, having noticed that the young composer was looking pale. "Forgive me, for rambling on. I should know better than to sing the praises of Mr. Romberg before another composer. I know that I do not like it when someone sings the praises of someone else's pianos. And I have kept you away from your work for too long. Have you finished your new sonata yet, Mr. Salomon? Would you be willing to let me hear just a little bit?"

Mr. Salomon stared at the smiling Mr. Kimml with a look that was close to horror. Rising to his feet, he said, "No. No, I ... I have nothing yet."

"Are you unwell, sir? You are looking very pale."

"I should like some air. Please excuse me." Mr. Salomon, who was feeling as though he could not breathe, walked unsteadily toward the door.

"Should I accompany you?"

"No. No, in a minute I shall be fine. Good day, sir."

After Mr. Salomon left, Mr. Kimml sat down at the pianoforte and began to play the sonata from the beginning. His assistant came forward to listen.

"It's very good."

Mr. Kimml was thoughtful as his hands came to a rest. "Yes, it is."

Mr. Salomon knew there was no point in returning to his room. Work was impossible when he felt that his head was about to explode. And at that moment he felt an intense need to get away from Cornhill Street as fast as he possibly could. He therefore hailed a passing carriage and climbed in.

"Where to, sir?" asked the coachman.

For a moment, the young man could not reply. He did not yet know London very well. Then he recalled that his mother had mentioned that Berkeley Square was a pleasant place, and he gave the coachman that direction.

Sinking back into the seat of the hired carriage, he tried to think calmly about what had just occurred. Yet how could he be calm? He could accept that, without his being consciously aware of the fact, he had overhead the first sonata — perhaps through an open window while he was taking a walk — and stored it in his brain, where its main elements were recalled when he sat down to write his own composition. But to do it twice, and within such a short amount of time, seemed too fantastic to be possible.

Then a comforting thought occurred to him, as his carriage slowly wended its way through London's crowded streets. Perhaps it was Mr. Kimml who had made the mistake. After all, Mr. Salomon had played his sonata for Mr. Tree. Perhaps Mr. Tree had played the sonata for Mr. Kimml. Then Mr. Kimml had gone to his concert, where he heard the new sonata by Mr. Romberg — and confused the two compositions.

By the time he came to this conclusion, his carriage had arrived at Berkeley Square. Mr. Salomon paid the driver and glanced about the small park, which was ringed by an orderly procession of elegant residences and shops. He had been let off near Gunter's Tea Shop, a confectionary that was famous for its fancifully flavored ices and frequented by the most fashionable members of London society.

For a few moments, Mr. Salomon forgot his own worries as he took in the charming scene. It was one of those miraculous days of autumn, when the Almighty displayed His compassion for His struggling creatures by commanding the sun to bestow one last day of warmth and light before the damp gloom of winter set in finally for the season. Several open carriages were parked in the square, opposite the tea shop, and a few waiters were hurrying from the shop to serve the gaily colored ices to the ladies sitting in their carriages, whose pelisses and bonnets were as brightly colored as their refreshments. A few gentlemen, elegant in their more somber close-fitting coats, gleaming riding boots, and narrow-brimmed top hats, attended the ladies. The company's carefree laughter filled the square, in pleasing counterpoint to the birds chirping in the park's numerous leafy trees.

It was a pretty world, and Mr. Salomon was not immune to its charms. What made it all the more tantalizing was the knowledge that he could be a part of it, in some small way. Although Mr. Kimml had mistakenly ascribed his new sonata to the pen of Mr. Romberg, the piano manufacturer had called the sonata a work of genius. He had only to apprise Mr. Harold Kimml of his mistake and present the sonata to Mr. Herman Kimml and he would be back on the path to fame and fortune. By this time next week, he might be laughing as cheerfully as the ladies and gentlemen in the park, his financial worries as forgotten as yesterday's scandal sheets.

And then he heard it.

From behind him, someone had struck the first chords on a violin. The introduction was followed by the jangle of a barrel organ and the sound of a woman singing. Mr. Salomon could only stare open-mouthed as the group passed by him, performing his sonata—his new sonata!—whose main theme had apparently already been set to words!

The group of musicians moved toward the carriages, where the fashionable ladies and gentlemen listened with delight. Windows that dotted the square began to open, and heads popped out to listen. Even Mr. Gunter's battalion of waiters stopped their running to enjoy the impromptu concert.

At the end, a child—perhaps the young daughter of the singer—sprang forward with an upturned tambourine to collect the coins that dropped down upon the group like beneficent raindrops on a parched land. Then the band of musicians left the way they came, passing a still-stricken Mr. Salomon as they departed.

The little girl held out her tambourine. When Mr. Salomon did not respond, she gave him a contemptuous look. And then they were gone.

A few minutes had already passed when Mr. Salomon thought to follow them and discover how they had heard the sonata. Dashing through the streets, he heard occasional strains of music over the clatter of the carriages and horses and followed them. But when he caught up with the players he was astonished to discover that it was a different group of street musicians who were playing his sonata to an enthusiastic crowd.

The musicians were also selling the music and Mr. Salomon purchased a copy. His eyes immediately went to the top of the page, where the name of the composer was written. He felt the world swim around him in a dizzying haze as the letters of the name of Mr. S. Romberg danced before his eyes.

He felt he must remain rooted to that spot forever, a pillar of salt, like Lot's wife. It did not matter that the hurrying crowds were passing by him, anxious to be on their way now that the musical performance was over. Let them jostle him and cast irritable glances at his immobile figure, which was blocking the path. He could not move. To walk, to take even the tiniest step, seemed like an impossible feat when he felt as though his very life had been knocked out of him.

"Mr. Salomon!"

The words came to him as though from a faraway land, the echo of an echo. The owner of that voice—Mr. Powell—alighted from his carriage, which had become stalled in the heavy afternoon traffic, and took the composer by the arm. He guided Mr. Salomon toward his carriage in silence, waiting until they were safely inside to speak.

"Do you require a physician, sir?"

Mr. Salomon looked at the man seated beside him. He vaguely recalled the face. That initial recollection was followed by the realization that the man had been at Lady Windsbury's party, that he had been seated beside Mr. Melamed.

"If you wish to be of service, sir, take me to the lunatic asylum. That is the only fitting place for someone like me."

Mr. Powell removed the crumpled pieces of paper from Mr. Salomon's hand. Seeing that it was a sonata written by Mr. Romberg, he correctly assumed that the young composer had experienced some sort of shock. Not knowing what else to do, he called out to his coachman, "Bury Street, Charles. Take us to Mr. Melamed."

CHAPTER XVI

IF MR. MELAMED was surprised to see Mr. Powell escort a pale-looking Mr. Salomon into his library, he did not embarrass the young man by showing it. He merely instructed his butler to bring his guests some tea. While they waited for the reviving beverage to arrive, he and Mr. Powell chatted about some mundane business matters. It was only after the tea had been poured out and the butler had closed the door behind him that Mr. Melamed lifted an inquiring eyebrow at the two gentlemen seated opposite him.

"I saw Mr. Salomon on Piccadilly Street," said Mr. Powell. "He looked as though he had taken ill, and so I brought him here."

"Are you ill, Mr. Salomon? I can recommend a very good physician."

"I am not ill, so please let us stop this farce. I have gone mad, Mr. Melamed. Your friend found me staring like a madman in the middle of a busy street, unable to move or speak, in the middle of a fit."

"There is a difference between experiencing a shock and a fit of madness," said Mr. Powell.

"True, but the shock was caused by the discovery that I am mad."

"How did this discovery come about?" asked Mr. Melamed.

Mr. Powell handed him the music, which he had kept stowed away in his coat pocket. Mr. Melamed saw the name of the composer and glanced in the direction of Mr. Salomon. "Should this tell us something?"

Mr. Salomon nodded his head. "I wrote that sonata. I tell you, I wrote that sonata — not Mr. Romberg! Now what have you to say?"

"Why then is it not your name that appears at the top of the page?"

"If I knew that!" Mr. Salomon threw his hands up in the air.

Mr. Melamed and Mr. Powell exchanged glances. It was evident that Mr. Salomon was under a great deal of stress, perhaps on the verge of hysteria. Yet they must get to the bottom of the mystery, if they were to be of help.

"When did you write your sonata?" asked Mr. Melamed.

"Last week."

"After Lady Windsbury's party?"

Mr. Salomon again nodded his head, this time more impatiently. "After Lady Windsbury's party."

"You wrote it at your home?"

"No, I have been given a room to use by the Kimml brothers. It is above Mr. Kimml's music publishing company, on Cornhill Street."

"Does Mr. Romberg also compose his music in this building?"

"Of course not. If he did, the Kimmls would know who he is, and no one knows who Mr. Romberg is."

"How can that be? Someone must know him. Otherwise, how can his music be performed and published?"

Mr. Salomon shrugged and again lifted his hands in exasperation. "I only know what I have been told. Mr. Romberg does not perform in public in England, either because he does not wish to do so or because he is currently in Europe and cannot do so."

"Have you any idea how it could have happened that you and Mr. Romberg have written the same sonata?"

"Not just one sonata, Mr. Melamed," Mr. Salomon bitterly replied. "Remember, please, what happened at Lady Windsbury's party."

"Very well, have you an explanation?"

"I have given it, sir. I am mad."

"That does not explain how you gained access to Mr. Romberg's work," said Mr. Powell. "I was at the concert on Saturday night, when this new sonata was first performed. I do not recall seeing you there."

"That is because I was not there."

"Perhaps you heard it being rehearsed?" asked Mr. Melamed.

"No. All last week I was in my room, above Mr. Kimml's establishment, lost in a delusion that I was creating a masterpiece that would make my name and fortune. I only left Cornhill Street to eat at Mr. Baer's coffee house or to go home to sleep. I did not stop at any concert hall to eavesdrop on rehearsals."

"There must be some explanation for how you heard these two pieces," Mr. Powell insisted. "You could not have both pulled the same notes from the thin air."

"Perhaps I have a twin brother that my mother never told me about, or a doppelganger. Yes, that must be it. Mr. S. Romberg is my doppelganger, my alter ego, my spiritual twin. Last week, we were both sitting in our respective rooms, hearing the same music, struggling over the same phrases, rejoicing over the same resolutions. The only difference being that he is quicker than I am when it comes to getting his work performed and published."

"I think Mr. Powell was suggesting that there must be a rational reason," said Mr. Melamed, whose logical mind rebelled at the thought of this sort of supernatural solution, even when it was proposed with cynicism by a distraught young man.

"If there is a rational reason I would be much obliged if someone could find it, before ..." Mr. Salomon quickly rose from his seat and went over to the bay window that looked over the street to collect himself. He had almost let slip the secret that was lingering in the back of his mind—that very soon he and his mother would be penniless. When he felt he could speak without revealing that secret, he returned to the two men and said, "I do not know if you can understand what a blow this is, or why it has unnerved me in the way that it has, and so I apologize for my behavior, which to you must seem extreme. I agree that there must be some rational explanation. Perhaps someday it will be revealed. Good day, gentlemen."

Mr. Salomon bowed and turned toward the door.

"Wait! You do not wish Mr. Melamed to help you?" asked Mr. Powell.

"Are you acquainted, sir, with Mr. Romberg or his publisher, Mr. Schumetti?"

"No," Mr. Melamed replied.

"Then how can you help me?"

Mr. Powell laughed. "Don't worry about that! Mr. Melamed has his ways."

Mr. Powell offered the use of his carriage to take Mr. Melamed and Mr. Salomon to Cornhill Street. Mr. Salomon's predicament intrigued him, and so he did not mind accompanying the two other men while Mr. Melamed made his initial inquiries.

On the way there, Mr. Salomon told the others what he knew about the Kimml brothers. "But I suppose you are already aware of this, Mr. Melamed, since it was you who recommended them to my mother."

Mr. Melamed did not mention that he personally knew nothing about the Kimmls, since the introduction had come about through Mrs. Baer. But since he had been the instigator of that introduction, through his initial promise to try and help the young composer, he now felt a personal obligation to extricate Mr. Salomon from his intolerable position. And if the Kimmls were somehow involved, he must discover what their involvement might be. But he did not mention this either, preferring to not cast suspicion on anyone so soon in his investigation.

Instead, Mr. Melamed expressed a wish to see with his own eyes Mr. Herman Kimml's establishment, both the inside of the building and its exterior, to better understand the place where Mr. Salomon had been doing his composing. So that the group would not draw attention to themselves, Mr. Melamed suggested that Mr. Salomon go up to his room, as usual.

After Mr. Salomon left them, Mr. Melamed said to Mr. Powell, "You will pretend to be a customer, while I take a look around outside."

"Is there anything I should do?"

"After I join you upstairs, we must find a reason to send Mr. Tree out of the room. Giving him a message for your coachman might be the easiest way. Then I want you to take a seat at the piano and start banging loudly on the keys — the wrong keys."

"You wish to see if Mr. Herman Kimml is as deaf as he pretends to be?"

Mr. Melamed nodded, and the two parted ways. While Mr. Powell ascended the stairs to the shop, Mr. Melamed searched out the alleyway that would lead to the back of the building. When he found it and retraced his steps, he glanced up to the small window that Mr. Salomon had described. It was closed — Mr. Salomon had mentioned that he had never succeeded in opening it — and Mr. Melamed threw a small stone, which tapped lightly against the pane. In a moment, the face of Mr. Salomon appeared through the dirt-streaked glass and the composer nodded his head. As previously arranged, Mr. Salomon returned to the pianoforte and began to play.

Mr. Melamed listened. He could hear nothing, except the noise coming from the other business establishments whose windows also looked out upon the back alleyway and the fainter sounds of city life coming from Cornhill Street. Those sounds would not be heard at night, yet he wondered how clearly Mr. Salomon's playing would be heard through that small window even then, since the window was always closed.

Satisfied that he had seen all there was to see outside, he joined Mr. Powell inside the shop. Mr. Powell was in conversation with Mr. Tree, who was seated at the piano, playing a piece by Mr. Johann Sebastian Bach.

"I shall be with you in a moment, sir," said Mr. Tree.

"We are together," Mr. Melamed replied. "Powell, your coachman wishes to know if he should wait for us or deliver the hat to your aunt."

"My aunt will be insulted if I do not accompany her birthday gift." He then turned to Mr. Tree and said, "Please tell my coachman to wait."

Mr. Tree did not take offense at being treated like a messenger boy. He had grown up amongst the gentry and was accustomed to their careless ways of treating anyone not in their station of life as a personal servant.

After Mr. Tree left, Mr. Powell sat down at the piano. "What do you think of this?" he said and began to randomly bang at the keys.

Mr. Melamed had noted that Mr. Kimml, who was seated at his desk at the back of the room, had looked up when he had entered the shop and had watched Mr. Tree leave. Yet that proved nothing. As the shop's proprietor it was only natural that he would be sensitive to the movements of his customers and staff. The air coming in from a just opened door, the change in light as a person stood by a window and blocked the sun might be enough to alert the deaf man that someone had entered or left.

Indeed, when Mr. Powell had sat down at the piano, Mr. Kimml had looked up and waved his hand and said, "You are welcome, sir. Play as long as you like." He then had returned to his work.

Mr. Melamed fought the temptation to raise his hands to his ears, while Mr. Powell continued to play. Even he found it painful to listen to the noise that was emanating from the piano. Yet Mr. Kimml, who surely once had a more sensitive ear than him, did not wince. When he did look up, it was to smile and wave. "Enjoy yourself, sir. It is a pleasure to see a gentleman play with so much gusto!"

Through the noise, Mr. Melamed could hear faintly footsteps on the stairs. He signaled to Mr. Powell to stop playing, and a few moments later Mr. Tree appeared.

Mr. Tree gave them a curious glance, and Mr. Melamed realized that the man must have heard the noise out on the street.

"My friend was showing me what he thinks of Beethoven's music," said Mr. Melamed. "I hope he did not scare the horses."

Mr. Tree smiled. "Beethoven is not to everyone's taste. May I demonstrate anything else?"

"Have you anything by Mr. Romberg?" asked Mr. Powell.

"Mr. Andreas Romberg? I am afraid not. I believe he is represented by Mr. Clementi's publishing house."

"I was referring to Mr. S. Romberg. I hear he has a new sonata."

Mr. Tree glanced from one gentleman to the other, before saying, "We do not carry the music of Mr. S. Romberg."

"Then I shall take this," said Mr. Powell, giving Mr. Tree a coin in payment for the piece of music by Mr. Bach that Mr. Tree had first suggested.

When Mr. Tree returned with Mr. Powell's change, Mr. Melamed said, as though the thought had only just then occurred to him, "Are you familiar with a gentleman named David Salomon. I believe he has rented a rehearsal room somewhere on Cornhill Street."

"He has a room in this building. May I say who wishes to see him?"

They gave their names and Mr. Tree, after giving a worried glance at the piano, climbed the stairs to the next floor. In the silence that ensued, Mr. Melamed listened.

"Do you hear him playing?" he said softly to Mr. Powell.

Mr. Powell shook his head. "These old buildings were built with thick walls."

When Mr. Tree returned, it was to show the visitors upstairs.

"Will you be requiring tea, Mr. Salomon?" he asked.

"Not for us," said Mr. Melamed.

"No thank you, then, Mr. Tree," said Mr. Salomon, who followed the shop assistant to the door, which he closed tightly after Mr. Tree had left. He then turned to the two other men and asked, "Well, have you discovered anything?"

"I do not think it is possible to hear you playing from outside," said Mr. Melamed. "Did you hear anything from the shop?"

"If you mean that great cacophony of noise, yes, I did hear that."

"But not the other times, when Mr. Tree was playing?"

"No, I rarely hear anything from the shop."

"Do you hear when someone goes up and down the stairs?"

"Only if I am not playing, or if I am not lost in thought."

Mr. Melamed looked about the room. It was obvious that there was no place where a person could hide in that empty space. "What is on the other side of this room?"

"I believe it is a storeroom where some of the music is kept. I have never looked."

"Please play something, while I do so."

Mr. Melamed went out to the corridor. He could hear Mr. Salomon playing inside the room. He could also hear Mr. Tree playing down below, and he hoped he was correct to assume that the assistant was with a customer. He went to the door of the storeroom and tried the knob. The door was not locked. He entered the room, which was similar in shape and size to the room where Mr. Salomon did his composing. Like the other room, only one small window illuminated the space. Unlike the other room, this one was crowded with cabinets and wooden boxes, in which, presumably, reams of music were stored.

He noted that the wall that adjoined the other room was hidden by a row of bookshelves, which reached from the floor to the ceiling and from one end of the room to another. Each shelf was piled high with manuscripts, which served to almost muffle completely the music coming from the other room, when both doors were closed. It would not be impossible, if a person listened closely, to transcribe the notes that Mr. Salomon was playing, but it would be hard work.

Mr. Melamed returned to the door and was about to leave when he noticed something lying on the floor, which had been concealed by the door when he had opened it to enter the room. He stooped down to pick it up and saw that it was nothing more than a piece of black gauze material, about the size of a handkerchief. It did not look important, but he stuffed it into his pocket anyway. One never knew and, since the piece of material wasn't covered in dust, it did show that someone had been in the room fairly recently. He then returned to Mr. Salomon's room, having completed his inquiry.

"If someone has been listening to you, Mr. Salomon, it appears they could have done so only from the corridor or the stairs, both of which seem unlikely since the person could be discovered at any moment."

"That is what I thought. No one has stolen *my* music."

Mr. Melamed thought for a few moments, and then he said, "I know that you and your mother are only recently arrived in England, but is it possible that you have made any enemies here?"

Mr. Salomon smiled wanly. "Other than you and Mr. Lyon?"

Mr. Melamed brushed aside the response. "Let us forget about what happened in Leeds. I can assure you that neither Mr. Lyon nor I wish to harm you. But is there anyone else who might?"

Once again, Mr. Salomon found himself caught between a desire to openly assist Mr. Melamed with his investigation and an equally strong desire to hide the true state of his financial position. He therefore did not mention Jonas Street, but he did say, "I did offend a musician in Leeds, a pianoforte player named Karl Grimm. I cannot believe, though, that he would take steps to harm me."

"Have you run across him in London?"

Mr. Salomon stared at Mr. Melamed. "Now that you mention it, I did see him once at Mr. Baer's coffee house. He didn't stay long, since he was looking for gin."

"Did he see you?"

"Yes."

"Did he say anything to you?"

"No, Mr. Baer suggested he leave before he felt tempted to make a scene."

"Have you pen and ink here? I would like to take down his description."

Mr. Salomon walked over to the table that served as both his dining table and desk, and opened the drawer. When he did so, he let out a gasp.

"Is something wrong, Mr. Salomon?" asked Mr. Powell.

By way of response, Mr. Salomon removed from the drawer a sticky pile of papers that were almost completely covered in black ink.

"It is my new sonata." He showed the obliterated score to Mr. Melamed and Mr. Powell. "Why? Why did someone destroy it?"

"Perhaps they wished to destroy any proof that your work was the same as the piece published by Mr. Romberg," said Mr. Melamed.

Mr. Salomon could not stop staring at the inky pages.

"It could be worse," said Mr. Powell, once again taking out the music that Mr. Salomon had bought earlier that day. "At least the score to your sonata still exists."

That, however, was cold comfort for Mr. Salomon.

CHAPTER XVII

THE HOUR WAS already growing late, and Mr. Melamed felt that nothing more could be accomplished that day. Mr. Powell therefore drove the two Jewish men to the Great Synagogue, where members of the community were already gathering for *Mincha*, the afternoon prayer.

"You will keep me apprised of what happens?" he asked.

"Of course," replied Mr. Melamed. "Do you think you could use your influence to send a letter to the Continent in a diplomatic pouch?"

"I could try."

"I would like to know if anyone has heard of a Mr. S. Romberg."

"I'll let you know if I find out anything," replied Mr. Powell, and then his carriage drove off.

Mr. Salomon had already turned, to make his way toward the synagogue, when he stopped. Standing in the courtyard was Mr. Samson Roth, who was speaking to a young man.

Mr. Melamed saw the pair, as well. He slightly pushed Mr. Salomon forward and nodded in the direction of Mr. Roth and his son Nathan as they passed by them, on their way to the synagogue's front door.

Mr. Samson Roth was not pleased by the sight of Mr. Melamed walking practically arm in arm with Mrs. Salomon's son. He hoped that the philanthropist had not changed his mind and decided to pursue Mrs. Salomon after all.

Nathan followed his father's gaze with interest. "Who is the young man? Mr. Melamed's long-lost son?"

"He is Mrs. Salomon's son."

Nathan raised his quizzing glass to his eye. "So that is the person who has replaced me in your affections and your purse."

"If you have something to say to me, say it now, or you will have to wait until after *Mincha*."

"Cannot we at least step to the side of the square, Father? Must all our family's sordid affairs become public?"

Mr. Roth glared at his son, but did as Nathan requested. When they had found a quiet corner, he said, "What mischief are you up to now, Nathan?"

"I am hurt, Father. Here I've come all the way to Duke's Place to see you and ..."

"I haven't time for this. Tell me what you want."

"Does Mrs. Salomon know that your property and your belongings now belong to a rather well-known moneylender?"

"I do not know what you are talking about."

"Now it is my turn to be abrupt, Father. Let's not waste time. I was forced to pay a visit to the same gentleman yesterday. He refused to lend me money, informing me that he had lent out as much money as he dared to such a shaky enterprise as Mr. Samson Roth & Sons. The only question now is if the lady knows that very soon you will be sitting in debtors' prison — unless she pays off your promissory notes. I assume she is wealthy."

"How much do you want?"

"She must be very wealthy." Nathan smiled and then named a large sum.

Mr. Roth angrily shook his fist in his son's face. "Have you gone mad?"

"Think it over, Father. It would be a shame to let a fortune slip through your fingers, just at the time when you need it most."

"If you think you can blackmail me, you are mistaken."

"We shall see who is mistaken, sir. And do give my compliments to Mrs. Salomon's son. Tell him he is welcome to my inheritance, since it is now nothing but bad debts."

General Well'ngone and Saulty came out from their hiding places, after Mr. Roth and his son left what they had thought was a secluded corner where their conversation would not be overheard.

"What a world," said the General, sadly shaking his head. "It almost breaks my heart to see fathers and sons speak to one another like that."

"And them being almost gentry, too."

"But we have work to do. You follow Nathan Roth and see if he'll lead you to his brother Martin. I'm going to keep my eye on David Salomon."

One might think that General Well'ngone would be an easy person to spot, even in London's crowded thoroughfares. Yet poverty is a curious thing. No one cares, really, about the poor children that one sees on the street. The orphaned child can do you no favor — offer you no loans or advancement at court. You will not marry your daughter to him, or take him into your business. And so he is invisible.

The General was also helped by the fact that Mr. Salomon was exhausted, after the long and distressing day. The musician walked home in a weary daze, oblivious to poor and well-to-do alike. Yet when he reached the door to his house, Mr. Salomon knew he must gather up what remained of his shattered strength. Unless his mother was out, she would want to know what happened with his sonata and Mr. Kimml. He must tell her the whole story.

Meanwhile, the General had hidden in a nearby stairwell, where he exchanged his large bicorne hat for a smaller cap. He also removed a box that, when opened, revealed a small cache of thimbles and needles and other sewing notions. Thus attired in his peddler's disguise, he set up shop on Mr. Salomon's street and hawked his wares for a few minutes. When he was certain that he had been seen, ignored and forgotten, he casually strolled to the end of the street and disappeared into the narrow alleyway behind the building, counting the houses until he arrived at the one belonging to the Salomons. There he found a hiding place, from which he could listen to the conversation going on in the family's back sitting room.

"I do not understand, David. How could you and Mr. Romberg have written the exact same sonata? Twice?" asked Mrs. Salomon.

"That is what Mr. Melamed is trying to find out."

"Mr. Melamed," she said bitterly. "I wish we had never come to London."

"We haven't had much luck, have we?"

"It is not a question of luck. Sometimes I feel ... I feel we are being chased by some evil spirit, some demon who has escaped from ... only God knows where."

Mr. Salomon went over to the window and gazed into the mews, whose walls had already disappeared into the darkness of the night.

General Well'ngone stooped down a little lower.

"Mother, you are certain that we paid Jonas Street what we owed him? There were so many debts to pay off before we left New York, and so little money to do it with. Perhaps we did forget him."

"Jonas Street! I am sick to death of hearing about Jonas Street!"

"Well, he is chasing us, and he certainly looks to me like a demon escaped from some nightmare." He paused and then said, "Tell me the truth, Mother? What happened to Father's receipt book? Did you forget it in New York?"

"I do not want to hear that receipt book or Jonas's name mentioned again in my house."

Mrs. Salomon swept out of the room, her face glowing with pent up rage.

Mr. Salomon did not follow her. Instead, he picked up his violin and vented his own anger and frustration on the object that until now he had always considered his friend. He did not use the bow to play, but plucked the unresisting strings with a sharp ferocity, striving for the ugliest sound he could pull from the sweet-tempered instrument, as though to say to his doppelganger, "Here, copy this — and see how much good it will do you!"

While he was thus engaged in his angry serenade, a rock came crashing through the window and almost hit the violin. After he recovered from his first shock, he stretched his head out the window to see who had been lurking in the darkness outside. He was too late to see much. He caught only the glimpse of a young person running after one, or possibly two fleeing adults. Then he heard the sound of a sharp whistle, after which he saw and heard nothing more.

General Well'ngone waited for a moment to see if anyone from the Earl's gang would answer his whistle. When that shrill blast was greeted with silence, he kicked a nearby railing, a handy substitute for kicking himself. He had been so engrossed in the conversation going on inside the house that he had not noticed that anyone else had crept into the mews. That was inexcusable for a person with his long experience in the streets. Then he had let those persons get away, without his so much as getting a glimpse of their faces. Another black mark on his record, he bitterly thought, as he retrieved his bicorne hat from its hiding place.

"I must be getting old," he muttered sadly, as he made his way back to Gravel Lane. "Pretty soon I won't be good for anything but honest work."

The Earl of Gravel Lane listened to General Well'ngone's tale with a mixture of amusement and perplexity.

"They are both in debt?" he asked. "Mr. Roth and Mrs. Salomon both have no money?"

"So it seems," replied the General. "Mr. Roth wants to marry Mrs. Salomon for her money, and it looks like she wants to marry Mr. Roth for his money. I wonder what will happen when they wake up and realize that all they've done is married each other debts."

"I should not like to be in the vicinity when that explosion occurs, I can assure you of that. Where is Saulty?"

"He hasn't returned yet? He was supposed to be following Nathan Roth, to see if the path would lead to Martin."

The Earl was thoughtful. "Why can't we find Martin Roth, General?"

"I don't know."

"A man can disappear in London for only so long. If he is well, someone will know of his whereabouts. If he is in trouble, either he turns up at one of the flash houses, or his body gets washed up on the shores of the Thames."

"We've been looking everywhere."

The Earl closed his eyes and retreated more deeply into his thoughts. "Perhaps that has been our mistake. Perhaps instead of looking for Martin Roth everywhere, we should try looking for him nowhere."

The General gave his superior a perplexed look, but said nothing. He would rather leave the Earl in a contemplative mood than risk raising his ire over the incident with the rock throwers. Yet when he tried to noiselessly tip-toe out of the room, the Earl of Gravel Lane stopped him and, without opening his eyes, said, "Nowhere, General. Put the word into your dreams. If you wished to be nowhere, where would you be? If you wished to be nobody, who would you be?"

Mr. Melamed was also in a pensive mood that night. It was after dinner, and Mr. Salomon was now sitting with him in his library. The young composer had just described to him the incident with the rock.

"It might have hit my mother," said Mr. Salomon.

"If your mother had been the intended target, the rock would have been thrown sooner. The object was meant to either hurt you or destroy your violin."

Mr. Salomon grasped the violin's case even tighter. Perhaps it was absurd, but after the incident he had been afraid to leave the violin unattended in his home. He had felt able to leave his home and pay a visit to Mr. Melamed because his mother was out for the evening, attending yet another supper and card party at Lady Allyn's.

Mr. Melamed noticed the gesture, which was a perfectly natural one for a talented musician to make. He himself did not play any instrument, but his wife had been an accomplished player of the harp and she had often spoken about the uniqueness of musical instruments, at least when they were made by an expert craftsman. Each instrument had not only a voice, but a soul, she would say, which is why an accomplished musician could not easily change one instrument for another. It took time to learn an instrument's personality — both its charms and its quirks — and sometimes the desired harmony between player and instrument could never be reached. No, Mr. Salomon would not want to lose his violin.

"What exactly was the quarrel between you and Mr. Grimm?" asked Mr. Melamed.

"I cannot say exactly, since my very existence seemed to offend the man. But I did refuse to include one of his compositions in the program. And he took offense at my interpretation of one of Clementi's sonatinas."

Mr. Melamed shook his head. It was true that musicians could be temperamental, but he could not imagine a musician destroying first another musician's composition and then his violin for such a commonplace reason. "What about the other musicians? Or someone else in Leeds? Was there no other incident you can think of?"

Mr. Salomon was silent. The rock had done more than shatter a windowpane and given him a momentary scare. It had brought the often violent world of his Father into his home. He therefore decided that he must be frank with Mr. Melamed and reveal the entire truth. He told Mr. Melamed about Jonas Street and the man's claim that the Salomons owed him money. "But I cannot see how this could have anything to do with Mr. Romberg. Jonas Street knows nothing about music. He could not possibly have sat outside my room and transcribed my sonata."

"He could, though, have thrown the rock and covered your musical score with ink."

"You think, then, that those incidents and the Romberg sonatas are unrelated?"

"I have not reached any conclusions yet," said Mr. Melamed. "I am only trying to understand your life. It might be worth it to you and your mother to pay off Jonas Street and put him on a boat to America, if you feel a mistake may have been made, especially if the man has a violent nature."

Mr. Salomon took a deep breath. "Unfortunately, we are not in position to do so."

"Your money is still in New York?"

"Our money is gone, Mr. Melamed. I was counting on the sales of my sonata to tide us over, until my career is more established." He paused, wondering how much he should reveal. A glance at Mr. Melamed's stony face convinced him that he must go on. "I do not mind teaching, but even that will be out of my grasp until my name is cleared. But I do mind my mother having to marry a man she cannot possibly love, simply to save us from the workhouse. You do not really know my mother, Mr. Melamed. She was truly an enchanting, affectionate creature before my father's business affairs turned sour. It is desperation that makes her seem cold and calculating at times. I do not doubt that she would try her best to make Mr. Roth a good wife, but I fear that it would kill her soul, which is why I cannot allow the marriage to occur."

Mr. Melamed did not say what he was thinking—that there were people who managed to retain their generosity and compassion even while in the midst of real and unexpected misfortune. He too much respected Mr. Salomon for trying to show his mother's character in a good light. Yet he also felt that the young man must be set straight, and so he said, "It is not for the son to tell his mother what to do."

"But it is up to me, as the only remaining male member of the family, to provide my mother with the financial security she needs to make a wise decision. We are straying, though, from the reason why I am here. You asked about other enemies I might have. I seem to have also offended Mr. Deare, although I cannot think why. Perhaps because I declined his offer to visit the factories in Leeds, he took offense. My mother tried to make up for my lack of tact by reading one of his boring pamphlets."

Mr. Melamed's attention alighted upon the name of Mr. Deare. "Did you meet Mr. Roth's two sons while you were in Leeds? One of them, Martin Roth, worked for Mr. Deare."

"I may have seen him, when we visited Mr. Deare's furniture shop, but he did not dine with us."

At the mention of the furniture shop, an unpleasant thought entered Mr. Melamed's mind, which he felt he must clarify. "Mr. Salomon, are you aware that fifty pounds went missing from Mr. Deare's strongbox on the day that you and your mother left Leeds?"

Mr. Salomon rose angrily from his seat. "And are you aware, Mr. Melamed, I had twenty pounds in my pocket on that day, my proceeds from the concert I gave in Leeds?"

Mr. Melamed smiled. "You are correct to be angry, sir. I had forgotten about the concert. Please accept my apologies."

Mr. Salomon gave a stiff bow. "Is there anything else I can do to assist you in your inquiries?"

"For the moment, just continue with your normal routine. But fix the broken windowpane as soon as you can—and stay away from windows from now on. And keep a lookout for anyone who might be following you."

Mr. Salomon refused the offer of Mr. Melamed's carriage to drive him home. The distance, which was not a long one, would not have been worth the effort of harnessing the horses. Yet as he walked he felt an increasing uneasiness with each step. He had the feeling that he was being watched, although there was no echo of footsteps behind him, no rustle of a branch disturbed by human hands.

When he reached his home, he gave a sigh of relief. Looking back at the dark and silent street, he whispered, "Mr. Doppelganger, goodnight."

But his attempt to lighten his depressed spirits failed when he saw what was on the other side of the closed door.

CHAPTER XVIII

THE SOUND OF a woman sobbing in the drawing room was the first thing to alert Mr. Salomon that something was terribly wrong. He ran to the door and discovered his mother kneeling on the Turkey carpet, her head buried in the cushions of the sofa, her shoulders heaving with the force of her anguished cries. A letter was clenched tightly in her hand.

Normally, Mr. Salomon would have gone immediately to his mother. But in those first moments he saw something else that made his blood run cold. Scrawled on the large mirror that sat above the mantelpiece was a line of music, the notes written in heavy black ink. Above the music was one word: Romberg.

The housemaid brushed past him, bearing a vial of smelling salts on a tray. Mrs. Salomon tried to push away the bottle, and as she did so she saw Mr. Salomon standing in the doorway.

"David, thank God you're home!" She rushed to him and collapsed into his arms.

He gently led her back to the sofa and sat her down, taking a seat beside her. Holding her trembling hands in his, which were also shaking, he said, "It's all right now, Mother. Please try to calm down."

He sent away the housemaid, after she had set down the tray. Mrs. Salomon slowly regained her composure and, removing her hand from her son's grasp, wiped the tears from her eyes with her handkerchief. "Where were you, David?"

"I went to see Mr. Melamed. I wanted to tell him about the rock that was thrown into the other room."

"Next time, tell one of the servants where you are going. I was frantic with worry."

"I thought you would still be at Lady Allyn's. You usually do not come home until late."

"The Dowager Duchess felt unwell during dinner. The party ended early."

Mr. Salomon looked down at the letter that his mother was still holding in her hand. "Bad news?"

"I am not sure. It was waiting in the entranceway when I returned home. Read it."

Mr. Salomon took the letter. The message was comprised of just two things. The first was an address. The second line read: "Ask if Mr. Samson Roth is familiar with the gentleman."

"The address means nothing to me," said Mr. Salomon, puzzled. "Does it mean anything to you?"

"It is the business establishment of a moneylender. I went there this evening, before I went to Lady Allyn's. But I was so careful! I left the carriage several streets before the man's street. Afterward I did the same thing. How can someone know I was there? How could anyone find me out so quickly?"

"What did you pawn, Mother?"

"My fur-lined cape."

"The one Father gave you for your birthday?"

"This is no time to be sentimental."

"I remember that night. I watched you and Father from the top of the staircase. You were going to some party, and you were wearing your new cape."

"We need the money. If your career as a composer is finished ..."

She realized too late that she could not have hurt him more if she had slapped him across the face. "Don't pay attention to what I say, David. It's the strain. This is how it began with your father, the anonymous notes, the insinuations, followed by the threats." She glanced over at the ink-stained mirror. "If Jonas Street did that ..."

"This cannot be his work. I doubt he can write a single note, let alone one whole line of music."

"Then who did do it?"

"I don't know."

Mrs. Salomon turned back to her son. "Mr. Roth must not find out that I have been to a moneylender."

"We cannot stop whoever wrote this letter from telling him."

"Then we must think of something to say, something that won't make it seem as though I did it because we needed the money."

"That should be easy, Mother," said Mr. Salomon, rising from the sofa and walking over to the mirror. He traced the opening notes of the sonata with his finger, and then stared fully into the reflection of his sad and weary face. "Just tell Mr. Roth what you have told me. The cape was a gift from someone who disappointed you. You have no further use for his gifts, just as you have no further use for him."

The next morning Mr. Salomon approached Mr. Melamed at the Great Synagogue and apprised him of what happened the night before. After the morning service, Mr. Melamed accompanied the composer to his home, where the two gentlemen stood before the mirror, trying to read some further meaning into the defaced surface.

"This has been written by someone who knows music," said Mr. Salomon, "someone who is accustomed to writing down musical notes."

Mr. Melamed nodded. Looking at the mirror gave him a strange sensation. There was nothing ugly about the musical score; he agreed with Mr. Salomon that it had been written by an accomplished hand. But the violence of the act—the invasion of the family's home and privacy, the accusation that was hurled, literally, into Mr. Salomon's reflected face—disturbed him more than he wanted to admit.

"May I destroy the mirror? My mother would prefer not to see it."

"I would not destroy it yet," replied Mr. Melamed. "Wrap it up and I will keep it at my home. I will have a new mirror delivered to you this afternoon."

Mr. Melamed then asked to interview the servants. The housemaid, a young woman named Mary, appeared in the drawing room first.

"The letter was delivered by a messenger, sir," she said in response to Mr. Melamed's question.

"Was there anything out of the ordinary about this messenger?"

"No, sir. He was just a boy."

"No one else rang the bell?"

"No, sir."

"What did you do with the letter, Mary?"

"I put it on the table in the front hall."

"Not in the drawing room?"

"No, sir. Mrs. Salomon doesn't like me to go in there, after I've finished my cleaning work, unless it's to bring in the tea."

"Were any of the servants upstairs, after Mr. Salomon left or when the bell rang?"

"No, sir. We were having our tea, sir, in the kitchen."

"No one came to the kitchen door? A peddler, perhaps?"

Mary thought for a moment. "There was someone ... no, that was the night before. He was selling thimbles and thread, sir."

"He did not return last night?"

"Not that I know of, sir."

The interview with the cook and the kitchen maid confirmed the broad outline of what Mary had said. There had been one ring of the bell that night. They remained in the kitchen while Mary went to the front door. When Mary returned she said the visitor had been only a messenger, and they went back to their tea. It was a very ordinary evening, and none of them suspected anything wrong had occurred until Mrs. Salomon returned home and they heard her scream.

"Have you any idea how the person entered my home?" asked Mr. Salomon, when the interviews were over.

Mr. Melamed examined the lock of the front door. "These old locks are not so difficult to pick, for someone acquainted with the art," he said. "Or the housemaid may not have closed the door properly, after the messenger left."

What he did not say was a certain fact that puzzled him more than anything else about the curious incident. However, he stored it in his mind, to retrieve later, when he had more time to think.

Mr. Melamed's next visit was to Gravel Lane, where the Earl was powdering his wig before a broken mirror.

"Good morning, Earl. Is there any progress concerning Martin Roth?" Mr. Melamed asked, skirting the banter that usually began their conversations.

"No," said the Earl, who could be just as terse as Mr. Melamed, when he wanted to — and when he was busy with his wig he was happy to not speak more than necessary.

"I have two more names to add to the list."

"It is lucky you were born to wealth, Mr. Melamed," the Earl said with a cynical smile. "A smart merchant would not give additional tasks to a man who has failed at the first."

"You'll find Martin Roth, Earl. I am certain of that."

The Earl bowed, in recognition of the compliment. Having finished with his wig, he turned his attention to tying his cravat, taking care to hide the stains of numerous meals past — which, unfortunately had been enjoyed by the previous owners of the worn piece of linen, and not him. "Who else are you looking for in this great metropolis of ours?"

"The first is a man named Karl Grimm. He plays the pianoforte. I believe he speaks with a German accent. He was recently employed at Leeds ..."

"And now is employed in making a nuisance of himself at many of London's finest gin houses. I believe we have one of his handkerchiefs somewhere." The Earl gave a vague wave of his hand.

Mr. Melamed smiled, despite himself. There was very little that escaped the Earl's notice. He had tried more than once to convince the Earl to use his talents in more honest endeavors, but the young man had always refused the offer with a disdainful laugh. Mr. Melamed was not sure if he totally blamed him. On Gravel Lane, the Earl really was like a king, albeit one of diminished fortunes. In the legitimate world, at least in the beginning, the Earl would have to bow and scrape to others, and receive very little wages in return for his hard work. For a man able to put off gratification until the future, the effort would be worthwhile. But in places like Gravel Lane, the idea of having a future was as foreign and, ultimately, unreal as the fabled gold storehouses of Timbuktu.

"I wish to speak with Mr. Grimm," said Mr. Melamed, returning his thoughts to the matter at hand. "Do you know where he lives?"

"We can follow him home one night and find out. Who is the second person?"

"Jonas Street. He is an American, shabbily dressed. He worked as a fur trapper on the American continent. He might be violent."

"In what way? You know I do not like to place my boys in unnecessary danger."

"I do not believe he has a weapon. He might throw rocks, or fists."

General Well'ngone gave a start.

The Earl glanced over at his second-in-command. "Do you know him?"

The General stroked his chin with his finger. "He might be the man who was sitting with Karl Grimm last night. And he might be the man who threw a rock at Mr. Salomon's window."

"You were there that night?" asked Mr. Melamed.

General Well'ngone looked at the Earl for instructions.

"The General was in the alleyway behind the Salomons' house on a private matter," said the Earl.

Mr. Melamed knew that the Earl of Gravel Lane was under no obligation to divulge his private affairs. And, to be honest, Mr. Melamed preferred not to know everything that the Earl and his gang were up to. He therefore only said to the General, "Would you know his face if you saw him again?"

"Which face, Mr. Melamed? I didn't say that the man who threw the rock and the man with Mr. Grimm were the same. I only saw the back of the man who threw the rock, and his companion, and it was dark."

"Then the man with Mr. Grimm, would you remember him?"

"Possibly. I would definitely remember his empty pockets. Making his acquaintance was a waste of my valuable time."

"It happens," said the Earl, magnanimously.

Having finished his business with the Earl of Gravel Lane, Mr. Melamed continued on to Cornhill Street, where he entered the curio shop of Mr. Herbert Kimml. Mr. Melamed was not acquainted with the Kimml brothers. He suspected that they might be members of the Jewish people, but he was not sure. They were certainly not members of the Great Synagogue, though they might pray at one of the other synagogues that had recently sprung up. On the other hand, not every new immigrant from Germany and Central Europe was a Jew, just as not everyone who enjoyed Mrs. Baer's roast beef and potato kugel at the coffee house was Jewish.

Mr. Kimml was at the counter when he entered, and the shop proprietor greeted Mr. Melamed with a cheerful good morning. "How can I help you, sir? Perhaps a musical sewing box for your wife or daughter?"

Mr. Melamed did not stop to explain that his wife had no more need of earthly things, or that his two married daughters were both living far away. Instead, he began the speech he had prepared beforehand and said, "I am here on behalf of a friend of mine, a well-to-do gentleman who would prefer not to be named."

Mr. Kimml's nod of the head implied that so far everything was understood.

"He would like to privately sponsor the publication of musical works by a young composer at the beginning of his career. He is very interested in music."

"I salute him, sir, for his noble sentiments and his generosity," said Mr. Kimml, with real feeling. "But for this, you must speak with my brother, Mr. Herman Kimml. He is the one who publishes music."

"I understand that your brother is deaf."

"That is correct."

"I would therefore prefer to state my business here and have you relay my friend's offer to your brother."

"Very well."

Mr. Melamed collected his thoughts for a moment. It was not natural to him to lie; usually when he conducted his inquiries he did it using his own name and appearance. But there was something about this problem that made him believe that his opponent was not acting according to those same rules. Therefore, a change of tactics was necessary.

"My friend is very impressed with the music of Mr. S. Romberg. Do you know if Mr. Romberg is a young man?"

"I am like everyone else," said Mr. Kimml. "I would be honored to meet Mr. Romberg and give him my compliments. But I have no idea if he is young or old or somewhere in between. And if your friend wishes to sponsor Mr. Romberg's music, he must speak with Mr. Schumetti, Mr. Romberg's publisher."

"I will tell my friend. Have you Mr. Schumetti's address?"

"He is as unknown as Mr. Romberg."

"Is there another young composer you can recommend?"

Mr. Kimml hesitated, before saying, "Let me ask my brother, sir. Is there a way to send you a message?"

"You may send a message to Baer's Coffee House, Sweeting's Alley."

"For what name?"

"Address the message to Mr. Asher Baer, the proprietor. I will advise him to look out for your message."

Mr. Melamed repeated the same performance at the establishment of the piano manufacturer, Mr. Harold Kimml, where he received a similar response. Then he directed his steps toward Sweeting's Alley.

Although Mrs. Salomon would have preferred that her son remain at home with her, Mr. Salomon found that he was too restless to remain inside. Therefore, after promising to return home before dark, he walked to Cornhill Street and ascended the stairs. Yet he found no peace of mind in that room either. He spent the morning wandering from the piano to the table and from the table to the window, before returning to the piano again. His mind, he discovered, to his horror, was totally blank. He felt as though some force had wiped it clean, like a child's slate, of every musical thought and note.

Since he could not work, he went back outside and directed his steps to a nearby circulating library. His mother, who was an avid reader, had paid for a year's subscription upon their arrival in London. He had been too busy with his music to pay the place a visit, but today he thought it might offer him a welcome distraction.

When he entered the reading room, he saw that there were perhaps a dozen elegantly dressed ladies and gentlemen scattered about the room. The ladies were mostly absorbed in reading the titles of the newer novels, while a few of the gentlemen were discussing an item found in one of the day's newspapers. Mr. Salomon was not looking for anything in particular and so he walked about the room, gazing at titles, hoping that something would attract his interest. As he passed a group comprised of two ladies and one gentleman, he thought he heard his name whispered, which was followed by a burst of laughter. His face reddened and he quickly went to another part of the room.

When that group had drifted away, he approached one of the clerks and said, "Have you anything about ghosts or spirits or ... doppelgangers?"

"We might, sir. There is the novel *The Monk*. It is very popular, though, and so it is not always available."

"I was looking for something more ... scientific."

The clerk thought for a moment. "If you will follow me, please, I may have something for you."

The clerk went to the other side of the room and ascended the library steps, until he reached one of the higher shelves. He then extracted a book, which he presented to Mr. Salomon.

"This is not a recent book, sir, but even today it is considered to be something of a classic."

Mr. Salomon looked at the book's title page, and read: *World of Spirits, An historical, physiological and theological treatise of spirits: apparitions, witchcrafts, and other magical practices, By John Beaumont, Gent.*

He was relieved to see that the book had been written by a gentleman, that he was not the only educated man to be interested in the topic. "Thank you, I shall take this," he said to the clerk.

Mr. Salomon was about to take a seat in the reading room, when he reconsidered. Gentleman author or no gentleman, this was not the type of book that a person would want everyone to know he was reading, and it was impossible to know who might walk through the door at any minute. He therefore walked back to his room and began to read there.

However, after just a short while his restlessness returned and he put away his book. He tried, instead, to play his violin, hoping this music would bring with it, if not inspiration, at least some peace of mind. But when he sounded the notes of Clementi's Sonatina, the music sounded dull and wooden to his ear. He was therefore relieved when there was a knock on the door, eager for anything to relieve the tedium of the unproductive afternoon.

Mr. Tree entered the room, apologizing for the intrusion.

"Not at all," said Mr. Salomon, with more than usual alacrity. "Have a seat. Would you like some tea?"

Mr. Tree declined the tea, but did accept the offer of a chair. "I did not hear music today," he said, to explain his visit. "Usually, when I open the door to let out a customer, I hear a few notes coming from your room."

"Some days are like that, I suppose," said Mr. Salomon, trying to sound unconcerned.

"Mr. Kimml was wondering if you have a sonata for us yet. We are almost finished compiling the new collection. If you do not have a sonata ready for publication, we will need to find one by someone else."

"I understand. When is the latest you would need it by?"

"We would like to have it by the end of this week. But if we knew you had something for us, we could wait until next week."

Mr. Salomon considered this offer for a few moments, before saying, "I wouldn't wait for a sonata by me, Mr. Tree. I am sure there are plenty of other composers for you to choose from."

"Come, come, Mr. Salomon, are things as bad as all that? Surely you are not still moping about what happened at Lady Windsbury's party?"

"You did not hear?"

Mr. Tree shook his head.

"I thought that perhaps Mr. Harold Kimml might have guessed and told you. Mr. Romberg has written a second sonata."

"Everyone knows that," said Mr. Tree, smiling. "Don't tell my employer but I purchased a copy of the music, and I sometimes play it when there is no one in the shop."

Mr. Salomon smiled, grimly. "That is very nice to hear, Mr. Tree, since I was under the impression that this sonata, too, was mine."

Mr. Tree stared at the young musician with a worried eye. His anxiety increased when he noticed the name of the book that was sitting on the table. "Perhaps you have been working too hard, Mr. Salomon. Why don't you take a holiday? Go to the country, or to the sea. Forget about music for a few days. Enjoy life."

Mr. Salomon shook his head. "I had a long holiday during the sea voyage to England. I was perfectly relaxed and refreshed before all this happened. Besides, someone broke into my house last night. I cannot leave my mother alone there until she has recovered from the shock."

"That's terrible, sir. Did they take anything of value?"

"No, quite the opposite — they left me a gift."

"A gift, sir? I don't know if I understand."

"They left a rock, which might have killed me if it had hit my head. And they wrote the opening bars of my sonata — or I suppose I should say Mr. Romberg's sonata — on my drawing room's mirror. A strange thing to do, wouldn't you say?"

"I'd say it was very strange. Did you call for a constable?"

"No, I didn't."

"If it should happen again, Mr. Salomon, I suggest you bring in the law."

"Has no one tried to break into Mr. Kimml's shop?"

Mr. Tree shook his head, and then he examined Mr. Salomon's face more closely. "Has something happened here, in this room?"

Mr. Salomon removed the ink-splattered manuscript from the drawer and showed it to Mr. Tree. "Someone did this."

Mr. Tree stared at the manuscript and shuddered. "If you don't mind, sir, I wouldn't say a word about this to Mr. Kimml. He is an elderly gentleman and very excitable. If he should think there was someone prowling about his premises, destroying musical scores, it would be very bad for his heart."

"I understand."

"But please keep me informed, Mr. Salomon. And I do suggest hiring a Bow Street Runner, if these incidents continue. Some of them are very clever, from what I hear."

"I have already hired someone, in a manner of speaking. He is a gentleman from my own community, Mr. Ezra Melamed."

"I am glad to know you have already taken steps. And I shouldn't worry about not being able to work this morning. A break-in is always unsettling."

"You are right, Mr. Tree. I should not let things affect me so deeply. But since they do, I should not expect my mind to function as normal. Still, if I could work ..." Mr. Salomon glanced over towards the corner of the room.

"The piano is waiting for you, sir," said Mr. Tree. "Do not let yesterday's events defeat you."

Mr. Salomon looked from the piano to Mr. Tree. "You are right. Thank you. Your conversation has revived me."

Mr. Salomon strode over to the piano and sat down. He closed his eyes and let his fingers hover over the keys. Then he began to play.

Mr. Tree listened for a few minutes, until a familiar call was heard from below.

"Mr. Tree! Customers, Mr. Tree!"

CHAPTER XIX

MR. MELAMED TOOK his usual seat at the back of Baer's Coffee House. This time, only Mr. Baer came over to greet him.

"Mrs. Baer is upstairs, with the children," the proprietor explained. Then he added, "It is a blow to her. She was hoping to have you married off by Chanukah."

"With all due respect to your wife, I believe it is better for the matchmaker to be disappointed than the bride or bridegroom."

Mr. Baer laughed. Then he said, "Do you prefer company, Mr. Melamed, or quiet?"

"Company, Mr. Baer. I need to make use of your common sense, if you do not mind."

"Let me bring the coffee, and then I and my common sense are at your service."

After Mr. Baer returned, Mr. Melamed explained the curious circumstances of the sonatas and other incidents. He concluded by asking, "Do you see a pattern?"

"The two sonatas obviously belong to the same group. To copy a piece of music requires skill," replied Mr. Baer. "Anyone can throw a rock, though, or dump a bottle of ink on a pile of papers."

"And the incident with the mirror?"

"That is curious, isn't it? To the extent that it was a break-in, it seems to belong with the rock and the ink. To the extent that the music was written with a professional hand, and that it was music from one of the sonatas, it seems to belong with the musical theft."

"There is something else about the mirror," said Mr. Melamed. "To throw a rock or spill a bottle of ink only takes a moment. To write on the mirror took time and it took light. Remember it was done at night. How could the person be sure that none of the servants would see the light? Or know that neither Mr. Salomon nor Mrs. Salomon would return before he had finished?"

"If he was aware of the family's habits, it could be done. But it would take someone with a cool head and a steady hand."

"From what I understand, neither Mr. Grimm nor Mr. Street possesses those qualities. I will know more when I meet them, of course."

"What do you hope to achieve from your ploy with the Kimmls?"

"An insight into their integrity. If they suggest the name of a young composer who is living and breathing and can be interviewed — and can prove that the music is his — then I would assume they are honest men. But if they claim to suddenly have access to Mr. Romberg, or they present their own mysterious figure, I shall be inclined to investigate them further."

Mr. Baer heard the door to his coffee house open and looked in that direction. Mr. Melamed looked there, as well. He recognized the shop assistant from the music publishing company, who was peering into the room, obviously in search of someone.

"That is Mr. Tree. Perhaps one of the Kimml brothers has sent him here with a message for me."

"Should I take the message or bring him over?"

"Bring him over. I should like to hear what he has to say."

Mr. Baer duly introduced himself and brought Mr. Tree over to Mr. Melamed's table. Mr. Melamed invited him to sit down, while Mr. Baer returned to his work behind the counter.

"I did not know it was you, sir," said Mr. Tree, having recognized Mr. Melamed from the day before. "Is it your Beethoven-hating friend who is the patron?"

"No," said Mr. Melamed, not wishing to involve Mr. Powell in the scheme. "Has your employer someone to suggest?"

"I have come on a different errand, sir."

When Mr. Melamed waited for him to continue, Mr. Tree said, "You see, I saw you on the street today, outside the shop. I thought that in addition to wishing to help your friend the patron, you might be interested in helping Mr. Salomon."

"Does Mr. Salomon require my help?"

"You know he does as well as I do, Mr. Melamed. And since you're an important man in the Jewish community ..."

"You know me?" Mr. Melamed scrutinized the man's face, but he could not remember meeting him before the other day.

"I used to be a servant in Mr. Samson Roth's home, sir. I believe you were a visitor there once or twice. A good servant has a good memory for faces and names."

"I see, and do you still have contact with the family?" Mr. Melamed tried to frame his question casually, but inwardly he was wondering if Mr. Tree had information about the whereabouts of Martin Roth.

"I have limited time, before I must return to Mr. Kimml's shop. I came to speak to you about Mr. Salomon."

"Very well, what can you tell me?"

Mr. Tree drew his chair nearer to Mr. Melamed. "I do not like to tell tales, sir, and I hope you will not take offense at what I have to say, seeing that I used to be a servant."

"You may speak freely, Mr. Tree. I cannot say that I will believe what you have to say, but I will listen."

"That's a fair answer, sir. And since I do not wish to waste your time, I'll come straight to the point. I am afraid that Mr. Salomon is very ill."

"In what way?"

Mr. Tree pointed to his head. "Up here, sir. His mind."

"Have you any evidence, Mr. Tree?"

"First, there are those sonatas. What man in his right mind would try a trick like that, try to pass off another man's work as his own? But let's leave that on the side for the moment and consider that ink that was spilled on his manuscript. I cannot say that my eye is on the staircase every second of the day, but it is my job to keep an eye on who goes in and out of the building. I haven't seen anyone strange prowling about the building or go up to Mr. Salomon's room — except for you, of course, sir, and your friend. But like I said, I knew who you were and so I didn't make a fuss."

"What exactly are you suggesting, Mr. Tree?"

"I am suggesting that it was Mr. Salomon who poured the ink over his manuscript."

Mr. Melamed could not hide his surprise. "Mr. Salomon?"

"I don't say he would do such a thing under normal circumstances. But when he is in a depressed state — well, I have seen other artists do even worse."

Mr. Tree looked about the room again, and then drew his chair even closer. "Then there's that business with the mirror. Mr. Salomon mentioned it to me this morning. It's very strange, Mr. Melamed, very strange."

"What is your opinion of the incident, Mr. Tree?"

"If I understand correctly, someone wrote several bars of music on the mirror with ink."

"That is correct."

"And they did the job well enough that Mr. Salomon was able to recognize the music."

"And so?"

"That takes time, sir, and light. How could someone from outside the family know they could do all that work in the drawing room without being disturbed?"

Mr. Melamed felt a queasy sensation in his stomach when he heard his own words thrown back at him by Mr. Tree. "You are suggesting that Mr. Salomon did this thing?"

Mr. Tree nodded his head.

"Why?"

"I am not a physician, sir. Perhaps Mr. Salomon has developed a fever in the brain. Perhaps he has been under a great deal of mental strain, and it has become too much for him to bear. So he has given himself over to the darkness of his soul and is trying to destroy his career with his own hands. Artists usually destroy themselves with drink. That is much more common. But Mr. Salomon is not a common man, as I am sure you know."

From somewhere in the streets of London, a bell tolled the hour.

"I must get back to work, sir. I hope you do not mind my talking to you. Like you said, it is your choice to believe me or not."

"Wait a moment, Mr. Tree. What about the sonatas? Could it not be that Mr. Salomon wrote the sonatas and, when in a depressive fit, put another man's name on them?"

"Oh, no, sir, I do not think that is the case. I am as sure that Mr. S. Romberg exists as you or me. I think that Mr. Salomon's troubles began when he came to London and discovered he could not write a single note. I do not know why that happened. I understand he had some success in New York. But something happened in London, sir, that caused these periods of delusion when he believes he is creating masterpieces when all is he doing is copying Mr. Romberg's work — which is followed by periods of disgust with himself afterward."

"You are referring to the mirror and the destroyed manuscript?"

"That is my meaning, sir. Discover what happened in London and you will discover the reason for his descent into these fits of madness. And please to do it soon, sir, before he is lost to us entirely. I saw a most disturbing book in his room today. Most disturbing."

"What sort of book, Mr. Tree?"

"A book about magic and demons, sir. I do hope that Mr. Salomon has not been dabbling in the black arts and tried to put a spell on Mr. Romberg, so he can steal that gentleman's compositions. I am very fond of Mr. Salomon, who has always treated me very kindly. But if he cannot himself compose music anymore, and his attempt at black magic isn't working, well you could see why his spirits would be troubled. Now I must go, or I shall lose my job."

The man left. Mr. Melamed sat in stunned silence.

Mr. Baer approached him warily. He sat down, but waited for Mr. Melamed to speak first.

"If what Mr. Tree says is true ..." Mr. Melamed then repeated the conversation for Mr. Baer, omitting only the man's comments about black magic, which he found too fantastic to believe until he had seen the book with his own eyes. "All of the pieces seem to fit, do they not, Mr. Baer? The shock of his father's death, the first knowledge of his family's debts, the pressure to succeed — could all this not be too much for a young man of a sensitive nature?"

Mr. Baer tapped a spoon against the table. "It could," he reluctantly agreed. "It could. But ..."

Mr. Melamed waited while the coffee house owner searched his mind for what was bothering him. Mr. Baer could sometimes be ponderous when thinking through a problem, but his solution was usually well worth the wait — and this time he once again did not disappoint. "The rock, Mr. Melamed, what did Mr. Tree have to say about the rock?"

Mr. Melamed thought back to the conversation and realized that this incident had not been mentioned. "It could be that Mr. Tree did not have time to state all his reasons. His time is not his own."

"If only someone had been there when the rock was thrown and had seen Mr. Salomon at the window. At least we would know that this incident was not done with Mr. Salomon's own hand."

"There was a witness," said Mr. Melamed. "General Well'ngone."

"Then we can say, in a manner of speaking, that the jury has still not rendered its decision. It is an impressive theory that Mr. Tree told you, but we must treat it as only one possible explanation. And if I were you, Mr. Melamed, I would go back to Mr. Herman Kimml. If I were a betting man, I would bet good money that he is not as deaf as he would like the world to believe."

Mr. Melamed was about to call upon Mr. Salomon when he was accosted by the pianoforte player, Mr. Grimm, who entered the door of the coffee house just as Mr. Melamed was about to leave.

"I beg your pardon, sir," said Mr. Grimm, lifting his crumpled hat slightly upward.

Mr. Melamed could detect a faint smell of gin on the man's breath, as well as a German accent, two facts which made him linger by the doorway instead of going on his way.

Mr. Grimm went over to the counter, after first looking around the room to make sure that no one he knew was seated at one of the tables, and said to Mr. Baer, "I believe this is a Jewish establishment, sir?"

Mr. Baer recognized the truculent intruder from before and replied, with his sternest voice, "It is, sir. Are you looking for someone?"

"I'm looking for someone named Melamed."

Mr. Baer glanced in Mr. Melamed's direction, and that gentleman stepped forward.

"I am Ezra Melamed. How may I be of service to you, Mr. ...?"

"Grimm, sir. Mr. Karl Grimm. My name is known in the courts of Europe."

"I am sure it is, Mr. Grimm. Have you eaten?"

Mr. Grimm looked longingly in the direction of the kitchen, which was off to the side of the counter.

"A plate of roast beef and some strong coffee, Mr. Baer," said Mr. Melamed, as he led the musician to his usual table at the back of the room.

"I thank you, sir," said Mr. Grimm, who did seem truly grateful to sit down and rest his weary limbs. "And please give my compliments to the gentleman patron you are assisting. I admire any man who wishes to make a contribution to the furtherance of the musical arts."

Mr. Melamed looked surprised. "You have heard, then, of my quest?"

"By a happy accident I saw Mr. Tree in the street. He said I might find you here."

"The music world seems to be small one."

"Men of talent have a way of finding one another, sir, if I may be so bold as to sing my own praises, since Mr. Tree is not here to do it for me." Mr. Grimm gave the door a nervous glance, to make sure that Mr. Tree had not reappeared to contradict his words.

"Then perhaps you are acquainted with Mr. Romberg?"

"I am."

At that moment, Mr. Baer arrived with the plate of roast beef and the coffee. Although Mr. Melamed was anxious to hear more about Mr. Romberg, he did not have the heart to delay the musician's repast, especially since it was evident from Mr. Grimm's hungry looks that he had not had a proper meal for some time.

"Please, eat," said Mr. Melamed.

"You will not join me?"

Mr. Melamed shook his head. "I have already eaten."

When Mr. Grimm finally set down his fork and knife, Mr. Melamed said, "We were speaking of Mr. Romberg. Is he in London?"

"I wouldn't know, sir. The last time I saw him was when we were both with the Hamburg Opera Orchestra. That would have been around 1794 or '95."

Mr. Melamed raised an eyebrow at the mention of a date that was almost twenty years in the past. "I was under the impression that Mr. S. Romberg was a younger man."

"I was speaking of Herr Andreas Romberg, sir, the well-known violinist and composer. It was a pleasure working with *him*, unlike some people who call themselves violinists and composers."

"You are not an admirer of Mr. S. Romberg's work?"

It took a few minutes for Mr. Grimm to reply, since he had been referring to Mr. Salomon, and not Mr. Romberg. "I suppose Mr. Romberg's music does have its good points, in some parts," he grudgingly admitted.

"And how is he to work with? Many artists are temperamental, or so I hear."

"I have never had the honor of making his acquaintance, sir. Mind you, I would not object to sharing the stage with him, should it happen that someone would like to sponsor a musical evening." Mr. Grimm gave Mr. Melamed a knowing glance as he removed several pages of music from his coat pocket. "This is only a small sample of my own work, sir, but if you would be so good as to show this to your gentleman patron ..."

Mr. Melamed looked down at the tattered pages and gave an inward groan. He had not intended to harm an innocent person when he first devised his plan, but now he saw that he had unfairly raised the hopes of the composer sitting beside him. Yet before he allowed compassion to gain the upper hand, there was still something he must find out.

"Mr. Grimm, I should not like to take these pages unless you assure me you have a copy sitting in your room."

"A copy? No, I do not have a copy. But I trust that you will treat these pages with the care and respect they deserve." Mr. Grimm tried to thrust the music into Mr. Melamed's hands, but the gentleman refused to take them.

"I cannot take an original. You can make a copy of one of your sonatas here. My patron is only interested in sonatas, you see, and if you present your best one that will be enough for him to judge."

Mr. Melamed called to Mr. Baer and asked if he could send for some already prepared musical paper, as well as pen and ink. When those writing supplies had taken the place of the plate of roast beef on the table, Mr. Melamed handed the pen to Mr. Grimm.

The composer took the pen with a shaking hand and, after dipping the tip into the ink, laboriously wrote out the first bars of his sonata. Mr. Melamed watched his progress, and it was soon clear from the lopsided notes that this was not the same hand that had written on Mr. Salomon's mirror.

After several minutes, Mr. Grimm set down his pen and sighed. "It is slow work, sir."

"If you would like to finish it at home, bring the manuscript when you are done. I will receive it the next time I am here."

Mr. Grimm looked relieved and started to put away his papers.

"By the way, Mr. Grimm, are you familiar with a man named David Salomon?"

Mr. Grimm stopped what he was doing and gave Mr. Melamed a startled look. "I may know him," he said, warily.

"I ask because you mentioned earlier that the musical world is a small one. A few days ago, someone entered the room where he had left his new sonata and poured black ink all over it."

Mr. Grimm could not prevent the sides of his lips from curling up into something like a smile. "That is too bad. As you say, sir, the musical world is small and there are many petty jealousies."

"You do not know who did this?"

"Me, sir?"

"I thought you might have overheard some other musicians discussing the incident."

Mr. Grimm returned to gathering up his papers. "No, I do not recall hearing anything about it."

"Then perhaps you have heard something about this. Two nights ago someone threw a rock through Mr. Salomon's window and almost shattered his violin. Do you know who did that?"

The musician was still thrusting pages into his pocket when he rose from the table and ran out the door.

CHAPTER XX

MR. MELAMED DID not follow the fleeing musician. His first concern was to seek out Mr. Salomon, to confirm at least part of the shop assistant's tale. While he ascended the stairs of Mr. Kimml's establishment, he exchanged a wordless greeting with Mr. Tree, who was showing out a customer from the shop.

Once upstairs, he paused outside the door of Mr. Salomon's room. He did not hear music.

"Come in!" Mr. Salomon called out, after hearing the knock at the door.

Mr. Melamed entered and noticed the young man's pale face. "I hope I am not disturbing you, Mr. Salomon."

Mr. Salomon, who was sitting at the table, where he had been reading, glanced over at the piano. "I was working on a new piece. But if I can be of assistance to you ..."

The young composer watched uneasily as Mr. Melamed walked across the room. He closed the book and pushed it to the side, before his visitor joined him at the table.

Mr. Melamed pretended not to notice. Before coming to the principal reason for his visit, he asked, "Are you familiar with the musicians who performed your sonata at Lady Mercer's birthday celebration?"

"No, I am not acquainted with Lady Mercer. Is it important to know their names?"

"I would like to know how they heard about the sonata. It would help to know where they got the music from."

"Yes, I see."

"If it would be awkward for you to try to find out their names, I can ask Mr. Powell to do it. I believe he is acquainted with Lady Mercer."

Mr. Salomon looked relieved. "I think that is the better way."

"Very well." Mr. Melamed's eye went to the book sitting on the table. "I see you have paid a visit to the circulating library. Have any interesting new books arrived?"

He reached over and picked up the book. After glancing at the title page and leafing through the pages, he said, "Are you truly interested in such things, Mr. Salomon?"

"If you had asked me that question a month ago, I would have said of course not."

"And now?"

"Now, how can I explain what I am going through to someone who has never experienced it?"

"I suggest you try."

"At first, after Lady Windsbury's party, I felt mostly shock and embarrassment. I generally try to avoid making a fool of myself in public."

"Those sentiments are very understandable."

"But lately something else has happened. I feel like the creative force inside of me is being drained out. At night I cannot sleep, during the day I cannot work. Even when I do have a few minutes of inspiration, a feeling of despair quickly comes over me. A voice whispers in my ear, 'What is the use, Mr. Salomon? When you are done, your composition will be spirited away to the rooms of Mr. Romberg. It will be published under his name, garner him even more fame. And you, sir, will be left with nothing. All of your hard work will be for naught.' Is it therefore any wonder that I should like to know what sort of spell this Mr. Romberg has placed upon me?"

"That is why you have borrowed this book, because you believe that someone has cast a spell upon you?"

"When I talk about it with you, it sounds ridiculous to my ears as well. But when I am here alone, or when it is late at night, and I can neither work nor rest ... Yes, I do feel that somewhere in this city there is someone who has found a way to enter into my mind and remove every creative impulse I have."

"I agree with you, Mr. Salomon, that someone is doing you harm. But again I tell you that there is a rational reason for what has happened, and we will discover what that reason is. For now, will you allow me to return this book to the circulating library?"

Mr. Salomon shrugged. "Do as you please, sir."

Mrs. Salomon adjusted her hat in the new mirror that was now sitting above the drawing room mantelpiece. She had been invited to accompany Lady Allyn and her daughter to Harding Howell & Co., the fashionable ladies' shop on the Pall Mall. It was not an invitation that Mrs. Salomon relished, since she already had a drawer full of bills from milliners, glove makers and the like. But she did not feel she could afford to lose the friendship of Lady Allyn either.

She heard a carriage pull up before her home, and then the ring of the front bell. A moment later, her housemaid entered the room to announce that Lady Allyn's carriage was waiting. Mrs. Salomon gave her reflected face one last look and said a silent prayer that Lady Allyn would not notice the dark circles under her eyes. Lady Allyn usually did not notice such things, since the woman was so absorbed in her own affairs that she seldom had time to notice anything else, but one never knew. That is why Mrs. Salomon had chosen her bonnet with especial care. It was better for the bonnet to be noticed than her tired face.

As Mrs. Salomon was going down the front steps of her home, the heel of her shoe caught on the pavement and she almost fell. A man came forward to catch her. It was Jonas Street.

"Careful, ma'am, you don't want to fall," he said loud enough for the ladies in the carriage to hear him. Then he whispered, "Though it would serve you right if you broke your neck."

"Don't make a scene here," she whispered back. She reached into her reticule for a coin—a small coin—and gave it to her supposedly unknown rescuer. "Come back later."

"You'll have the cash?"

"Later!" She broke away from him and climbed into the carriage.

Jonas Street watched the carriage drive off. He slipped his hand into his pocket, where a key was sitting. He then glanced at the front door of the Salomons' home. He climbed two of the steps and then he stopped. The step seemed to disappear from beneath his feet, while the world swirled around him at a dizzying speed. It was the second time that day that the sickening spell had overcome him. He therefore cautiously retraced his steps and disappeared down the street.

Mr. Samson Roth did not often frequent Harding Howell & Co., but his written requests for payment for the silk goods he had supplied had been met with silence. He therefore had paid a personal visit to the shop's head clerk, who pleaded the shop's inability to pay its debt at the present moment. The sad fact was that once it became common knowledge that a merchant was in financial trouble and might become bankrupt, his customers—the merchants he had sold his goods to on credit—no longer felt a need to pay off their debts; they preferred, instead, to keep in the good books of the suppliers they would need in the future.

Mr. Roth was leaving the shop when he spotted Mrs. Salomon drive up in an elegant carriage, a sight that revived his despondent spirits. The introductions were made, and Mrs. Salomon asked for and received permission to join Lady Allyn and her daughter inside the shop a few minutes later. Then Mr. Roth and Mrs. Salomon began to stroll down the Pall Mall.

After exchanging a few pleasantries about the weather, which had turned overcast and damp, Mrs. Salomon said, "I did not know your silks were sold at Harding Howell. I must tell Lady Allyn to ask for them. She is giving a ball next month and must have a new dress."

"I would be honored to have one of my silks present at Lady Allyn's ball," he replied.

"It must be wonderful to be a silk merchant. You must see so many beautiful designs. Although I assume your silks sell so quickly you hardly have time to notice anything but the money rolling in."

Mr. Roth did his best to give a carefree laugh. "And you ladies, who have so many gowns in your cupboards, never have time to notice the money rolling out."

Now it was the turn of Mrs. Salomon to mask her true feelings and laugh gaily. "Are you quizzing me, Mr. Roth, to see if I am a spendthrift?"

"Heaven forbid! As a silk merchant, I would never criticize a lady for owning too many gowns. If ladies stopped buying my silks, where would I be?"

"At the moneylender's, I suppose," said Mrs. Salomon, with her most lilting voice, although from the corner of her eye she was watching carefully for any change in Mr. Roth's expression. She had given him an opening to ask about her visit to the moneylender, now she would see what he would make of it.

There was a pause. Then Mr. Roth laughed heartily. "It is not fair, Mrs. Salomon. How the other ladies must envy you. To have everything—beauty, wealth, and wit—no, it is not fair."

Mrs. Salomon did not apprise him of his one mistake. She merely accepted the compliment demurely.

They parted ways after returning to the entrance of the shop, each satisfied that the brief conversation had been a success. Mr. Roth, impressed by the sight of Lady Allyn's carriage and the assumed knowledge that Mrs. Salomon could afford to shop at such an elegant emporium, decided to go at once to the coffee house to inform Mrs. Baer that he was ready to ask for Mrs. Salomon's hand in marriage—something he wished to do before his son Nathan acted on his threat to reveal his debts.

Mrs. Salomon, for her part, felt that a man who sold silks to someone like Lady Allyn must be a man of means. As she passed the shop's department that sold furs, she did feel a moment's hesitation. After all, her late husband's furs kept many a wealthy lady warm on a cold winter's night. But she chose to believe that Mr. Roth's carefree manner was the mirror of a bank account that was also worry-free. She too therefore decided to contact Mrs. Baer at the first possible moment—which must be before someone informed Mr. Roth of her recent visit to the moneylender's pawnshop.

Mr. Roth did not delay. He arrived at Baer's Coffee House not long after Mr. Melamed had departed. When he asked to speak with Mrs. Baer about a private matter, Mr. Baer was not surprised. He showed the silk merchant to a table and went to get his wife.

The conversation between Mr. Roth and Mrs. Baer was brief and to the point. He assured Mrs. Baer that his house would provide a comfortable haven for both Mrs. Salomon and her son, until Mr. Salomon was ready to marry and establish his own household. He further assured her that his business had had an excellent reputation for many years.

"Have you any debts, Mr. Roth?" asked Mrs. Baer, who could ask for such personal information in her role as matchmaker.

Mr. Roth smiled. "An excellent question, ma'am, and I am pleased that you have Mrs. Salomon's interests at heart. As a man of business, I of course have a few outstanding notes, just as I hold the notes of several merchants who must pay me."

"And your annual income, Mr. Roth? What may I tell Mrs. Salomon?"

Mr. Roth could feel beads of sweat pop out on his brow and he hoped that the matchmaker did not notice. "I believe that Mrs. Salomon and I have already come to an understanding regarding our respective fortunes."

Mrs. Baer did not press the question. She would find out if this was true when she spoke with the lady. But when Mr. Roth left, she found herself going over the conversation in her mind—and each repetition brought with it a more intense feeling of apprehension.

"Something is not right here, Mr. Baer," she said to her husband. "I can feel it in my bones. And you know that my bones are seldom wrong."

Mr. Baer knew better than to disagree.

"Have you heard nothing about Mr. Roth's financial affairs at the Great Synagogue?"

"The synagogue is a place of prayer, not of gossip, Mrs. Baer," said her husband, doing his best to appear shocked.

Mrs. Baer gave her husband a look, which conveyed more clearly than words that she was not fooled. Although it was true that the Talmud did say that women had received nine out of the ten measures of speech given to the world, she knew that men used part of the remaining one measure for gossip, too.

"Then I shall have to search out the truth myself."

"What do you intend to do, Mrs. Baer?"

She went to fetch her shawl and money for the hired carriage. "I am going to the Earl of Gravel Lane. If anyone in London knows who has taken up residence on Queer Street, it is him."

The Earl was not accustomed to receiving female visitors in his squalid abode, and so he greeted the appearance of Mrs. Baer with less than his usual assurance.

"Honored, ma'am, I am sure," he said, while painfully aware that Mrs. Baer was examining every stain and tear of his clothes with a Jewish mother's disapproving eye. When that eye reached his flea-bitten wig, he instinctively raised his hand to protect it. "How may I be of service?"

"If I were your mother, may she rest in peace, I would say that you could be of service by casting aside your ridiculous pretensions and predilections for a life of crime and becoming a respectable member of our Jewish community, instead. But since I am not your mother, I won't waste my breath."

Mrs. Baer was about to take a seat when she noticed the layers of caked dirt on the chair and changed her mind. "I have come about Mr. Samson Roth. What do you know about the state of his financial affairs?"

"Why do you assume I know anything about them, Mrs. Baer?"

"Earl, you may choose to live in this foul den, but I do not intend to linger and breathe in this damp, infested air a moment longer than I must. Either you tell me now, or I'm taking you with me to the coffee house, where you can tell me all about it while you're washing our customers' dirty dishes. Mr. Melamed has been far too lenient with you, and it's about time that someone taught you a lesson and made you do some honest work."

The Earl looked with horror at Mrs. Baer. "Frankly, ma'am, I would rather be scalped by Indians. What exactly do you wish to know?"

"Is he in debt?"

"Up to his eyebrows."

"Thank you. That is all I came for."

"I beg to disagree. I think you should be interested in the state of Mrs. Salomon's financial affairs, as well."

"She is also in debt?"

"Yes, but only up to her ears, from what I hear."

"You should have said something."

"What? And dashed the dreams of the happy couple?"

Mrs. Baer gave him a dirty look. Then she removed a coin from her purse and put it on the table.

"What is that for?" asked the Earl, glaring at the coin with disdain.

"I do not expect to receive my information for free."

"Consider it a gift, Mrs. Baer. I only interested myself in the affairs of Mrs. Salomon because of the marital trap that you were laying for Mr. Melamed."

CHAPTER XXI

MR. GRIMM RACED back to the lodgings that he shared with Jonas Street. Although the two had little in common, one of the things they did share — their almost empty pockets — made splitting the cost of the small room they had rented by the week advisable. The pianoforte player sometimes found work teaching piano to the children of some of London's less wealthy merchants, until the parents discovered his partiality to strong drink. As for Mr. Street, he found that his former work as a trapper could be adapted to serve the interests of some of London's criminal elements, although his heart was not in crime. By pooling together their meager earnings, they managed to keep alive from week to week.

They also shared their respective grudges concerning the Salomons, and it was concerning this matter that Mr. Grimm was so anxious to converse with Mr. Street. This person had not yet returned, however, and so Mr. Grimm took up a place by the window to await his arrival. He must speak with Jonas about his conversation with Mr. Melamed, and tell the American that their plot had been found out.

While he waited, a tangle of wild thoughts raced through his gin-addled mind. He had not meant to actually hurt Mr. Salomon, he decided. It was really all the fault of Jonas Street that he had ever become involved, and once he did he had merely gone along. But since he was the taller of the two men, he had thrown the stone.

But he had not meant to do anyone any actual physical harm, he muttered to some invisible barrister of the law. He had only meant to help his friend, Jonas Street, convince the Salomons that they must pay the debt they owed to the trapper.

What was his interest in the matter? he could almost hear a robed and wigged judge ask. Only a small fee, to be received when the money was in Jonas Street's pocket. Nothing more.

And he hadn't hurt anyone, or stolen anything. He must remember to stress that. So there were no grounds to transport him. And Australia was no place for an artist like him, a musician who had once performed at the most elegant courts of Europe. The law must understand that.

Martin was out for one of his walks, when he heard a familiar voice call after him. Unlike in Leeds, this time he ran.

"Martin!" Nathan shouted after the fleeing figure. "I have the money!"

Several people walking down the street turned their heads, curious to hear more of what promised to be an interesting conversation. Martin felt torn between disdain and interest in what his brother had to say. Then he made his decision and continued to run.

"Follow the money!" General Well'ngone instructed Saulty and another boy, who immediately took their positions to watch the next movements of Nathan Roth. At the same time, the General and the others with him ran after Martin.

Martin was not as familiar with the labyrinth of back alleyways of London's poorest quarters as the General and his companions. He therefore was not aware that General Well'ngone was chasing him in the direction of Gravel Lane. When they did reach that street, the General whistled and the boys stationed outside the Earl's residence sprang to attention. Martin, who had been running from General Well'ngone more out of instinct than out of reason, now realized that he was trapped, without understanding why.

"Take him to the Earl," the General commanded, after pausing to catch his breath.

When Martin was thrust into the room, the Earl turned and greeted him with a warm smile. "Mr. Roth, you are just in time for tea."

After having received the news that the elusive Martin Roth had been found, Mr. Melamed arrived. The Earl graciously gave his room to Mr. Melamed, so that Mr. Melamed could conduct his interview in private, and went with the General to another part of the building.

"Where have you been hiding, Martin?" asked Mr. Melamed.

"I have not been hiding anywhere, sir. I was not aware that you were looking for me."

Mr. Melamed placed Mr. Deare's promissory note on the table.

"I told Mr. Deare I would pay him back and I will, when I have the money. I do not expect you to pay my debts, Mr. Melamed."

"Are you working?"

"Yes."

"Where?"

Martin hesitated. "I am not allowed to say."

"Can you tell me, then, where you are lodging?"

"I am not allowed to tell that either."

Mr. Melamed shook his head. "It will not do, Martin. I have already paid Mr. Deare his money. Your debt now rests with me. What assurance can you give me that you will not disappear again, if I let you go now?"

Martin's eyes grew wide. "You're not going to send me to debtors' prison, are you?"

Actually, Mr. Melamed had no intention of doing that. But he did wish to impress upon the young man that the matter was serious. A knock at the door interrupted their conversation, before he could say more.

General Well'ngone entered. "Excuse me, gentlemen, but Mr. Nathan Roth called and said he had an important message for Mr. Martin."

The General placed a hastily folded piece of paper on the table. Martin opened it up.

"It's money," he said, at first not believing his eyes. He quickly counted the banknotes, which amounted to exactly fifty pounds. He then pushed the money in Mr. Melamed's direction and said, "Here is your money, sir."

Martin then noticed that there was writing on the page, which had been written in faint pencil. He could not read what was written in the dim light, nor did he wish to read the letter in the presence of others. He therefore said to Mr. Melamed, "May I go now?"

"Yes, of course," said Mr. Melamed, who wished to learn more about what Martin was up to at his mysterious place of work and lodgings, but knew he could make no further claim upon the young man.

Martin did not wait to return to Mr. Tree's lodgings to read the message from his brother Nathan. The letters were legible in the sunlight, and so he found a doorstep where he would not be disturbed. The note was not long, but its contents were bitter.

I had some luck with cards – did not I tell you a person cannot always be unlucky?

Unfortunately, these banknotes will very likely be all you will ever receive from either Father or me. Father is ruined. His last hope was to marry a lady of fortune, but it seems that the lady is as much in debt as he. It therefore no longer matters to me if I am disinherited or not. You may act as you please.

I leave for the Continent this week – another scheme! When next you hear of me I shall either be a man of great fortune, or hanged.

Till then, I remain your affectionate brother,
                    Nathan

Martin folded the letter and put it in his pocket. It was an odd thing. An hour earlier he had been certain that he never wished to see his brother again. Yet now, when it was almost certain that his wish had come true, he felt curiously sad and alone.

He could not yet come to terms with the news about his father's financial ruin. That was too much of a shock to assimilate in a matter of minutes.

"Martin?"

The young man looked up, surprised to hear the familiar voice. Then he realized that it was not his brother but Mr. Tree who had spoken.

"I had need of some fresh air," he said to Mr. Tree. "The exercise was beneficial. I believe I have solved one of the problems of your invention."

"You've said that before, Martin. Sometimes I wonder what I am paying your wages for."

Martin looked over at his companion. There was a bitter tone in Mr. Tree's voice that had not been there before. "I did warn you that it would take time, John."

"And that time is running out. I have heard rumors—credible rumors—that someone else is working on something similar to our invention. If they should find out, before us ..." Mr. Tree angrily thrust his closed fist into his other hand. "I thought you were a clever man, Martin. Isn't that what you told me? That you were clever? Why did you lie to me? Was that right to lie and take money from an honest man's pocket, take food from his larder?"

Martin's face turned red. In Mr. Tree's angry words he could hear echoes of the many rebukes he had received from his father. "I am working as fast as I can, John."

"No more walks, Martin. From now on, you must work day and night, until the thing is done. Do you understand me? Otherwise, you go back on to the streets, where I found you."

"I understand."

Martin and Mr. Tree continued walking.

Saulty and his companion casually strolled after them.

When Mr. Melamed returned to his home on Bury Street, the fire had already been lit in his library. Soon afterward the butler entered with the tea tray, which he wordlessly placed on a table. Then he just as silently exited the room.

The hot water lost some of its warmth as Mr. Melamed stood by the window, looking out on the autumnal scene, which was fast fading into darkness. The fifty pounds that sat in his coat pocket felt heavy, as though the banknotes had been made of lead. It was not the money that he cared about. For some reason, in the back of his mind he had always thought that Martin Roth might hold the clue to the mystery of Mr. Salomon and the sonatas. Now it appeared that Martin's disappearance was not a chapter in a broader story, but merely a separate tale of its own. It also appeared that Mr. Melamed was no closer to solving the mystery of those sonatas than he had been from the first.

The muffled jangle of the front bell roused him from his melancholy reverie. A few moments later, his butler reentered the room, with a letter.

Mr. Melamed took the letter and, noticing the foreign postal markings on the outside, carried it to his armchair. There were actually two letters. One was from his married daughter who lived on the Continent, where she and her husband had become followers of a Chassidic rabbi. The other letter was from the rabbi.

He set aside the letter from his daughter; he preferred to defer that enjoyment until after dinner, when he hoped that his spirits might be improved. The other reason for reading the rabbi's letter first was that more than once he had received guidance from this person, albeit of a hidden nature.

The rabbi began by thanking Mr. Melamed for some generous contribution that the philanthropist had made several months earlier. This was followed by some general news about the Jewish community and news about the political situation, including the Congress of Prague, which had taken place in June of that year and produced no lasting results. Russia, Austria, Prussia, England, France — almost all of Europe was still at war, a fact that the rabbi bemoaned.

I am not naïve about the difficulties involved in making peace, after so many years of bloodshed and violence. Does not the Jerusalem Talmud ask, in the tractate Nedarim, Chapter Nine: "How can we be expected not to take revenge and not even to bear a grudge against someone who has hurt us?" Yet see how the Talmud responds, in contradistinction to much of the rest of the world. Let us say that a man cuts his hand with a knife, while chopping meat. Shall he then cut the hand that wielded the knife, in retaliation for what it has done? Who would do such a thing?

Our lives are all connected, just as the right hand is connected to the left. We are part of the other, and the other is part of us. The hurts we inflict on another are hurts we will eventually inflict upon ourselves. We must find the hidden string that connects one life to another. Only then can we sound the chord that heralds peace.

The letter ended with the familiar blessings and good wishes. Mr. Melamed sat for several minutes gazing at the fire. He knew from experience that the rabbi was not making comments about the political situation simply to fill the page. There was a message for him about the problem he was working on here in London.

He thought back over the events of the past several days. Those thoughts kept returning to Mr. Herman Kimml's music publishing company. He recalled what Mr. Baer had said earlier, at the coffee house, although Mr. Melamed was not convinced that the solution lay with Mr. Kimml. But he had missed something there, he was sure of it.

The teapot was already quite cold and forgotten when Mr. Powell's carriage arrived at Bury Street and Mr. Powell entered the room. Casting a glance at the untouched tea things, that gentleman said, "You have not forgotten the exhibition at the Royal Academy? You said you would accompany me to the private viewing."

"I had forgotten, to tell you the truth. But I am happy to see you. And I shall be very happy to have my thoughts engaged by something other than Mr. Salomon and his sonatas."

CHAPTER XXII

DESPITE HIS DESIRE to think of something else, Mr. Melamed did not use his time at the art exhibition in vain. Although most of the talk was about the art on display, a painting that depicted a scene of a musical family gathered around a pianoforte provided him with an opportunity to begin a discussion about the current musical scene in London. Everyone admired Mr. S. Romberg's compositions, but no one knew the man personally. The composer's publisher, Mr. Schumetti, was equally elusive.

"How then does the music reach the hands of the musicians who perform it?" Mr. Melamed asked.

A young gentleman, who was smartly dressed and had the air of being someone in the know, shrugged expressively and said, "My dear sir, how do scandal sheets written by an anonymous author appear out of nowhere? If you pay a printer for both his work and his silence, the job will be done. Young boys, who care little about what words are printed and even less about who wrote them, take the printed sheets from the printing house and sell them to the eager buyers. It is done every day."

"You sound like you have intimate knowledge of the business," someone in the group joked. "Which scandal has come from your pen?"

The young gentleman smiled, basking in the momentary attention, and then drifted away.

Later, Mr. Melamed turned the conversation to the Kimml brothers and their respective businesses, and here he received an interesting piece of news.

"They've been given a run for their money by Muzio Clementi," said a Mr. Jordan, who was a member of the recently formed Philharmonic Society of London.

"The composer?" asked Mr. Melamed.

"Clementi also has a music publishing company. He manufactures pianos, too. He had a setback when his warehouse was destroyed by fire five or six years ago, but now he is doing rather well. He has sole publishing rights to Beethoven's music here in England, and he has made some interesting improvements to piano manufacturing."

"He is successful, then?"

"Many people believe his instruments have the best sound in the world — and they are priced accordingly."

"Is the market in England not large enough for more than one manufacturer?"

"It is, but Clementi has the lion's share. The others must share the scraps."

Mr. Melamed and Mr. Powell discussed this information on the way back to Bury Street.

"It appears to be a double blow for the Kimmls," said Mr. Powell. "I am sure Clementi is making a nice packet of money from selling his own music and those works by Beethoven. The German's music is not to my taste, as you know, but there are many people who do like it. So one can see why the Kimmls would want their own brilliant new composer."

"But why the mystery? Why not publish the music under Mr. Salomon's name, and the name of their publishing company?"

"If they invent a composer, they don't have to pay Mr. Salomon for his work. Remember, if both the music publisher and the piano manufacturer are being put out of business by Muzio Clementi, the family might be desperate for cash."

When Mr. Melamed was seated once again in his library, with a glass of wine by his side and pen, ink and paper before him, he tried to do as the Chassidic rabbi had written in his letter and draw a connecting string through all the seemingly unconnected pieces of his puzzle.

At the upper left-hand corner of the page, he wrote the names of the three Kimml brothers, Herman, Herbert and Harold. Their business was music and so they had the ability to steal the sonatas, print them and distribute the music to both professional musicians and those who performed in the street. They had a motive, as well, if their business was on the decline. He made a note next to their names to ask the Earl of Gravel Lane if he knew anything about that.

Opposite their names, he wrote the names of David Salomon and his mother. Their finances were in a desperate strait, a circumstance which had put pressure on the young man to quickly make his name and establish his career. It could be as Mr. Tree had said; Mr. Salomon might have one of those diseases of the mind where, when he lapsed into a fit of despondency, he engaged in behavior that was destructive to the very career he was trying to establish.

Or, perhaps he wasn't so mad after all, thought Mr. Melamed, setting down his pen. Perhaps the young man had a very sane and lucid reason for publishing his work under another man's name. Lady authors often masked their identity under the cloak of anonymity. But why would he do such a thing?

The name of Jonas Street appeared before his eyes and he wrote it down. He had not yet met this person who was supposedly dogging the Salomons and claiming that they owed him money. Was Mr. Salomon hiding his success from Jonas Street so that he could avoid paying the man?

Mr. Melamed discarded the idea. The desperation of Mrs. Salomon to marry well was all too real. He had seen it in her eyes on the evening of Lady Windsbury's party.

He also had observed the young man on the night of the public fiasco. A disturbed person might destroy his work in private, but as Mr. Salomon had himself said, he would never knowingly set himself up for public ridicule, which is what had happened in Lady Windsbury's drawing room. Mr. Salomon's reactions on that night—his shock, his embarrassment—were perfectly natural under the circumstances, and Mr. Melamed did not believe that those strong emotions had been feigned.

Mr. Grimm's name was joined to that of Jonas Street. Mr. Melamed did not know how the two had found each other, but he was almost certain that they were behind the incident of the rock. Perhaps they had been behind the incident of the ink, as well. Those actions, which were both crude and spiteful, required neither great intelligence nor skill—and therefore seemed to fit the unlikely pair perfectly.

That left the Roth family. Although his intellect suggested that they were only a postscript to the main story, Mr. Melamed's intuition still urged him to include them in the circle of connections. Yet rather than try to connect the father and two sons to the other names on the page, his mind kept wandering back in time. Mr. Melamed had not known the family well, but he vaguely recalled that once they had been a family like many others. Mr. Samson Roth, whose father had been a rather unsuccessful greengrocer, worked hard to establish his own business in the silk line. His wife had been a pleasant, hard-working woman who often helped Mr. Roth in the silk merchant's first shop. Their marriage was quickly followed by the births of their two sons. It was a perfectly normal story that was repeated any number of times everywhere throughout the world. But then something had happened. Mrs. Roth turned bitter. Mr. Roth turned against his sons. Did any of this have anything to do with the sad tale of Mr. Salomon?

Mr. Melamed heard the great clock in the hallway chime the hour. It was one o'clock in the morning. His butler would not retire for the night until he did, despite his many attempts to persuade the servant to not wait up for him. He therefore made a note to himself that he must discover who was printing the music, for despite what the young gentleman had said at the Royal Academy exhibition, there had to be a way to trace the music bearing Mr. Romberg's name back to its source. Once that was discovered, perhaps the other pieces of the puzzle would fall into place, and the connections between these seemingly unconnected people would become clear.

CHAPTER XXIII

MR. POWELL ARRIVED at Bury Street while Mr. Melamed was still at breakfast. Helping himself to a cup of coffee, he said, "A letter from the Continent was awaiting me when I got home last night. My musical acquaintance has heard of an Andreas Romberg and a Bernhard Romberg. He ran across them in Hamburg a few years ago. They are cousins, he believes."

"But he has not heard of an S. Romberg?"

"No, although that proves nothing. This S. Romberg could be anywhere in Europe."

"If he is not in London. Can you do me a favor and find out who were the musicians playing at Lady Mercer's birthday celebration?"

Mr. Powell grimaced. "If I do that I shall have to explain why I did not attend. Is it that important?"

"We must find out how the musicians get the music."

"Then I suppose I should speak to the people at the Philharmonic Society as well."

Mr. Melamed nodded.

"And what are you going to be doing, Melamed, while I am running all over London?"

"I shall be paying a visit to some printers on Fleet Street. Then I intend to go to Saffron Hill, to see what I can find out from the Italian street musicians," said Mr. Melamed, smiling, since he knew that Mr. Powell never "ran" anywhere, if he could help it. His comfortable carriage would take him wherever he needed to go. "Of course, if you would rather change places ..."

Mr. Powell quickly finished the last of his coffee and rose to go. He had absolutely no desire to pay a visit to Saffron Hill, one of London's most dangerous neighborhoods.

Mr. Melamed was not eager to go there either, which is why he directed his carriage to go to 183 Fleet Street first, hoping he could obtain the information he needed there.

When he arrived at the printing establishment of Mr. William Norbert, he gave his card to an employee of the firm. A few minutes later, he was shown into Mr. Norbert's office.

Mr. Herman Kimml would have felt at home in the place. The printer's desk was piled high with manuscripts in various stages of production, and the printer himself was engrossed in checking the margins of a sheet of paper, when Mr. Melamed entered the room.

Mr. Melamed had made the acquaintance of the printer while trying to clear the name of Mr. Franks, when that gentleman was wrongly accused of spying for the French. Mr. Norbert now greeted his visitor and gestured to Mr. Melamed to take a seat, although there were the usual question marks in the printer's eyes as he did so.

"Looking for anonymous pamphlet writers again?" asked the printer.

"Not pamphlets, Mr. Norbert, music. I am looking for music that is being printed at the request of a Mr. Schumetti, or a Mr. Romberg."

"Music? That's not my line of business."

"Do you know whose line it is?"

"Before I say yes or no, you might want to tell me what this is all about."

Mr. Melamed explained. The printer shook his head.

"I am sorry, Mr. Melamed, but I cannot help you—and I don't think anyone else will. If we divulged the names of the people who paid us to keep quiet, we'd lose an important part of our business."

"Even if the person has done something against the law?"

"Engage a Bow Street Runner to rummage through the storeroom of every printer in London, if you like. But no one will talk to a private citizen, such as yourself."

Mr. Melamed saw that the printer's eyes were drifting back to the printed sheet he had been examining. Taking the hint, he left Mr. Norbert to his work and hailed a carriage.

Before going to Saffron Hill, Mr. Melamed decided it would be wise to change his clothes. His well-cut coat and spotless boots would be much too noticeable in that part of town. When he arrived home, he was surprised to hear his butler say that Mr. Powell was in his library, waiting for him.

"What are you doing here, Powell? Surely you haven't already been to see Lady Mercer and the Philharmonic Society?"

"No, I decided to visit the latter first, since I thought they also might know about the musicians who performed at Lady Mercer's party."

"And did they?"

"Yes."

Mr. Melamed waited. "Well, did you get their names?"

"There was no need."

"Why not?"

"According to the Society's secretary, the music for the first sonata appeared on their doorstep, with a note."

Mr. Powell handed Mr. Melamed the page. On it was written, "With the compliments of Mr. S. Romberg and Mr. Schumetti, who would be pleased to have your musicians perform this work."

"And the second sonata?" asked Mr. Melamed, after reading the note.

"The same thing."

Mr. Melamed considered this information. "I suppose the publicity was what they were after. The money would come from sales of the music."

"What did you discover, Melamed?"

"That printers will print anything—except the names of the people who cause so much misery in the world through their lies and gossip-mongering."

"Then you're off to Saffron Hill?"

"Yes, after I change my clothes."

"Have you anything that might do for me?"

Mr. Melamed regarded his friend with renewed appreciation. "Do you intend to come with me?"

"I am a former army man and you are not. I would never forgive myself if I let you enter that thieves' den alone and you never came out."

After the two gentlemen had exchanged their elegant clothes for ill-fitting garments that had seen better days, some of which Mr. Melamed had kept in his closet for precisely such occasions and some of which had been stored in boxes in the attic, Mr. Melamed and Mr. Powell set off for the outer boundary of Holborn in a hired carriage. They then proceeded on foot for the rest of the way.

Despite their costumes, the two were very aware of the suspicious, hostile stares that followed them from the doorways and the entrances to narrow and gloomy alleyways as they walked down the muddy street. Mr. Melamed did not have a clue as to where they should go or how they were to begin a conversation with the poor people who lived in that sorry place. But the One Above was with them and sent them, seemingly out of the blue, a dog.

This dog came running out of one of the dilapidated buildings, followed by its owner, who nearly knocked down Mr. Melamed in his hurry to capture the fleeing animal. Mr. Powell immediately sprang into action and joined the chase. Mr. Melamed followed them, and between the three of them they were able to catch the dog, who accepted defeat with grace as its owner tied a piece of string around its collar.

"*Grazie, signore,*" said the man, to Mr. Powell, with real warmth. Turning to Mr. Melamed, he said *grazie* again. And then, after taking closer note of the faces of the two strangers, he said, more warily, "Thank you, the dog she no like to learn her dance."

"I don't blame her. I'd say it's a bit early in the morning for dancing lessons, too," said Mr. Melamed, trying to disguise his voice so that it resembled the rougher tones of Holborn's streets.

The Italian laughed, and once again there was a warm smile on his face. "Say, that's good. You an actor or a juggler or what?"

Since Mr. Melamed had never mastered the art of juggling and did not want to take a chance on whatever "what" might imply, he said, "An actor, when there's work."

"And when there's not?" The Italian eyed Mr. Melamed closely.

"Signore Schumetti told us we could find some work here, selling his music." Mr. Melamed nodded in Mr. Powell's direction. "My friend is an actor, too."

The Italian shrugged. "That I don't know."

"You perform don't you, with your dog?"

"Sure, with my barrel organ. I play, the dog dances, the people laugh, and I collect the coins till the constable comes and chases me and my dog away. That's my life, until I can go back to Italy. Where do you want to go back to?"

"Nowhere," said Mr. Melamed. "London's my home. Are you sure you've never heard of somebody called Signore Schumetti?"

The Italian shrugged. "People come and go. Nobody asks for names."

"Who would know? Somebody has the music. We just want to sell some for a few days, till we get another job. Otherwise, we're out on the street."

Mr. Melamed removed from his pocket the black piece of gauze he had found in the storeroom at Mr. Kimml's music publishing company. He had not wanted to take along one of his own handkerchiefs, whose quality and pristine white color would have given him away at a glance. But he was glad he had brought along something, because the street's potent smell of sewage and rotting food was beginning to affect him.

The Italian shrugged again. "*Scusi*, but my work." He tugged at the dog and the two went back into the building.

Mr. Melamed and Mr. Powell were still considering what to do next when Mr. Melamed felt a tug at his coat. He turned and saw a child of about ten or eleven standing behind him. The child nodded his head in the direction of one of the alleyways and started to walk away. The two gentlemen followed him. At the end of the alleyway was a door, which the child opened. He waited until Mr. Melamed and Mr. Powell had passed through.

The two men heard the door close behind them. The sound of a heavy bolt being closed soon followed.

"Well, we've walked right into their trap," said Mr. Powell. "We'd best find another way out before it is too late."

While Mr. Powell explored their options for a quick escape, Mr. Melamed began to explore the contents of the warehouse. The room held a variety of things—shoddily made wooden dolls with garishly painted faces, cheap cooking pots and cutlery, various types of musical instruments in equally various states of repair. He was about to inspect the contents of a wooden box sitting on the floor when he heard footsteps outside. A moment later the bolt was shoved aside and the door opened.

A different Italian man walked in. This person, who was about thirty years of age and of sturdy, muscular build, stared at Mr. Melamed with an unpleasant expression on his face. He did not see Mr. Powell, who had hidden behind a tall cupboard, prepared to attack the Italian, should that man try to harm Mr. Melamed.

"Who are you? What you doing here?" said the Italian.

While Mr. Melamed wracked his brain for a reply, he slowly wiped his face with his black handkerchief.

The Italian stared at the handkerchief. "Where you get that?"

Mr. Melamed knew that he must appear as tough as the other man, if the interview was to be a success. He therefore stood his ground and said, "Where do you think?"

"You're not Schumetti. What happened to Schumetti?"

"He's having tea with Vivaldi. What's it to you if Schumetti comes himself or he sends me to do his business for him?"

Mr. Melamed offered a silent prayer that the Italian would reveal what that business was, since he did not know how much longer he could continue to play his part.

The Italian scowled, but he was now less threatening. "Why you not say in beginning that Schumetti sent you?" He then took some coins out of his pocket and counted out a few, which he shoved in the direction of Mr. Melamed.

Mr. Melamed returned the handkerchief to his pocket. He scowled down at the coins, as though he expected to receive more.

"Business not good yesterday," said the Italian. "Rain, she fall on the ladies. They run to carriages before they pay my musicians."

Mr. Melamed took the money. "How many did you sell?"

The Italian opened the wooden box. "Count, if you want."

Mr. Melamed did not bother to count the remaining copies of the second sonata by Mr. S. Romberg, which were sitting in the box. Instead, he quickly leafed through the pages. "Where is the music for the other sonata?"

The Italian shrugged. "Gone. Tell Schumetti we need more."

"At least we now know that the black handkerchief is some sort of signal," said Mr. Powell, after the two gentlemen were safely seated in a hired carriage. "Where did you get it?"

"A storeroom in Mr. Herman Kimml's building. Someone from Mr. Schumetti's operation must have dropped it there."

"I suppose Cornhill Street is our next stop, after we have changed our clothes?"

"If you have more important things to do, Powell, do not let me detain you. Your accompanying me to Saffron Hill was more than enough help for one day."

"The only thing on my agenda for the afternoon is picking up a few novels for my dear aunt. Your investigation is much more entertaining."

Mr. Melamed smiled, but inside he was far from feeling amused. He could imagine the Italian becoming dangerous, if provoked. That could mean that Mr. Schumetti, whoever he was, might become violent, too.

Mr. Tree was with a customer when Mr. Melamed and Mr. Powell entered Mr. Kimml's shop on Cornhill Street. The customer, who was a young man, wore a bored expression on his face, despite the fact that Mr. Tree was playing a lively composition.

"It won't do," said the young man, shaking his head. "My pupils want Mr. Romberg and only Mr. Romberg."

"Then why come here, Mr. Clarke? We do not sell the music of Mr. Romberg."

"Because all of London is waiting for his next composition to arrive, and I must have something new to give my students in the meantime. Have you nothing in a similar style?"

"Let me see if we have anything in the back room." Mr. Tree walked over to a door and opened it, leaving it slightly ajar.

Mr. Melamed noticed that Mr. Kimml's eyes followed the assistant. Not for the first time Mr. Melamed found himself thinking that the music publisher did not miss much.

While Mr. Tree was still out of the room, Mr. Melamed walked over to Mr. Clarke and said, "Mr. Romberg will be glad to hear that all of London is waiting for his next sonata."

The music master's face lit up. "Do you know him? Do you know when the next sonata will be in the shops?"

"Excuse me, there is something in my eye," Mr. Melamed said. He then removed a small mirror from his pocket. Instead of looking at his eye, he watched the face of Mr. Kimml, who had returned to poring over his manuscripts. "My friend, here, recently had the pleasure of making Mr. Romberg's acquaintance. Isn't that so?"

Mr. Powell took his cue, and said, "Mr. Romberg said he hopes to have a new sonata ready soon."

The music master was very excited to hear this news. However, Mr. Melamed was less enthusiastic with the results of his experiment. As far as he could tell, Mr. Kimml had not reacted at all to Mr. Powell's supposed news. It really did seem that the music publisher was practically deaf.

Mr. Tree exited the back room and returned to the piano with a few pieces of music. "Mr. Clarke, do you think any of these will do?"

"I shall wait for Mr. Romberg," said Mr. Clarke, brushing aside the offered musical scores, before heading out the door.

Mr. Tree watched him go and sighed.

"What? No sale?" asked Mr. Kimml, who had again looked up from his work.

Mr. Tree shrugged and then shouted, "Romberg!" The shop assistant then turned back to Mr. Melamed and stared at the piece of black material that Mr. Melamed was using to wipe his brow. Mr. Melamed noticed that Mr. Kimml was staring at the black handkerchief as well.

"Is anything wrong?" he asked.

"Has someone in your family died, sir?" Mr. Tree asked with hushed tones, looking suitably solemn.

"No, I am not in mourning. I seem to have misplaced my other handkerchief."

Mr. Melamed put the handkerchief back in his pocket. The smile returned to Mr. Tree's face. "I am relieved to hear that, sir." He then turned to Mr. Kimml and shouted, "No one died."

Mr. Kimml's face also broke into a smile. He said, waving his ear trumpet in Mr. Melamed's direction, "To your continued good health, sir! And your family!"

Mr. Tree then said, "Now, gentlemen, how can I be of service?"

Mr. Powell did not accompany Mr. Melamed to his next stop. The hour was approaching when he must put in an appearance at Rotten Row, the popular spot for promenading in Hyde Park, if one was a member of the fashionable world. Since Mr. Melamed was not a part of that world, he was soon confronting General Well'ngone, on the General's own turf, which was certainly a rotten row, but hardly fashionable.

"You're getting to be a regular visitor to Gravel Lane, Mr. Melamed. Pretty soon you're going to want a room of your own here."

Mr. Melamed offered a silent prayer to the One Above that he should never find himself in such sorry circumstances. When he was seated in the Earl's room, he said, "I want a watch set on the building that houses Mr. Kimml's music publishing company. I want at least two of your boys to be there around the clock, twenty-four hours a day — more, if you can spare them. I would also like a watch set on a warehouse at Saffron Hill."

The Earl looked at him with surprise. "I agree to Cornhill Street. You must find someone else to go to Saffron Hill."

"Your boys are afraid to go there?"

"I should hope so," replied the Earl with aplomb. "Those Italians carry long knives. I would not expose my boys to the danger."

"Very well." Mr. Melamed placed a pouch upon the table. "This is money for the boys to buy food and whatever else they need."

"Will they be looking for anything in particular?" inquired the Earl.

"Yes. They will be looking for someone carrying a black handkerchief — like this." Mr. Melamed showed the Earl the piece of black fabric.

"It belongs to Mr. Romberg?" asked the Earl.

"To him, or to Mr. Schumetti. I shall be satisfied if you find even one of them."

To give the Earl his due, he was not lazy. When he received a job, he responded with alacrity. After Mr. Melamed left, the Earl summoned his boys and gave his instructions.

General Well'ngone and Saulty, accompanied by two of the younger boys, were given the first watch. When they arrived at Cornhill Street it was already dark. But, they noted, a light still shone in Mr. Kimml's shop. A visit to the back of the building revealed that a fainter light glowed in the room used by Mr. Salomon.

"You and the boys find hiding places inside," the General said to Saulty. "When you hear the bells chime the half hour, check on the others to make sure no one has fallen asleep."

"What if Saulty doesn't come to check?" asked a small boy named Marcus, who looked like an ordinary street urchin but was able to run very fast, a talent that came in handy in their line of business.

"I won't be the one to fall asleep," said Saulty, giving the younger boy a dirty look. "But what about you, General? It's going to be a cold night. I don't mind relieving you later and letting you take a watch inside."

The General stuck his hands into his coat pockets. He was the only one of the group who had a warm coat. It was his most treasured possession—indeed, it was one of the few things he owned—and he would rather endure the cold and drizzle than give it to another to wear, even for a few hours. He therefore said, "I don't mind the weather. Just make sure you stay awake and alert all night."

They parted, and the other boys soon found opportunities to sneak inside the building without being seen. The General removed his peddler's box of thimbles and thread and from time to time called out his wares as he walked up and down the nearly empty street.

Mr. Herman Kimml was the first to leave. Stopping to gauge the extent of the drizzle, he wrapped his woolen scarf more tightly about his neck before continuing on his way. Mr. Tree made an appearance about thirty minutes later. By then the drizzle had turned into a true rain and he hesitated before dashing into the street, minding to avoid the puddles that were already starting to form.

Inside the building, Mr. Salomon was vaguely aware of raindrops hitting the roof above him. But his real concentration was on the page of music that was propped up on the pianoforte. Unlike the other two pieces, this sonata had not come easily to him. Indeed, he felt as though he had to wrestle with every note.

At the moment, he was struggling with a certain musical phrase in the second section of the piece and the continuation would not come. He played the troublesome section again — and again — hoping that the repetition would create a breakthrough, much like a battering ram could create a hole in an ancient city's wall.

Saulty, who was stationed near to Mr. Salomon's room, was heartily sick of hearing the same few bars of music played again and again. If that was art, he would have none of it and stick to the ordinary organ barrel players who gave their performances on the street corners and in the city's parks. He was therefore happy to see the door to Mr. Salomon's room open, and see the composer close the door for the night.

He watched as Mr. Salomon descended the stairs. Marcus and Levi, the other members of that night's company, watched Mr. Salomon's progress, too, from their respective hiding places. When the front door closed behind Mr. Salomon, they relaxed and made themselves more comfortable. But even though they performed their assigned task with alert dedication, their sleepless night was for naught. Nothing disturbed their peace, except the occasional sound of footsteps, which belonged to the General, who was shivering outside.

CHAPTER XXIV

MARTIN ROTH COULD not concentrate. The work on Mr. Tree's invention was tantalizingly close to being completed. He had worked out the last mechanical obstacle, and now he only needed to finish building the thing, which, with his talented fingers, should not take very long. But he had come across a disturbing item in the morning's newspaper. His father's bankruptcy had been announced, along with the news that Mr. Samson Roth's personal belongings were to be put on the block, with all proceeds from the auction going to pay his creditors. The house's furnishings would be on view this week.

The young man wondered how his father was bearing up, but he did not know if his presence would be welcome. If there had been little affection when times were good, what could he expect when times were bitter?

Yet he could not work when he knew that in another part of London strangers were walking through his childhood home, appraising the value of the dining table where he and his family had eaten their meals, the pianoforte that his mother had played, and even the contents of the cupboards that held their clothes. He therefore left Mr. Tree's room, despite that man's previous warning, and walked to his father's house.

The person from the auction house looked Martin over with disdain. Martin, who was dressed in his laborer's clothes, did not mention that he was a son of the house and the employee did not ask for his name. The person informed him that Mr. Roth was not at home, but that he could leave a message inside.

Martin entered the house, which held so many memories for him, and wandered from room to room. He avoided the people who had come to view the family's belongings; it was too painful to hear their comments about whether or not a piece of furniture was in or out of fashion, or whether the stains on a carpet might be able to be removed.

He was relieved when he entered his father's study and found that he was alone. Not that this room held fond memories for him. This was the room that he had been summoned to when he and his brother were about to be punished for some youthful prank. The cane that his father had used to strike him must still be somewhere in the room—and the auction house was more than welcome to sell that!

Yet he no longer felt anger toward his father—not for the lost years of his childhood, when they might have had a happier home, and not for the loss of his inheritance, which now appeared to be irretrievably gone. As he sat down at his father's desk, he could only feel pity for the man whom he had once held in such fear, sadness for his fall.

Instinctively, Martin ran his fingers across the top of the desk. Also instinctively, he began to study the table with a professional eye. He had learned much during his apprenticeship in Leeds, and he could recognize a fine piece of work when he saw one. These desks usually had a secret compartment or two, and he decided to divert his morbid thoughts by trying to discover the desk's secret before it was sold and transferred from his home. He didn't expect to find a fortune buried in some dark recess—if there had been one, his father would have known about it and used the money to pay off some of his debts. No, his motive came from a different source. So many times he had stood trembling before that desk, while awaiting his father's wrath to explode upon his small body. For once, he would be the master of the desk and make it yield to his touch.

To his disappointment, the desk's secret was surprisingly easy to discover. One of the drawers was actually a double drawer. When the spring mechanism was released the top compartment lifted up and revealed a second tier underneath. There were still a few old letters sitting on the bottom of the concealed compartment. Martin assumed that his father had forgotten about their existence, since the desk's other drawers had been emptied of their contents.

He decided to take the letters and return them to his father, rather than let a stranger discover them, and he was just about to put them in his pocket when he heard a disturbance in the hallway. A moment later his father rushed into the room, with the man from the auction house and Mr. Melamed following.

When Mr. Samson Roth saw the letters in Martin's hand, his body began to tremble with rage and his face turned a bright shade of red. "Thief! Those letters are mine!"

The elder Mr. Roth lunged forward and raised his hand to strike his son. He was prevented from doing such a terrible thing by Mr. Melamed, who had grasped him from behind.

Martin, in his shock, let the letters fall to the floor. As he bent down to retrieve them, he saw that one of them had come open. At the bottom of the page was a signature written in a large and legible hand, the name of the letter's author: Moses Salomon.

Mr. David Salomon arrived at Cornhill Street that morning eager to work, which was a glorious feeling after being in a brown study for so many days. As sometimes happened, his brain had worked out the musical problem while he was sleeping and the solution had been given to him as a present while he was sipping his morning coffee.

He barely noticed his surroundings while he walked from his home to Mr. Kimml's establishment. It therefore was not remarkable that he did not notice the new batch of boys sent by the Earl, who were already in their hiding places. The boys noticed him, though, and they became more alert when he entered the building and ascended the stairs.

Mr. Salomon worked throughout the morning and much of the afternoon. It was only when he was almost faint with hunger that it occurred to him that he really must get something to eat. When he returned from Mr. Baer's coffee house, Mr. Tree was in the process of seeing an important customer to the front door.

The Earl's boys—a different group, for they were on the late afternoon shift—watched as Mr. Tree and Mr. Salomon ascended the steps together.

"You are looking well today, Mr. Salomon. Does this mean your work is progressing?"

"I believe it is."

"I am happy to hear it. Good day, sir."

The boys watched as Mr. Tree entered the shop and as Mr. Salomon entered his room. They watched customers go into the shop and go out. They watched the closed door that led to Mr. Salomon's room. It was boring work, and they saw nary a trace of a black handkerchief. But at least they knew a good dinner would be waiting for them after they were back at Gravel Lane and had made their report.

Mr. Grimm had barely left his post, except to get some dinner and some gin, and he could not understand what had happened to Jonas Street. In his worst fears, he saw the American standing in Bow Street, pleading with the magistrate on duty that he was innocent and it was Mr. Grimm who was at fault. Subsequently, Mr. Grimm had played out many scenes in his mind when he had skillfully forced Jonas to retract his lying words and admit the truth. The fanciful scene always ended with the magistrate begging his pardon and procuring for him an invitation to perform before the Prince Regent.

Thus were his fancies, but when he saw the real Jonas Street stumble down the street, Mr. Grimm forget all his animosity and gave a sigh of relief.

"Mr. Street, where have you been?" he asked, when Jonas tumbled into the room. "What has happened, sir? Are you ill?"

Jonas replied by collapsing on to his bed. "I have had the fever, Mr. Grimm. I have been very bad. Even now I am very weak."

Mr. Grimm responded in the only way he knew how. He went to the gin house and brought back a bottle of the liquor, some of which he poured into a cup. "Here, Mr. Street, this will bring you back to health."

Mr. Street drank the cup's contents in one gulp and then collapsed back on to the bed. After a few minutes he said, "Thank you, Mr. Grimm. I feel a bit better."

"I am happy to hear it, sir, because I have bad news."

"Can it not wait until morning? I would like to sleep."

"They know that it was us who threw the rock at Mr. Salomon."

Jonas Street struggled to raise himself to a sitting position. "Who knows?"

"The Jews."

The American trapper was silent as he ran his still shaky fingers through his straggly hair. "It was only a rock," he finally said.

"You don't know the Jews," replied Mr. Grimm. "They'll say we didn't just throw a rock. They'll say we broke into the house and stole the lady's jewels. They'll say ..."

"Be quiet!" Jonas shouted. Then he said, more quietly, "Let a man think for a minute."

When Jonas had finished thinking, he turned to Mr. Grimm and said, "I have it, Mr. Grimm. I know how to get my money. I just need to get my strength back, and then I'll be on my way back to New York."

Mr. Melamed put down the last of the letters and was silent. He had brought Mr. Samson Roth to the coffee house so that they could talk in relative privacy. After what he had just read, he was glad that he had done so — and that he had instructed Martin Roth to return to his place of work.

"Another man would have done the same," said Mr. Samson Roth, with a belligerent tone of voice. "You were born to wealth. You don't know what it is to be poor, to have to scrape and save every penny. Our Sages were right. Never judge a man until you have been in his place."

"Don't quote the Talmud to me," Mr. Melamed replied, sickened by the other man's words. "Not every man would betray his friend as you have done."

"Moses Salomon should never have left his money in my care. It was too big a temptation," Mr. Roth persisted.

"He did not leave money in your care," said Mr. Melamed, pointing to the letters that were sitting on the table and which spelled out the whole sorry tale. "His money was invested in the Funds. Your only responsibility was to see that the money was reinvested when his shares came due. Instead, you took those shares, cashed them in and used them to start your own business."

"I intended to pay him back."

Mr. Melamed picked up the final letter—the one where Mr. Moses Salomon had begged his former friend to send him his money, which he thought was still safely invested.

Samson, I cannot understand your delay. My creditors are at my throat. I cannot turn to the right or the left without seeing their angry faces. I must have the money or—or I do not know what I shall do. Answer me. Your silence is killing me. I cannot hold out much longer.

"I cannot understand how you could have ignored such a desperate plea," said Mr. Melamed, placing the letter back on the pile. "By the time he was in trouble and needed his money, your business was established and you were a wealthy a man. Why didn't you send him the money? You had it. You knew it wasn't yours."

"You sound like my wife, may she rest in peace." Mr. Roth's voice reeked of cynicism. "She judged me, too. But I say it's a fine thing when a man's wife reads his personal letters, and then throws them in his face, as if a woman can understand anything about business other than how to spend her husband's hard-earned cash."

Mr. Melamed did not reply. He had not known Mrs. Roth very well, but he now understood why her final years had been so bitter. He assumed that she had not divulged her secret to her children. But once the relationship between husband and wife was poisoned, the children could not help but be infected by the toxic atmosphere, too.

"Well, is the community going to help me, or not?" asked Mr. Roth.

"Help you with what?"

"Pay off my creditors, so I don't have to go to debtors' prison."

Mr. Melamed stared at the man. In truth, he had gone to Mr. Roth's house that morning with the intention of helping him. His plan had been to buy several pieces of furniture at their full value, so that Mr. Roth would receive a decent amount. The furniture would be given to needy families in the community. But the letters, with their tale of heartless betrayal, changed everything.

"I suggest you first turn to your friends for help, Mr. Roth. If you have any."

CHAPTER XXV

WHEN GENERAL WELL'NGONE made his report to the Earl, after yet another uneventful evening's watch, he finished by saying, "How much longer should we do this? I know that Mr. Melamed is paying us handsomely for the work, but I don't want the boys to get too used to living off the fat of the land. Once they get accustomed to being inside all day, they'll find it hard to be out on the streets."

The Earl nodded. And when Mr. Melamed arrived later in the morning to receive a report from the Earl, the young man rendered an opinion that the watch should come to end.

"I understand that Mr. Salomon is working on a new sonata," Mr. Melamed replied. "I want to keep a watch on the premises until the sonata has been performed by him and publicly attributed to his name."

"Very well, Mr. Melamed. It's your money."

Mr. Melamed took the hint and placed a few more coins on the table. "What do you know about the business affairs of the Kimml brothers? Have they been selling any of their possessions? Are there any rumors afloat?"

The Earl pointed to the musical sewing box, which was still sitting on his mantelpiece. "That is a token of appreciation from Mr. Herbert Kimml, in lieu of banknotes, for a service I rendered him. I would have preferred to receive the banknotes, but he didn't have them — though that might have been a temporary lapse. I haven't heard that the brothers will be exchanging their shops on Cornhill for living quarters on Queer Street any time soon."

Mr. Melamed accepted this information without experiencing feelings of disappointment. By now he was used to all his ideas leading nowhere, except to a dead end.

"Your boys are certain that no one has gone up those stairs other than Mr. Salomon?" he asked, as he prepared to go.

"Allow me to make one small correction. No one has gone up or down the steps other than Mr. Salomon and Mr. Tree. Mr. Tree brings Mr. Salomon his tea some days."

Mr. Melamed looked at the Earl. "Who is this Mr. Tree? What do you know about him?"

"Not very much. He seems to be one of those dull men who have no vices to speak of."

"Does he have family?"

"If he does, he doesn't live with them. He's ..."

The Earl stopped in midsentence.

"What is it?" asked Mr. Melamed.

"He is sharing a room with Mr. Martin Roth. I wonder ..."

While the Earl was thinking his thoughts, Mr. Melamed's thoughts went back to his earlier conversation with Martin Roth and the young man's reluctance to reveal either his place of work or where he lived.

"What are you thinking, Earl?" Mr. Melamed asked, for the young man had begun to smile.

"I was right. I told General Well'ngone to look for Martin Roth nowhere, that we would find him with nobody."

"I don't understand."

"There are tens of thousands of Mr. Trees living in London right now, Mr. Melamed. They're born, they live, and they die without anyone other than friends and families ever knowing that they spent time in this world. They are the nobodies who sweep your streets and sell you your cheese and drive your hired carriages from place to place, and make as much impression on your mind as a fallen leaf that you trample beneath your boot." The Earl stopped to straighten his wig, which had gotten a little askew when he got carried away with his unexpected burst of poetic speech and tossed his head a little too enthusiastically. "Mr. Tree is a Mr. Nobody par excellence—which of course does nothing to explain why he is sharing his lodgings with Martin Roth."

"You will find out?"

"Really, Mr. Melamed, is it necessary to ask?"

Mr. Salomon took one last look at his completed sonata, before he blotted the page to remove any excess ink. In truth, he did not feel that this sonata was of the same caliber as the other two that he had recently composed. It was impossible to work at such a frenetic pace without the quality suffering. But it was a respectable piece of work, at least in his opinion. And there were parts that he felt were truly very good.

He took out his pocket watch to check the hour. He had promised to perform at a charity concert at the Jewish orphanage, and he should be on his way. He would not play his new sonata, but something already well known, he decided as he put his manuscript in his pocket and picked up his violin case. Bach was always popular, at least with the ladies. As for the children, they would probably be more interested in their special tea, no matter what he played.

As he walked in the direction of the orphanage, he passed a small band of street musicians. They seemed to be everywhere these days. The Italians could be identified by the sound of their barrel organs, even before one saw their faces. The German immigrants preferred their horns and drums.

This group was from Italy, and they had attracted quite a crowd. Mr. Salomon listened with the others, despite the hard knot that was forming in his stomach, since it was his second sonata that they were playing—the one that had been set to words and was now a popular song that could be heard almost everywhere.

Mr. Salomon looked at the smiling faces in the crowd and wondered if one of them belonged to his nemesis, Mr. S. Romberg. Was the man enjoying his success—the knowledge that his name was on every lip, his newfound riches?

The composer could no longer bear to stay and listen to the song, whose melody now grated on his ears. As he walked away, he wondered if the day would ever come when he could forgive Mr. Romberg, whoever the man was, for having stolen his music. Or would he be condemned to experience forever the same feeling of rage whenever he heard those two sonatas played?

When Mr. Salomon arrived at the orphanage, he was informed that the concert was in progress and was shown to a place at the back of the room. Mr. Maurice Muller, the orphanage's director, smiled and nodded a greeting, and the little man made a gesture towards the audience of Jewish ladies, who had come out in full force to show their support of this worthy endeavor.

The orphanage's children sat at one side of the room, where — as Mr. Salomon had suspected — they were looked longingly at the platters piled high with cakes and sandwiches of bread and butter. The musician made a mental note to play something short, so the children would not have to wait too long for their tea.

The young lady playing a piece by Mozart on the orphanage's donated and rather battered pianoforte sounded her final note. The audience applauded politely, giving her time to make her curtsy and walk back to her seat, since all the mothers in the audience knew how many hours the little girl had spent in trying to master the composition. They, too, had children and had suffered along with their offspring through many wrong notes.

Mr. Salomon was about to approach the front of the room, when Mr. Muller signaled to him that his turn had not yet come. Instead, Mr. Muller announced that Miss Harriet Franks was going to treat the ladies and children to a very special song, assisted by Miss Rebecca Lyon, who would turn the music's pages.

The two young ladies took their places and gave each other a smile, before Miss Franks began to play. After a few moments, Harriet's initial flutter of nervousness vanished and her playing became more confident. Soon she was swept up in the music and the audience murmured their appreciation.

Miss Lyon turned her attention from her important task of keeping an eye on the music, so she would know exactly when to turn the page, to take a peek at the audience. She was happy for her friend's success and she wanted to describe to Harriet the pleased smiles on the ladies' faces, after the concert.

Miss Lyon smiled at her mother and at Mrs. Franks, who was of course smiling broadly, since she was very proud of her daughter. The young lady smiled at a few other ladies that she recognized, and then her eye alighted upon the face of Mr. Salomon — and stayed there. There was something in the young man's face — a look of pain and horror — that held her transfixed, as though they were now joined by some invisible cord.

"Rebecca," she heard Miss Franks whisper, as though from some faraway place. "Rebecca!"

When Miss Lyon did not respond, Miss Franks turned the page of music herself and continued to play. She stopped and realized that something was very wrong only when Miss Lyon ran out of the room.

"Rebecca! What's happened?" she called out after her friend. Then, after gathering up her music, she ran out of the room, too.

Miss Lyon ran out of the orphanage and looked about the courtyard. Miss Franks joined her soon after and asked, "Rebecca, why did you run out of the room like that?"

"It's Mr. Salomon. Oh, Harriet, if you had seen his face."

"Was he taken ill?"

"I don't know. But he can't be allowed to wander about alone in such a condition."

"Where is he?"

The two young ladies looked about, but could not see anyone who looked like Mr. Salomon. Then they spied him standing in a doorway on the other side of the street, his back against the wall and with his hands covering his face.

They raced across the street, but when they reached Mr. Salomon they were not sure what to say. They suspected that the young man was crying, and they were hesitant to intrude upon him at such a private moment.

But he sensed their presence and, after wiping his eyes with his handkerchief, was enough recovered to turn and face them. "Please accept my apologies, Miss Franks, for disturbing your performance. You play very well. You should continue with your lessons."

"We were concerned that you had taken ill, Mr. Salomon," said Rebecca. "Shall we call for a physician?"

"No, I am fine now. But, Miss Franks, may I ask, what music was it that you were playing?"

"It is a new composition by Mr. Romberg," said Miss Franks, who then showed the music to the young man. "It only arrived in the shops yesterday. I spent all last evening practicing. Mr. Salomon, are you certain that you are not ill?"

Mr. Salomon was staring down at the title page, where the name S. Romberg once again danced before his eyes.

By then Mr. Muller and Mrs. Franks and Mrs. Lyon had arrived upon the scene. The physician who attended the orphanage's children, Mr. Gabriel Taylor, who happened to be there attending to a sick child, also was part of the group of adults. Mr. Taylor took one look at Mr. Salomon and said, "My rooms are this way, sir."

Mr. Salomon did not resist when the physician took him by the arm and led him away.

CHAPTER XXVI

"WELL, MR. TAYLOR, what do you have to say about my strange tale?" said Mr. Salomon, after he had finished explaining the reason for his odd behavior.

Mr. Taylor was only a few years older than the composer and had had a harrowing experience of his own not that long ago. That experience (which is recounted in full in the chronicle of London's Jewish community called *Tempest in the Tea Room*) had convinced Mr. Taylor that he should leave London and establish his medical practice elsewhere—a decision he rescinded only after repeated requests to return by Mr. Melamed and others convinced him that he truly was needed in London. Because of all this, he regarded Mr. Salomon with a sympathetic eye, despite the strangeness of the composer's tale. "I can see how it might be tempting to believe that Mr. Romberg is your doppelganger, but I agree with Mr. Melamed. The truth will turn out to be more prosaic. Why are you not willing to entertain the possibility that this Mr. Kimml is the culprit?"

"It does not make sense. If he thinks my work is good enough to steal, why wouldn't he want his publishing company to publish it and receive the glory?"

"To avoid paying you?"

Mr. Salomon dismissed the idea with a shrug. "By the time he pays the fees of the boys who sell the copies to the street musicians, who also pocket a share of the proceeds, I don't believe he saves that much. And remember, if he had the sole right to sell my music, everyone would have to come to his shop. Once they were there, Mr. Tree could convince them to buy a few other pieces. He is very good at what he does."

"Then we must leave the solving of the mystery to Mr. Melamed. I am more worried about your health, sir. I suggest you leave London for a few weeks, have a change of scenery and forget about music for a while."

"Someone else already suggested that," replied Mr. Salomon.

"You do not think it will help?

"If there were a place in the world where there was no music, it might. But if wherever I go I will be followed by Mr. Romberg, what is the point of fleeing?"

"There must be somewhere where his name is not known."

Mr. Salomon considered this thought for a morose moment, and then he rose from his chair and reached for his violin case. "Yes, perhaps there is."

Mr. Taylor watched the composer leave with an uneasy feeling. Then he wrote a note to Mr. Melamed, urging strongly that for the next few days Mr. Salomon must not be left alone. His life might depend upon their careful watching.

The curtains were still drawn in Mrs. Salomon's room, despite the late hour. The shock of discovering the truth about Mr. Samson Roth—the knowledge that once again her attempt to escape from her financial woes by marrying a wealthy man had come to nothing—had been a blow from which she had not yet fully recovered. Her head ached terribly, and everything irritated her. She had scolded the housemaid who had brought her morning tea for clattering the cup and saucer and instructed the girl to remain down in the kitchen until she rang for her. Now, even the silence of the empty house was getting on her nerves.

Tired of tossing and turning on her bed, she rose and went to her dressing table. After arranging her hair and covering the graying strands with her white cap, she reached for her morning dress and slipped it on. She was just about to ring for the housemaid when she thought she heard the house's front door open. Going to the door of her bedroom, she called out, "David? Is that you?"

There was no answer, and so she went out into the corridor and once again called out, "David?"

When she could see the face of the figure slowly ascending the dimly lit staircase, she gave a gasp.

"No, it ain't Davey," said Jonas Street. "So you can stop your hollering."

"How dare you break into my house!"

"And you can stop your jabbering, too. Today is pay day, Mrs. Salomon. Either you give me the money or I'm taking all your pretty jewels."

"My jewels? Is that what you've come for?" Mrs. Salomon began to laugh. "You can have them, Jonas.

With my compliments! I had to sell my real jewels to come to London. Everything I own now is paste!"

Jonas stopped his laborious ascension and stared up at Mrs. Salomon's laughing face.

"You'll never get your money, Jonas. Never! I'm broke. Do you hear me? I'm broke, just like you."

Mrs. Salomon began to laugh hysterically into the face of the American trapper, who had by then reached the top of the staircase.

"Nobody laughs at Jonas Street."

"I do! I laugh at all of you! I laugh at the entire world, because it's all so funny!"

"We'll see how funny you think it is after I break your son's hands."

He turned to go and Mrs. Salomon grabbed him by the arm. "You wouldn't dare!"

"Try and stop me."

He tried to yank away his arm. There was a struggle. A moment later, the trapper's body tumbled down the stairs, not stopping until he landed in a heap at the bottom.

When Mr. Salomon opened the door to his home he walked into a scene of utter chaos. Mrs. Salomon was still standing at the top of the staircase, gripping the banister with all her might. The servants, who had come running at the sound of the noise, were huddled together in the corridor, crying. The last thing Mr. Salomon saw was the man lying on the floor, whose face was hidden from him. He went over to the man and gently lifted the injured person's face. Then Mr. Salomon looked up at his mother.

"David, thank God you've come. I don't know how he got in, this ... this intruder. I was so frightened ... seeing a strange man on the stairs that I ... I screamed, and he must have become frightened, too, because he slipped ... and then he fell. Is he dead, David? What shall we do?"

"We must call for a constable and a physician, Mother."

Mr. Salomon turned to the cook, who was the oldest member of the staff, as well as the calmest, and instructed her to find a constable and send a message to Mr. Taylor that his services were required at once. He then told the other two servants to go back to the kitchen and prepare two strong pots of tea — one for Mrs. Salomon and the other for themselves.

When they had gone, Mrs. Salomon ran down the stairs and grabbed her son by the arm. "You believe me, David, don't you? It was an accident. He broke into the house. He wanted to hurt me. He wanted to hurt you, too. He was going to ruin your career."

"Did you push him?"

"Push ...? He lost his footing — there, on that step. I'll show you."

Mrs. Salomon turned to go back up the steps. She paused before Jonas's prostrate body.

"Don't bother, Mother. And, please, stop with the lies."

"It was an accident. I didn't push him, David. He slipped. That's the truth."

"If that's your story, stick to it."

Mr. Street did not die, but he was badly injured. Mr. Taylor conferred with Mr. Melamed, who had been summoned by Mr. Salomon, and the philanthropist arranged for Jonas Street to be taken to a place where he could be looked after until he recovered.

The constable took down Mrs. Salomon's description of the events. The servants verified that they had not heard the front bell ring, nor heard anything, until the noise of someone thumping down the stairs alerted them that something was wrong upstairs. The constable ended his investigation by declaring that Jonas Street had gotten what he deserved for breaking into honest people's homes and trying to steal their possessions.

Mr. Melamed was about to leave the Salomons' home when he saw Mary coming down the hallway, with her suitcase in her hand.

"You are leaving?" he asked her.

"If you please, sir, tell Mrs. Salomon that I have decided to leave."

"Without your wages?"

The housemaid looked down at the floor. "I do not care about the wages, sir. This is not a house for me."

"I can understand your being upset by what happened today, Mary. I cannot understand your forgoing money that you have rightfully earned—unless you have received payment from elsewhere."

The servant girl looked up at him with startled eyes. "How did you know, sir?"

"Never mind how I know," said Mr. Melamed, who had only realized the solution to the problem of the mirror that moment. "Perhaps you will do me the favor of telling the truth about what happened on the night when someone wrote on the mirror."

Mary hesitated, and then she said, "He frightened me, sir."

"Who?"

"The man who rang the bell."

"The messenger?"

"No, sir. There was no messenger. Whoever delivered the letter dropped it in the letter box, without ringing the front bell. This was someone else, a gentleman, I think."

"You could not tell?"

"He was a foreign gentleman, sir. He spoke with an accent, and he had a funny name. It sounded like one of those Italian names, sir."

"Can you recall what the name was?"

Mary looked down at the floor, while she thought. "I think it was shoe something. They have such funny names, sir, I did not catch it all."

"What did this man look like?"

"I don't know, sir."

"You don't know? Did you not see his face?"

"No, sir. That's why he gave me such a fright. His face was all covered by a black piece of cloth. His face must have been horribly scarred, underneath. I was terrified that he might show me, if I didn't do as he asked."

"I see," said Mr. Melamed, wishing very much that he had pressed the housemaid to speak the truth sooner. "What happened next? Did he leave his card?"

"No, sir. He asked to be shown to the drawing room. He said he would wait there until Mr. Salomon returned home. I did not want to do it, sir, to have him in the house, because he frightened me. But ..."

"He gave you money?"

Mary again glanced down at the floor. "Yes, sir."

"And told you to keep quiet?"

"Not exactly, sir. But after what happened, with the writing on the mirror, and Mrs. Salomon so hysterical and Mr. Salomon looking so pale—well, I couldn't say I let the man into the house, could I?"

Mr. Melamed was at first at a loss as to what to do next. He felt that he had failed, badly, and he did not like to fail. He only knew that he must bring his investigation to a successful end before more violence occurred. He therefore retraced his steps to Gravel Lane.

"I want you, the General, Martin Roth, and whoever else you think will be of use to meet me at Mr. Kimml's music publishing company," he said to the Earl. "And bring some tools."

"What sort of tools, Mr. Melamed? I hope you do not intend to bury someone?"

"On the contrary, we are going to dig up the entire place, if we have to. But we will discover the secret of that room, and we will do it today."

When they were all assembled, Mr. Melamed first turned to Martin Roth. "Martin, you know how to search out a piece of furniture's secret places. See what you can find hidden in this piano."

Martin did his best, testing every inch of wood, but it was no use. "It's only a piano, Mr. Melamed."

"Very well, then, we will start to tear up the floor—and we start here. Someone help me to push the piano over to the side."

"We'll do it," said the General, stepping forward. "Give me a hand, Saulty."

To their surprise, despite their huffing and puffing, the pianoforte would not budge. Martin lent a hand, and in the end Mr. Melamed did as well, to no avail.

Martin bent down to discover the problem. "It's nailed down to the floor. Someone bring me a spade."

While he began to loosen the nails, the General and the other boys took their tools and began to pry up some of the other floorboards. Within minutes, the Kimml brothers—who had been having their afternoon tea together, in Mr. Herman Kimml's shop—were in the room, demanding an explanation.

"Either you produce Mr. Romberg or show us his hiding place, of your own free will, or we will tear up the entire building," said Mr. Melamed.

"I do not understand, sir," said Mr. Herbert Kimml. "How can we produce Mr. Romberg? We have no idea who he is."

"Boys, keep working."

"Do something! Stop them!" yelled Mr. Herman Kimml, waving his ear trumpet in the air. "Call for the law! This is an outrage! Mr. Tree! Mr. Tree!"

"Really, sir, I think you will regret this," said Mr. Harold Kimml. "There is nothing in this room except for what you can see with your own eyes."

"We shall see," said Mr. Melamed.

Mr. Tree arrived at that moment and looked about the room with dismay.

"Mr. Tree, find a constable!   Find a hundred constables!" yelled Mr. Herman Kimml. "Well? What are you waiting for? Go!"

However, Mr. Tree did not go. He remained where he was, staring at Martin Roth, who was removing the last of the nails. When he realized that several pairs of eyes were upon him, he ran over to the piano, gave it a shove, jumped into the hole that was revealed in the spot where the piano had once stood — and disappeared.

The General and his boys were after him, a few seconds later, flying down the heretofore hidden spiral staircase that connected the room to a storage room located on the floor below. At the same time, Mr. Melamed flew down the main staircase. But they all reached the front door just moments too late. Mr. Tree, who had used those first few seconds to his advantage, had already flown out the door and disappeared into that great metropolis of anonymous citizens and forgotten souls, otherwise known as the city of London.

CHAPTER XXVII

MR. MELAMED WAS examining the spiral staircase with the Earl of Gravel Lane and General Well'ngone. At the bottom of the stairwell they found a supply of candles, as well as paper, pens and ink. There were also several pieces of black gauze cloth, similar in size to the one he had found in the storeroom on the upper floor. He surmised that that handkerchief had fallen out of Mr. Tree's pocket, without his being aware of it, when the shop assistant had visited the storeroom on some legitimate errand that was part of his duties in Mr. Kimml's shop.

The black handkerchief, with its suggestion of a pox-marked face hiding beneath it, had been a clever touch. Mr. Melamed could imagine that few people on Saffron Hill, or even on Fleet Street, would wish to come too close to Mr. Tree, and the risk of infection, while the shop assistant was doing his business, under the guise of Mr. Schumetti.

"He could sit on the steps near the top very comfortably," said the General, demonstrating. "No one would see the lit candle, so he'd be able to write unobserved."

Mr. Melamed looked up to the top of the staircase, which was now open to the room above. "Martin, push the piano back in place, and play something. It doesn't matter what. I just want to hear the sound."

Martin did as instructed. The sound was not perfectly clear, of course, but the notes could be heard. Then they heard Martin shout, "Shall I stop playing, Mr. Melamed?"

"Yes!"

Above them, they heard the sounds of the piano being pushed aside and Martin's face peered through the opening. "I do not understand, Mr. Melamed. What exactly is Mr. Tree being accused of?"

"Apparently, he sat on this staircase while Mr. Salomon was composing his sonatas and, when the sonatas were nearly completed, copied them. Then he had them printed up and sold them under the name of S. Romberg. Why he did such a thing, I do not know."

Martin sighed. "I do."

"I have no further interest in the matter, Mr. Melamed."

Mr. Melamed looked with exasperation at Mr. Salomon, who seemed to have retreated into his own world. The composer had expressed little interest when Mr. Melamed told him about what had just occurred at Mr. Kimml's premises. The news of Mr. Tree's treachery had been greeted with silence. Now Mr. Salomon was sitting in his drawing room, staring into space, doing nothing.

"Mr. Roth has asked that you be there, Mr. Salomon, when he demonstrates his invention. It will take only a few minutes of your time. He promises."

Mr. Salomon reluctantly joined the others on the street. They made a strange sight, for not only were the Earl and his boys standing on the pavement with Martin, but the Kimml brothers had come along, too. Together they all trudged to the lodgings that Martin had shared with Mr. Tree.

Mr. Tree, of course, was not there to greet them. But Martin had a key, and so he was able to let them into the room.

It was a good-sized room, yet there was not much room for all of them to stand, by the time they were all inside. The reason was because of a very large object standing in the center of the room, which was covered by several white sheets.

"If you please," said Martin, "make yourselves at home. It will take me only a few moments to prepare."

While the others waited in silence, Martin removed the coverings from the object and something that looked similar to an upright pianoforte was revealed. However, this instrument had a double keyboard, one on top of the other. It also had a rectangular cabinet that sat on top of the keyboards, but which was much smaller than the cabinets that were sometimes found on top of pianos.

"This is a kind of piano," Martin explained to his guests. "The bottom keyboard works as a regular keyboard." He then demonstrated what he meant by playing a few bars of music. "Now, watch this."

Martin went behind the instrument, crouching down behind the cabinet so that he could not be seen by the others. A few moments later, the keys of the upper keyboard began to move, by themselves, and the sound of Mr. Salomon's second sonata filled the room.

"Giblets! The thing's haunted!" Saulty cried out.

The Earl and the General also watched the moving keys, untouched by a human hand, with something akin to amazement mixed with fear. Mr. Salomon, for his part, did not know what to be most astounded by, the instrument or the fact that the thing was playing his music.

It was Mr. Harold Kimml who broke the spell. "Bravo! Bravo, sir, bravo! Now, tell us how you did it."

The music stopped, as did the movement of the keys, and Martin reappeared. "It took me some time to solve the problem," he said, as he removed the front panel of the cabinet.

"A music box!" Mr. Herbert Kimml exclaimed with delight, when a pinned drum similar to the mechanisms used in his musical sewing boxes was revealed.

"That was one piece of the puzzle," said Martin. "Mr. Tree did the pinning, using Mr. Salomon's sonatas for his model." Martin then turned to Mr. Salomon and said, "I am sorry, sir. I did not know that it was your music. Mr. Tree assured me that it was written by Mr. Romberg, who had given us his permission to use his music for our invention."

"How do the keys move by themselves?" asked Mr. Melamed. He had stepped forward to examine the strange instrument, but could not discover the secret.

"That, sir, was a problem that kept me up for more nights than I care to say. I devised a system of rods that connect the drum to the keys. There is one rod for each key. When the rod is pushed down, its corresponding key is pushed down as well. But it's really the drum that is playing the notes, like any other musical box." He paused and looked at the still-puzzled faces. "It's a bit difficult to explain, and to be honest I have not yet perfected the machine."

The Kimml brothers gathered around the instrument and excitedly discussed its merits and faults. Even the Earl and his boys stepped forward to get a closer look, now that they had been assured that the thing was not haunted and they would not encounter any ghosts. Only Mr. Salomon did not join in with the general enthusiasm for the mechanical thing.

When Martin caught his eye, the young composer said, rather stiffly, "It is an amazing thing you have created, Mr. Roth. I salute your ingenuity."

"Thank you, Mr. Salomon."

"What do you call it? Has it a name?"

"Not an official name. But I have my own name for it. The Doppelganger, because of the two keyboards."

"An interesting name," said Mr. Salomon. "But what I still cannot understand is why you had to use my music for your invention. Why could you not have used a piece by Bach or Haydn? It would have accomplished the same thing."

Martin's cheeks turned red. "I am afraid that was my fault, sir. You see, Mr. Tree had promised to pay me my wages. And then we had to buy things. We needed wood for the cabinet. I broke one keyboard, when the rods pushed down too hard. I believe he stole your music to finance the making of his invention. He thought if he could invent a piano that could play by itself—that could make music without any effort on the part of people—that everyone would want to buy one. He thought it would make us rich and famous. That was his dream."

"I see," said Mr. Salomon. "His dream."

Mr. Melamed was seated at his usual table at Baer's Coffee House. He was waiting for Mr. Salomon to arrive, to join him for a meal. He was not hungry, but he wanted Mr. Salomon to eat something. He suspected that the young man had not had anything since breakfast and that, after the strain of the day's events, he was near to collapsing. Besides, Mrs. Baer had always claimed that her chicken soup could cure almost anything. This would be an excellent opportunity to prove the truth of that statement.

But Mr. Salomon had insisted on taking care of some private business first, and Mr. Melamed had hesitated to treat the grown man as a child. Now, Mr. Melamed waited at his table, anxiously watching the door each time it opened, hoping that the person who entered would be the composer—for he had spoken with Mr. Taylor and heard the physician's fears that Mr. Salomon might, in his depressed state, attempt to take his own life.

At last, Mr. Salomon appeared in the doorway, and Mr. Melamed gave a sigh of relief that his belief in the essential sanity of Mr. Salomon had not been misplaced. As planned, Mr. Asher Baer brought over a platter filled with nourishing food not long after Mr. Salomon had taken his seat. Then Mr. Baer slipped away, so that the two men could converse in private.

"Mrs. Baer will be offended if you do not at least taste what she has made," said Mr. Melamed, nodding toward Mr. Salomon's untouched dish.

Mr. Salomon shook his head and continued to stare into space.

"Come, Mr. Salomon, the future is no longer so bleak. The Kimmls have agreed to publicize the news that the mysterious Mr. Romberg never existed, that the music is yours. I am certain that Mr. Tree will not dare to play more of his tricks. We all know that you are not mad and never were."

"That was his intention, with the mirror? To drive me mad?"

"Not to actually do it, but to make you appear that you were losing your mind, to deflect attention away from himself. After all, he needed you to continue writing, until he had completed his machine. I assume that was why he also spilled the ink on your manuscript."

"That was done by Mr. Tree?"

"Mr. Grimm knew nothing about it. When Mr. Street is able to speak I think we will receive the same answer from him. It therefore must have been done by Mr. Tree. He was the only one who could know with certainty when you were in the room on Cornhill Street, and when you were not."

Mr. Salomon gazed down at the strong black brew sitting in his coffee cup. Then he pushed the cup away, unable to stand the sight of more darkness in his world.

"And what about the invention?" he asked. "What will become of Martin Roth's work?"

"I believe that the Kimml brothers want to purchase the piano and display it in Herman Kimml's shop. It will cause a sensation, they claim, and bring them more customers than Clementi — and bring you even greater fame, since it is your music that the thing will be playing."

When Mr. Salomon did not respond, Mr. Melamed added, "There is no reason why you cannot put this ordeal behind you and go forward."

"You forget one thing, Mr. Melamed. Unlike the Doppelganger, I am not a machine."

"I do not understand your meaning."

"When I decided to devote my life to music, I hoped that my violin and my compositions would bring something positive into the world. That my music would uplift people's spirits, inspire them to accomplish great things. Instead, it has brought out the worst in people. It has inspired only lies, hatred and greed. I am not prepared to continue my career on those terms."

Mr. Salomon then took out a wad of banknotes and placed it on the table. "I have pawned my violin. Please use this money to help pay for Jonas's medical care."

"Are you not being rash, Mr. Salomon? Tomorrow you may feel differently."

Mr. Salomon shook his head. "There is no more music inside of me. It's dead."

"If that is how you feel, it is not my place to try to change your mind. Still, I was hoping that you would perform at least one more concert. Mr. Street's care will be expensive. This money will help, but there is also the problem of his sister. My idea was to organize a concert, where the proceeds would go to a fund to help the two of them."

"Surely there are other musicians in London that you can ask."

"Yes, there are. But it is not their world that has been shattered. You are the one in need of repair."

All of London seems to be sitting in the audience of the magnificent hall that Mr. Powell has procured for the charity concert taking place this evening. The Lady Windsburys and Lady Allyns of the world have, of course, received the choicest places. Yet the Lyon and Franks families do not mind that they have been seated, along with Mr. and Mrs. Baer and Martin Roth, in a more secluded part of the room. They still have a fine view of the stage, and they eagerly await the start of the musical performance. The Earl of Gravel Lane and General Well'ngone are there, too, for the Earl has become very fond of music after acquiring his little musical sewing box.

There are a few people missing from the assembly, who might have otherwise attended if our tale had ended differently—or if they had made different choices in their lives before our tale began.

Mr. Samson Roth has recently set up residence in the debtors' section of Newgate Prison, although Mr. Melamed is quietly organizing a communal fund to help the man, who seems to finally be cognizant of his error. Mr. Roth's son Nathan has apparently already left for the Continent, for he has not been seen or heard from again.

Mr. Grimm is also no longer living in London. Mr. Powell found the man a position as organ player at a small farming community in Wales. It does not matter that Mr. Grimm has never played that instrument. The community has only a pump organ in their place of worship, a mechanical instrument that requires very little skill to play, which suits Mr. Grimm's rapidly deteriorating talents perfectly.

Mrs. Salomon is also not here. She has not yet recovered from her recent traumatic experiences, and Mr. Taylor insists that she must have rest, preferably somewhere that is far away from London. It was therefore arranged for her to travel back to Leeds and the home of Mr. and Mrs. Deare to recuperate there for several months, and she has already departed. Although the loss of such an interesting personality was regretted by many members of London's Jewish community, there is at least one home on Devonshire Square that does not mind — and it is not because that lady once referred to Miss Rebecca Lyon and Miss Harriet Franks as "chattering" girls. This Narrator has too much sensibility to take offence at a comment that is so obviously far from the truth. Rather, there are certain persons in the community — those who have a fuller knowledge of what has transpired than others — who feel that her son, Mr. Salomon, might more easily regain his own equanimity and establish his career if he does not have the additional daily burden of his mother's care to weigh him down.

Mr. Street, of course, is still recovering from his fall.

As for Mr. Herbert and Mr. Harold Kimml, they are busy behind the scenes, trying to help the musicians get ready for the performance—but, in their excitement and eagerness to be of use, creating more chaos backstage than calm. Since Mr. Tree is not there to assist Mr. Herman Kimml to hear, that gentleman has been forced to wave his ear trumpet more often than usual, until he has resigned himself to finding a quiet corner by the side of the stage where he can at least see the musicians perform, using his memory to hear the notes being played.

Mr. Tree had seemingly disappeared forever, although there are some who say that he—like other persons of dubious scruples before him—must turn up some day at Bow Street; if he does not get his just reward at this earthly court of law, there is always the court of law in Heaven.

Mr. Melamed is standing at the side of the hall with his friend Mr. Powell, anxiously awaiting the beginning of the concert—and anxiously awaiting its end. It is not that he has lost his taste for music. Rather, he hopes that he has not been wrong to press Mr. Salomon to perform so soon. In plainer words, despite his outward mature and dignified appearance, he is inwardly as nervous as any Jewish mother waiting for the moment when her cherished child will take the stage and perform—praying that the child will succeed while, at the same time, harboring a secret feeling of dread, since disaster is equally possible.

At last, the musicians appear on the stage. As at the concert at Leeds, Mr. Salomon has chosen to begin the recital with the Sonatina by Mr. Clementi. He will perform his own compositions later, as the highlight of the evening.

The first two movements of the Sonatina are performed and performed well. Then the Rondo begins, more slowly and more stately than the London audience is accustomed to hearing. Once again there is a swell of murmuring, which stops when the first chord of Mr. Salomon's violin is heard—for, yes, Mr. Melamed has redeemed the violin, with money from the Jewish community's Free Loan Society, a debt that Mr. Salomon intends to repay.

Mr. Salomon comes forward, still playing, but even Miss Lyon, who is not an experienced musician, can see and hear that something is wrong. Whereas before, in Leeds, Mr. Salomon's movements had been graceful and fluid, he now appears stiff and wooden. His music also seems devoid of life.

The little company seated at the side of the room exchange nervous glances. But then, thanks to the great kindness of the One Above, a change occurs. Mr. Salomon has become more relaxed, more attentive to his violin and what the music is saying to him. He seems to have forgotten that there is an audience, that there are such things as sadness and disappointment in our lowly world, and is letting the music transport him to a better, more elevated place.

The musician catches Mr. Melamed's eye for a moment and gives a slight nod of his head, to show that he is now fine; the music has brought him back to life.

Miss Rebecca Lyon and Miss Harriet Franks exchange a glance, as well, relieved to see that Mr. Salomon has recovered. They settle into their seats to enjoy the rest of the evening, along with the others.

And, Reader, you may say what you will about the value of progress and the wonder of mechanical instruments that can perform music without a human hand's touch. But if you had been in this concert hall on this night, this Narrator believes that you would agree with her about this: No experience can compare to those divine moments when the musician, the music and the listener are connected by a sacred golden thread, which binds them tightly together with sublime cords of joy and love.

If you enjoyed **The Doppelganger's Dance**, please let others know by leaving a review at your favourite online bookseller. Thanks so much!

ABOUT THE AUTHOR

Libi Astaire is an award-winning author who often writes about Jewish history. In addition to her Jewish Regency Mystery Series featuring Ezra Melamed, General Well'ngone and the Earl of Gravel Lane, she is the author of *Terra Incognita*, a novel about modern-day descendants of Spain's crypto-Jews; *The Banished Heart*, a novel about Shakespeare, secret Jews and 1930s Berlin; and several volumes of Chassidic tales. She lives in Jerusalem, Israel.

GET COZY WITH ANOTHER GREAT
JEWISH REGENCY MYSTERY

"A more unique and colorful cast of characters would be difficult to find." – Amazon.com

Tempest in the Tea Room

Poison and missing jewels make for a baffling brew in this first volume of the Jewish Regency Mystery Series.

The Moon Taker

Murder comes to Gravel Lane — and with Mr. Melamed away, it's up to General Well'ngone and the Earl of Gravel Lane to catch the killer.

The Vanisher Variations

Things are far from bright in Brighton when a wealthy lady vanishes, and a reluctant Mr. Melamed is called in to find her.

Matzah Mia!

When a sack full of counterfeit coins is found in a matzah bakery before Passover, it could mean hanging for the baker — or his opera-loving son.

The Wreck of Two Brothers
After a Dutch diplomat is found murdered in the Great Synagogue, suspicion falls upon a young Englishman with the same name. Is it a coincidence? Or is there some fatal connection between the two men?

Fancy's Favorite
The struggle for fame and fortune isn't just tough when you're an up-and-coming boxer in Regency England — it can be murder.

Lyre, Liar!
When a London dinner party results in two deaths, Mr. Melamed must solve a baffling mystery where no one and nothing is what it seems.

Jewish Regency Mystery Stories
Enjoy these three intriguing tales: *Too Many Coins, General Well'ngone in Love*, and *What's in a Flame?*

Jewish Regency Mystery Stories, Vol. 2
The Jewish holidays of Chanukah, Purim and Shavuos provide the background for *The Melancholy Menorah, Costumed Foolery*, and *The Petrified Psalm*.

Jewish Regency Mystery Stories, Vol. 3
Join the Lyon family and their guests on June 21, 1815, as they tell stories while awaiting news that the messenger from Waterloo has finally arrived.

Also by Libi Astaire:

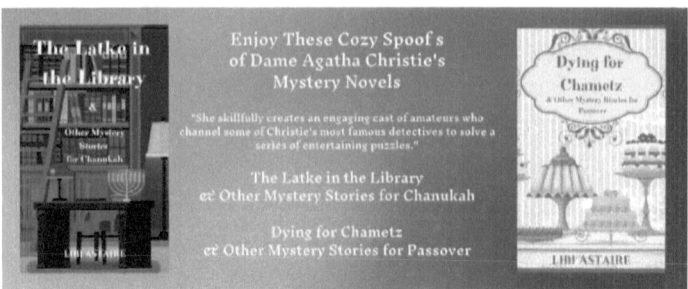

The Latke in the Library & Other Mystery Stories for Chanukah

"Fun and Clever" – Amazon.com

Oy vey! When elderly mystery writer Agatha Krinsky has to move into an assisted living facility, she discovers a body in the library. But the staff won't take her seriously, and even her luncheon companions — Herschel Perlow, Miss Eppel, and Ronny and Rubles Bernfeld — are more interested in talking about their earlier careers than helping Agatha solve her mystery.

Dying for Chametz & Other Mystery Stories for Passover

"An outstanding book with charming and funny characters and beautifully woven Jewish ideas" – Amazon.com

Barnet Court's connoisseurs of crime are back! Join retired Jewish detectives Herschel Perlow, Miss Janice Eppel, Ronny and Rubles Bernfeld, and author Agatha Krinsky as they tackle new mysteries to solve in this humorous, Passover-themed homage to Dame Agatha Christie.

Terra Incognita

"Masterfully weaves deep well-developed characters with historical underpinnings that make this a must read" — Amazon.com

Sant Joan Januz. A village locked away from strangers' prying eyes. But when Vidal Bonet, a young man with big dreams, tries to turn his sleepy Catalan village into a world-class resort, he unwittingly stumbles upon a long-buried family secret that threatens to destroy everyone he loves.

The Banished Heart

"A surprisingly GREAT read" — Goodreads.com

Who controls a person's identity; a society's notion of who is noble and good – and who should be shunned and despised?

For Paul Hoffmann, an aspiring Shakespearean scholar in 1930s Berlin, disturbing questions about his long-buried Jewish identity have suddenly become a matter of life and death — and to his dismay, it's a despised moneylender named Shylock who seems to have the answers.

Everby: Theo's Tale
"Beautiful writing, fascinating story line, lots of food for thought" – Amazon.com

When Theo — a misfit with a passion for music — is rejected from a top music school, he feels like he has nothing left to live for. His awful day gets even worse when he falls into Everby, a "Post-Catastrophe" kingdom where hope and happiness are banished in a cynical struggle for wealth and power. There he unwillingly gets caught up in court intrigue. But Theo is no storybook hero. Or so he thinks, until tragedy forces him to realize that in Everby there are only two options: Die or dare to dream again.

Day Trips to Jewish History
"Her descriptions of her discoveries in Spain and Portugal are fascinating" — Amazon.com

Who was the New World's first Jewish author? Why did some medieval moneylenders cover their hair? Which Jewish woman became queen of a North African people? And who was one of the most daring heroes of the Holocaust that you've never heard of? Join journalist and historical novelist Libi Astaire for a journey to some of the lesser-known — but fascinating — people and places in Jewish history.

For more information about these and future books, visit Libi's website at libiastaire.weebly.com

ABOUT THE AUTHORS

As a fantasy novel and horror movie enthusiast, NICK TAYLOR enjoys writing as an outlet for her creativity. The works of Tolkien have inspired her and remain some of her favorite novels. She is a video gamer by nature but also enjoys jogs outdoors, animals, and renaissance festivals. Nick currently lives in Texas where she hopes to acquire her registered nursing degree and is the mother of two beautiful children ages ten and twelve.

ALISHA PAYNE loves to read and has always had a fondness for creative writing. She loves reading a whole range of genres and authors from Tolkien to James Rollins, and blames her love for reading on her mother, who introduced her to the worlds of Pern and Xanth. Alisha is a former Petty Officer of the United States Navy, which is where she met her wonderful husband. She currently resides with her family in Virginia.